M000042884

Presence: Smoke and Fire

Charity Becker

Blysster Press

Email the author at optycal@optycal.com
Charity Becker
PO Box 1242
Port Orchard, Wa. 98367
Website: http://www.optycal.com
Facebook:http://www.facebook.com/charitybecker.author

"Presence: Smoke and Fire" Printing History
Blysster Press paperback edition June 2011

Blysster Press

A new kind of publisher for a new kind of world.

This is a work of fiction. Names, characters, places, and incidents either are the product of the author's imagination or are used fictitiously. Any resemblance to actual persons, living or dead, events, business establishments, or locales is entirely coincidental.

All rights reserved
Copyright © 2011 Charity Becker
Cover Art and Design by Charity Becker © 2011

No part of this book may be reproduced or transmitted in any form or by any means, electronic, mechanical, or otherwise including, but not limited to, photocopying, recording, or by any information storage and retrieval system, without permission in writing from the publisher. For information, contact Blysster Press at info@blysster.com

ISBN 978-0-9826818-5-5

Printed in the United States of America
www.blysster.com

If you purchased this book without a cover, you should be aware that this book is stolen property. It was reported as "unsold and destroyed" to the publisher, and neither the author nor the publisher has received any payment for this "stripped book."

Dedicated to my dear friend April. My promise is golden, you know that, so let your soul be free from worry or regret. I love you, April, never forget that.

THANK YOU

To my daughters, Katherynn, Celeste, and Ivy. Every day is an adventure with you three around. Thank you so much for loving me and for making me want to be a better person.

To the Blyssterites and my friends—too numerous to name individually—Can you believe I've made it this far? Your support has buoyed me in the toughest of times. Those of you who stayed true to me, I am forever indebted to you.

To Mickie and Nia for your input, your red pens, and for your friendship. I adore you both, and I appreciate all you have done for me.

To Jen and Erica, super-ultra-mega-awesome street-teamers and rabid fans. You two are so damn cool, and you don't even know it!

To Regina for your enthusiasm over the books and characters, and for your exuberant introduction! Never lose that lively, exciting personality.

To Roger D. Batson MS, NCC, LPC (lovingly referred to as Psych) for your extensive guidance in understanding PTSD and domestic violence. Because of you, survivors have a voice, hope, and a future.

And as always, to Born. I'm amazed by you. Your unending support and love carry me onward and upward. Without you, Mina's story may never have been told.
STARFISH!

Presence series, listed in order:

Presence: Awakening
(released March 2010)

Presence: Wolf Moon
(released 2010)

Presence: Smoke and Fire
(released 2011)

~~~~

Find other fiction, non-fiction, and artwork
by Charity Becker by visiting her website:
http://www.optycal.com

ONE

~~

Walter Garrot's heart exploded somewhere between Sidney Avenue and Kitsap Street, leaving a hole in his chest the size of a child's head. Or so the paramedics claimed.

Flipping through the report, I couldn't help but wonder why I was here. No doubt, a spontaneously exploding heart was weird. But Walter Garrot's situation seemed more like a Discovery Channel kind of weird. For *me* to get a call, it usually leaned more toward the Science Fiction Channel.

I'd recently become the Port Orchard police's unofficial expert on everything odd. It didn't take long for me to realize that *unofficial* is just fancy-talk for, "You're not getting paid, but can you pretty please pull our asses out of the fire anyway?" My *talents* were still under scrutiny by the powers that be, but that didn't stop them from asking for my help when the bizarre stuff slapped them in the face.

"What do you make of it, Ms. Jewel?" Detective

Richards asked.

He sat across from me in the coffee shop, large hands folded on the table between us, his dark eyes watching my every move. Months ago, when I'd first met the detective, I'd felt like I was under suspicion every time he turned that penetrating gaze on me. It was as if he could just stare the truth out of me, whether I knew anything or not. But now I was used to it, and I hardly noticed the weight of his gaze anymore.

"Well," I said between sips of coffee, "I'm not entirely sure why you called me. If you ask me, which you *did*, this looks like a medical anomaly. There's nothing paranormal about it."

I closed the file with my free hand and pushed the folder closer to the detective without looking past the initial report and witness statements. I knew what I'd find if I flipped a couple more pages in, and I really didn't want to see it; the statements had been graphic enough.

"You think it's a medical anomaly?" Detective Richards said with a slow shake of his head. "Our medical examiner says otherwise." He placed a hand flat on top of the folder. "She won't touch the body again. She says it makes her skin crawl just thinking about it."

"She's in the wrong line of work then, isn't she?"

He shrugged broad shoulders. "I'd have said the same thing if I hadn't been there when she ran out of the building shrieking like a banshee."

Setting my mug on the table, I glanced down at the closed folder again. Dr. Goodson was possibly the most calm and cool-headed person I knew. Normally, she was completely unshakable. For her to get spooked by a body, it *had* to be something awful.

I licked my lips and looked up to see the detective grinning. Great. I only got *that* look when he knew he'd won. Detective Richards had learned early on how to get my attention. Weird shit? Call Mina!

"She ran out the door still wearing her autopsy gloves and apron," he added, like chocolate sprinkles on top of the preternatural sundae.

I love chocolate sprinkles.

I raised an eyebrow and grinned at the detective. "The janitor must have been thrilled," I said. "What the hell got into Dr. Goodson, anyway?"

Detective Richards flashed a victorious smile, then had the grace to put his professional face back on as he opened the folder. He riffled through a few papers, then produced a three-page statement signed by Dr. Goodson.

"It says right there," he said as he tapped the page, "when she touched the wound she felt something creeping up her arm. She didn't get the usual. . . *visions*, just this feeling like something was moving its way up her arm and she had to get away from it."

The detective's hesitation on the word *visions* wasn't lost on me. It wasn't new for Richards to be uncomfortable with the things I dealt with every day. Even after knowing each other this long he still couldn't wrap his mind around the supernatural. We'd had plenty of arguments over the impossible becoming the possible. *I* knew it was all true, but proof be damned, *he* wasn't willing to believe it just yet. For now I'd leave it alone. The time would come though that he'd either need to accept the changes or. . .

Well, he'd better just accept the changes, because the alternative wasn't very pleasant.

"I don't suppose she's had a psych evaluation recently," I asked, skimming the medical report.

"She's as sane as they come, Ms. Jewel, but she hasn't left her house since the incident."

"Yeah?" I said with a smirk. "Running out of the

building screaming sure sounds like a sane person's response to me. *Totally* normal."

Detective Richards raised one bushy eyebrow, but said nothing as he pushed the folder toward me. Of course, he didn't need to say anything. The look that he gave me said, "No more stalling." When he looked at me that way, I didn't argue.

My smile melted into a grimace as I flipped through the papers, one by one, my gut tightening in anticipation with each turn. A lump had formed in my throat by the time I'd found the photos, which was probably a good thing considering my stomach wanted to empty its contents right then and there.

The ragged, blood-soaked edges of Walter Garrot's clothes were a sight, but they were nothing compared to the tattered chunks of flesh clinging to the steering wheel. Soft bits had fallen all down the front of his freshly pressed Armani slacks, and sat in his lap, glistening in the flash from the camera.

I rubbed my temple, thankful that at least the pictures were black and white. It was too early in the evening to stomach a full-color photo of a gaping chest wound. Then again, for me, it was always too early for that. But I'd thought about it too long. Suddenly my imagination added the missing color, and a whole new level of discomfort hit me square in the gut.

I shut my eyes and counted to ten, attempting to gather my composure—and swallow down the coffee trying to climb back up my throat. Puking on the evidence wasn't very professional. Not to mention an awful waste of good java.

Something weird was going on and I was supposed to be the go-to gal for this type of shit. If I didn't pull myself together more bad things could happen, and before I knew it I'd be up to my eyeballs in bloody police photos and too many questions.

One deep breath in, slowly out, and I didn't puke. Good. Step one complete.

I opened my eyes, concentrating on the small details of the pictures. Individually, they weren't as bad as the whole scene put together. Individually, each one was interesting, but safe. If I didn't look at the pictures as a whole, maybe I could pretend it wasn't a bloody corpse I was staring at in the middle of this quaint little coffee shop on a beautiful spring evening.

Yeah, right.

I took another deep breath and forced myself to calm down and to look at the case from a distance. I didn't know this guy. Garrot wasn't a friend or a loved one. I'd never even seen him walking the streets of Port Orchard before. His demise should mean nothing to me other than supplying me with an interesting case to be solved. And maybe some fresh nightmare fodder—as if I lacked that.

And that did it. Looking at this as just another case helped me pull my emotions out of the equation. Finally able to separate myself from the horror of the event, I took in the details of the photographs and added what I saw to what I'd previously read in the reports.

The shape of the wound, the tatters of shirt, and the splatter pattern of blood all held clues. But to *what* exactly?

The hole in Walter's chest didn't go all the way through his body, and according to the report, the car seat was untouched, so no gunshot to the back. The body fragments were all thrown out toward the front of the car, so definitely not an attack from the front. Both the driver's door and the passenger's seat were clean, so no attack from either side.

All signs pointed to the impossible. His heart had

gone *ka-boom,* and the force of the blast had thrown everything forward through muscle, bone, and Nordstrom's finest.

Rolling my bottom lip into my mouth, I squinted at the photo and tapped my fingers on the table, my mind racing with questions and a few possibilities.

"What are you thinking, Ms. Jewel?"

"Hm?" I glanced up, then quickly back down to the photo so my train of thought wouldn't get derailed now that it was going in the right direction.

"You look thoughtful," Richards said. "Have any ideas? Anything you'd like to bounce off me?"

"I was just wondering what was so special about this guy," I said quietly.

"What do you mean?"

"What was so special about Walter Garrot that someone had to make such a scene out of his death? Why not keep it under wraps?" I looked up at the detective. "Why not do it at home in a way that wasn't so. . . over the top?"

"*Do it?*" he asked, as he dug inside his tweed suit jacket with one hand. "No more medical anomaly?" He pulled a notebook and pen from his inside pocket and began scribbling. "You think someone *did* this to Garrot?"

His chocolate eyes flicked side to side as he wrote. When he looked at me again his face was blank, hinting at nothing. The perfect cop face. The weight was still there, that penetrating, knowing feel, but nothing else I could read.

"Don't *you* think someone did this to the poor S.O.B?" I asked.

"That's why I called you, Ms. Jewel. This whole case reeks of. . ."

"Weird?" I said with a smirk.

He frowned. "That's not what I meant."

I grinned and wiggled my eyebrows up and down. Then I reached across the table and poked his shoulder. "I was just giving you crap, Richards."

He rolled his eyes up. "When are you *not* giving someone crap?"

I lifted my coffee cup in a silent *touche'* and grinned before I took another sip.

He smiled, an affable expression, and one I didn't get from him often. We weren't friends, and probably never would be, but he trusted my opinion on matters of the strange, even if he didn't necessarily believe in it himself.

Much to my chagrin, I'd become a bit of a local celebrity in the past year and a half. I'd helped recover dozens of missing persons, many of whom had some kind of odd, supernatural twist to their cases. Most of the locals refused to believe the *supernatural* part and focused on the *odd* instead. Semantics. I didn't see much of a difference, but hey, whatever made them feel safe at night. Eventually though, just like Detective Richards, they'd *have* to believe.

The past few months had seen more and more gifted people coming out. Psychic gifts weren't mainstream by any stretch of the imagination, and they weren't readily accepted either, but a few brave souls had come out in the open, admitting what they were, and showing others what they could do. Psychic abilities were still regarded as a novelty by most people, and just plain evil by some.

I hadn't personally *come out* so much as made people wonder about the way I solved my cases. None of them ever made national news, but the local papers loved to grab interviews with the rare client who was willing to talk about their story. I'd never admitted to anyone that I was anything more than a good private investigator with unorthodox methods, but I didn't get squeamish when the news articles came out questioning just how I'd solved that last "unsolvable" case. Some of the theories kept me laughing for days.

Dr. Goodson was one of the gifted who'd recently come out to the public. How she did her job each day was beyond me. You'd think being able to see what happened just by touching objects or people would discourage her from going elbows-deep into murder victims' bodies. But Dr. Goodson loved her job and went to it each day knowing she was making a difference. Not just that she helped solve murder cases, but that she was showing the world that psychic gifts and unexplainable occurrences weren't things to be feared.

Until Walter Garrot burst onto the scene, that is.

Detective Richards waited quietly, his smile having faded back to the blank cop face I'd come to know so well. He was on the fence with what he believed. He trusted me, but only when it got his cases solved. He didn't like to talk about it more than he had to, and he didn't like to admit he'd called me in for help. That suited me just fine; I had no desire to put myself on the front page, and generally avoided reporters like they carried the black plague. As long as they talked *about* me, and not *to* me, I could handle the media.

"Who could have done this, how, and why?" Detective Richards asked after I'd been quiet for some time.

"I was wondering that myself," I said. "How? I'm not really sure. Microwaves? Too much cell phone use? Some high-tech implant? But then you wouldn't need me; you'd have called some super spy or techie genius. As to *why* Garrot went *boom*?" I paused, scratched my head, then said, "I'd love to give you an answer, Richards." I slid the file back to the detective. "Right now I've got a big heap of nothing, but if I come up with anything I'll give you a call."

"That's all I ask, Ms. Jewel."

If he was disappointed in my lack of quick answers, I couldn't tell. His face was still neutral, like we'd been discussing the weather instead of exploding body parts. He collected his papers and gory photos, arranged them neatly in the file, then nodded his good-bye.

I was left sitting in the coffee shop, recovering from the experience while I eves dropped on the other patrons. Many of them were discussing the big story of the day. Apparently, some huge, exotic snake had been set loose in the Kitsap Mall. The whole place had been shut down while Silverdale animal control tried to find it. I didn't see how that was big news, but then again, I knew a lot stranger things went on right under their noses.

For instance, there was a Lycan in the restaurant right now. A real live werewolf was sitting in the booth behind the guy with the brown bowler hat. However, none of these people knew that. None of them would ever suspect that little Mina Jewel was a Lycan and could turn at any moment and rip their faces off.

Of course, I'd never *do* that. Not unless they did something nasty to deserve it.

Personal rule number one: Only eat bad guys.

The bell above the door jingled and I glanced toward the front of the restaurant. Timothy, my friend, house mate, and fellow Lycan, waved and came toward me. I saw the heads turn as he passed each table, and the smiles creep over faces.

Women always gave Timothy a second glance, and who could blame them? He was an eye-catcher with that bright auburn hair and those sparkling blue eyes. Six-feet four-inches of stud. He wasn't the smartest man to grace the planet, but his naivety lent him a certain little-boy charm that some women found irresistible. He didn't really do it for me, but I could see the attraction.

"I thought I'd find you here," Timothy said as he slipped into the seat Detective Richards had recently vacated.

"That's because I'm always here," I replied.

His smile faltered. "When you're not working."

"Technically, I'm still working now."

Timothy frowned. "Why are you here then?"

"I just needed a change of scenery," I said as I clasped my hands over my head and stretched my arms up. My back cracked with the movement and I winced. "I stopped in for some coffee to wake my ass up, then I got spotted and made to look at disturbing crime-scene photos. You know, typical day for me."

Timothy didn't return my playful smile. I wasn't in the mood for more melancholy, so I didn't bother asking what his issue was. Instead I asked, "Did you need something?"

"Beckett wanted to see you." Timothy lowered his voice and added, "He's down at HQ waiting for you. He's been there for an hour."

"Beckett?"

I reached in my purse, pulled out my new cell phone —which was more like a tiny computer than a phone—and checked the calendar on the screen. Today's date was blinking, and a note flashed up on the screen every few seconds reminding me to meet Beckett an hour ago. There were also six missed calls. Guess I'd turned off the ringer and hadn't realized it. Damn touchscreen technology.

"Ah, shit!" I said. "I forgot all about him."

"We noticed."

I scooted to the end of the booth. Timothy watched me rummage through my purse and tuck five dollars under my coffee mug for the waitress. With his forearms resting on the table and his chin on his arms, he rolled his eyes up to meet mine, looking every bit like a lost puppy.

Before I stood, I leaned in close and asked, "Did you need something else, Timothy?"

He sat up, sighed dramatically, and shook his head. The shake sent his mane dancing around his face. He looked up at me through a shaggy curtain of hair.

Moody again? No surprise; he'd been moody off and on for weeks, but I didn't have time to sit and psychoanalyze the werewolf. What the hell did he have to worry about, anyway? His only real responsibility in the world was to keep my house clean. Granted, I could be a slob, so cleaning my house could easily be a full-time job. But still, it wasn't that tough of a life. Timothy's biggest worry in the last month had been which fabric softener to use on my unmentionables.

I shook my head, patted his arm, and left the gloomy Lycan to pout by himself in the coffee shop.

TWO

~~

Presence HQ was housed in the basement of Page's Pages—though *basement* didn't quite cover what was below the quiet book store at the edge of town. A sprawling, multilevel maze of twisting, brick-lined tunnels secretly spread out under half of downtown Port Orchard. I'd only been in a few of the upper tunnels in the handful of years I'd been with Presence. Quite frankly, that was plenty for me. What I'd seen down there was enough to keep me supplied with nightmares for several lifetimes. I wasn't about to go looking for more.

The cavernous meeting room was lit by small rectangular bulbs stuck in the walls and spaced so far apart the light couldn't quite reach the whole room. In the center of the polished stone floor stood an equally-polished long wood table. No chairs, no papers, no phones, pencils, or pens. Just a big lonely table and a green reading lamp reflecting off the liquid-looking surface and the gold-embossed symbol of our organization: An elegant capital *P* surrounded by swirling lines and shimmering dots.

Beckett leaned against the table, his arms crossed over his chest. He wore his typical tailored black tuxedo like it was a part of him. Beckett was one of those men who seemed to take up the whole room just by being there. He was wide and thick with dark, smooth skin free of any distinguishing features. No freckles, no blemishes, no scars, not even stubble on his squared chin. He wore his black hair in shoulder-length braids ending in white beads that clicked against each other when he moved.

Beckett could have palmed my face and crushed my skull with little more than a flinch, but I wasn't worried when he came toward me with one hand extended. Beckett may have been big and imposing, but he was one of the most gentle and soft-spoken men I'd ever known.

We shook hands and he turned back to the table. He pointed a finger to the right of the table, and just like that, a well-padded office chair rolled smoothly out of the shadows as if an invisible servant had run up to him pushing the chair. The chair stopped in front of Beckett and he settled into it. He then looked up at me and gave a slow single nod.

I grinned, raised my hand, and called a chair for myself—although mine wobbled slowly toward me as if *my* invisible servant was missing a leg and both arms. The chair jolted, rolled forward one more inch, then stopped. I'm pretty sure it was my shin that stopped the chair and not my *amazing* control.

I sat in the chair and crossed my legs, my right ankle resting on top of my left knee. I'd been accused of sitting like a man more than once, but I didn't really care. In jeans, sitting like a "proper" lady meant cut-off circulation and pinched skin in places most people don't *want* pinched.

Beckett sat with his back straight, his hands folded in his lap, and his attention all on me. His voice was a deep bass, but gentle when he said, "You should make time for practice every day, Mina."

"Telekinesis has never been one of my stronger gifts," I said quietly. It was a lame excuse, and I knew it.

Beckett knew it too. He shook his head slowly, the beads in his hair clicking softly against one another. "All the more reason to make time for your practice. You could be so powerful if you'd just *try*. I'd hate to think that all the things I've taught you are going to waste."

"Way to lay the guilt," I said as I looked away from his stern gaze.

Technically, I was his boss. But Beckett had been with Presence for much longer than I had, and he knew a lot more about psychic gifts and supernatural goodies than me. Truthfully, I felt like I was only second in command because my father had been the founder of the underground society and had ruled it for so long. It also helped that Justice, the current leader, was also my live-in boyfriend.

A shrill beep echoed through the room, and Beckett turned his thick wrist to look at his watch.

"God!" I said, suddenly remembering why I was there. "I'm so sorry I'm late. I forgot all about the antique show."

"It's fine," he said. "It's just started. If we leave now we can still get there in time to peruse the offerings. They're open until nine this evening."

"I can't," I said with a shake of my head. "My caseload's too heavy. I've got a bunch of missing teens. Some kind of rave gone bad or something. I'm not sure yet. I've been up all night working on it."

Beckett looked disappointed, but he nodded and

offered, "Anything I can help with?"

"I don't know," I said with a grin. "Spend a lot of time at raves?"

He smiled, shaking his head. "Sorry. Not really my thing." He raised his arms out to the sides and looked down at himself. "I don't blend in very well with the younger set."

I grinned wider, imagining calm composed Beckett at a rave surrounded by young people high on every drug imaginable. Maybe he'd even have one of those giant, light up baby pacifiers hanging from a brightly-colored string around his neck.

I laughed and said, "Don't worry about it. Hey, why don't you grab Oliver and Beth-Anne before you hit the show? They love that crap. They'll probably be more fun than I would anyway." I added softly, "Sorry again, Beckett."

"I understand." Beckett nodded and stood, straightening his jacket. "Before I go," he said, "Justice was here not long ago looking for you."

"Yeah," I said, my smile dropping away. "I'm not surprised. I haven't seen him since yesterday morning, and I didn't have time to answer his emails this afternoon."

"He seemed distressed. . ."

"He's fine," I said with a small shake of my head. "I'll send him a text before I go back to the office to be sure, but he's *not* distressed."

"Perhaps you should go home," Beckett said. "Maybe spend some time with your sweetheart before you forget what he looks like."

Sliding down my seat a little, I took in a deep breath, steeling myself for the inevitable. "Yeah, you're probably right."

It wasn't that I didn't want to see Justice or to spend any time at home; I really did need that recharge. It was just that things in my personal life hadn't been so great lately. I wasn't pointing fingers or trying to place blame, but home wasn't as relaxing as it should be. Admittedly, it wasn't *always* bad, but it wasn't always good either. There were some issues that needed to be addressed, and I was too chickenshit to bring them up. Then again, so was Justice. For months we'd been playing this immature game of pretending everything was just fine, and it was taking its toll on us both. Despite my efforts to keep things between just us, I suspected our issues were taking their toll on our work and our friends, too. But I wasn't sure how to stop it.

Beckett tipped his head toward me and smiled softly, as if he understood my trepidation, but he didn't ask. Without another word he left through the big metal door, leaving me to decide whether to go home and face a possible emotionally devastating situation, or to be a coward and just send a text.

~ ~

The fact that Justice was standing on my front porch when I drove up to my house meant Beckett had called ahead to let him know I was on my way. I'm not sure how I felt about Beckett's meddling in my personal life. He meant well, but some things really should just stay between the parties involved. Nobody in Presence knew all the crap that had been thrown between Justice and I lately in the privacy of our own home. Sure, they probably had their assumptions, but nobody really knew the truth, and I wanted to keep it that way.

But Justice didn't appear to be annoyed or angry. In fact, he looked quite eager to see me, so maybe things wouldn't be so bad. One could always hope.

He stood with his back against my front door, his right ankle crossed casually over his left. He held a single white daisy, twirling it round and round in his long, pale fingers. A breeze blew his black hair over his right shoulder and across his chest, the ends brushing the banister on the other side.

I got out of my car, walked around to the passenger's side, and leaned my back against it. Smiling, I folded my arms across my stomach and waited. Justice took the cue and came slowly down the steps and across the yard, giving me plenty of time to watch him move toward me, knowing I'd enjoy the view. He stopped in front of me and bent to lay a soft kiss on my forehead.

I sighed and closed my eyes as Justice pulled me closer, folding me into his arms. A rare peace moved between us on the warmth of our bodies, and for a moment I just breathed him in, all my anxiety starting to melt away at last.

"I've missed you," he whispered.

With my head snuggled into his chest, his silken hair caressed my face. I could just wrap myself in that hair and twirl it around my fingers for hours. And on good days I sometimes did just that. But before I could sink into that beautiful hair, the house phone rang, interrupting the sweet reunion.

My shoulders went tense at the sound. "Dammit," I whispered, pushing away from Justice.

At first he didn't let go. He didn't hold me tight or prevent me from moving, but he didn't let go either. He left his arms wrapped around me and he stared down into my face, his bright yellow eyes almost pleading. The phone rang a second time and I pushed harder to get away. He released me with a frown. I went up on tip-toes, kissed his cheek to ease his worry, then turned and jogged to the porch and up the steps. As I reached for the doorknob, a skinny black cat ran out from under the porch and took off into the woods.

"You know," I shouted after it, "I'm gonna pet you one of these days, you stupid cat!"

"It'll take more than a few meals for that stray to let *you* touch it," Justice said as he came up the steps behind me.

"Ingrate," I grumbled, and pushed the door open.

The bedroom phone was the closest, so I turned left and jogged down the short hall, took another left, and snatched the receiver off my dresser.

"What?" I said as I dropped my purse and keys on the floor next to me.

"Hey, it's Alex."

A twinge of pain shot through my temple, and I pressed my forehead against the cool wall, my visions of a relaxing evening crumbling away at the sound of my assistant's tentative voice.

"What's up?" I asked.

"I've got a lead."

"Alex," I said with a heavy sigh. "I just got home. I've been wearing the same clothes since yesterday, I haven't slept in God-knows how long, and the last meal I had was a bagel at ten yesterday morning—unless you count the buckets of coffee I've been drinking since then. Can't this wait until the morning?"

"No," he said softly. "No, I think you should take a look at this."

THREE

~~

Alex Rivers sat behind towers of notebooks and legal pads. At first glance his desk looked like a hurricane had blown through, but I knew the stacks were actually arranged in alphabetical *and* chronological order. They were even color-coded, like everything else on his desk. It was a good thing we each had our own private office. The sight of *my* desk probably would have given Alex an aneurysm.

I dropped into the chair he reserved for his clients, folded my hands across my rumbling stomach, and watched him stacking and arranging notes for a few minutes. If he had that many notebooks out at once, he'd probably found a good lead. Even so, I didn't really want to be at work again so soon.

I slouched and slid down the seat as I said, "What's so important that you had to call me all the way back here?"

"I got a call just after you left," he said, avoiding my angry eyes. "It seemed like just the break we've been looking for, or I'd have saved it for tomorrow."

"And?" I snapped. "Let's not mince words, Alex. I'm beat. What do you have?"

"Mrs. Johansson found a note in her son's bag. I had her bring it down, and after looking it over I thought you'd want to see it for yourself."

He opened his desk drawer and shook a blue file folder loose from the others, then opened it and tugged a wrinkled note from the inside pocket. He held it by the corner with his pointer and thumb, as if the note was coated in something unpleasant. To Alex, it probably was.

I smirked and reached for the note, thankful *I* wasn't a touch-psychic.

"Gonna be 1 helluva party!" I read aloud. "Meet up at the spot 2 hook up *wit* the rest." I gave a short laugh and said, "What ever happened to grammar and spelling?"

Alex shrugged.

"Did they quit teaching 'The Three Rs' in public school to make time for self-esteem workshops and Uzi-loading 101?"

Alex stifled a grin, then looked back at the files on his desk. "What do you think about the note?"

"I think it could have waited until tomorrow," I said, placing the note on the corner of Alex's desk.

The bottom fourth of the paper hung off the edge of the desk. Alex eyeballed the note, and the skin above his right eye twitched a few times. I grinned and flicked the paper with my fingers, wiggling my eyebrows.

Alex narrowed his pale eyes, then he looked away and said, "I don't know. It seems like a pretty big clue to me."

He wasn't taking any of my bait, and though I was glad he was so intent on getting this meeting over with, it annoyed me that I couldn't shake him. He'd interrupted my evening and I wanted at least a taste of retribution for that.

Childish, yes, but these little games kept me sane. Sort of.

"I mean," Alex continued without looking at me, "I'm sorry I interrupted you at home and all, but I thought you'd want to see this after the dead-ends we've hit on these cases."

A slew of missing teens, endless calls from worried parents, and not a single lead. Until now. I grunted and scowled. How could I stay annoyed at my assistant for doing his job? Yes, I was exhausted and he'd called me all the way back down here, but he'd found an honest-to-goodness lead. A lead that could bring six missing kids home to their parents—*tonight* if we were lucky.

"You're right, Alex," I said, grabbing the note from his desk. I slumped further into the seat and tried to relax my tense muscles. "Just that this week's marathon work session has got me all worked up. I know it hasn't been easy on you either. Sorry for the hard time."

"It's fine," he said with a wave of one hand. "I'm tired too, but it's worth it." He nodded once. "We'll get this solved. Don't worry, Mina."

Apologies out of the way, I looked at the note again and tugged at one of my long curls. "So, there was a party."

"Just a regular party, though?"

"Probably a rave. But where? Did any of the other kids have notes like this one?"

Alex shook his head quickly, making his blond bangs sweep across the bridge of his freckled nose. He kept his hair shaved along the sides and back, but let those straight, golden bangs grow long enough to cover his brilliant blue eyes—and the facial tick that caused him so much anxiety. The tick was more prominent when he was stressed, but even relaxed it could sneak up on him at any time.

The haircut, his smooth skin, and especially his freckles made Alex look a lot younger than his twenty-five years. Young and innocent. But I knew better. Underneath that harmless appearance was a man who'd seen too much pain and suffering.

"My guess is," he said, tossing his head to the right to dislodge a strand of hair from the corner of his eye, "the other kids got texts instead of paper notes."

"Why didn't Evan get a text? Why'd he go all *old school* and get a hand-written note?"

Alex gave a quick laugh, shaking his head wildly. "His mom wouldn't let him have a cell phone. She said she was worried he'd use it for 'bad things.' Her words."

"Poor baby," I said, rolling my eyes. "All right then, what else do we have? Looks like a girl's handwriting. We have any girls from Evan's school go missing around the same time?"

"Missy Edwards," Alex said with an energetic nod. He flipped through a purple notebook until he found the page he wanted. "Missy was reported missing a few hours after Mrs. Johansson called us about Evan."

"Could be the same party, and maybe Missy was the hostess?" I chewed the end of my hair, then said. "Call the Edwards and ask for a handwriting sample. We'll compare the two."

"Pretty basic stuff," Alex said.

"Sure, but we have to start somewhere."

Alex gave a weary sigh and flipped to the front of the purple pad. He picked up the phone, punched some numbers, and watched me from across the desk.

"Mrs. Edwards?" he said in his best professional voice. "Alex Rivers, Jewel Investigations. . . No, I. . ."

His cheeks went scarlet and his eye twitched. He looked away from me, and his voice was a shade softer when he said, "Listen, Mrs. Edwards, we'd like to. . ."

A moment later Alex turned to me, lips pursed,

holding the receiver out for me to take.

I stuck my tongue out at Alex and tucked the phone between my ear and shoulder.

"Mina Jewel," I said.

"Ah! Ms. Jewel," Mrs. Edwards said. "I was wondering when we'd hear from you again. Did your office boy give you my message?"

"Office boy?" I scrunched my nose and grinned at Alex. I gave him a playful wink and said into the phone, "You mean Alex?"

Alex looked indignant for a moment, then began aggressively shuffling notebooks, trying his best not to meet my teasing gaze.

"Yes, that's it. Alan."

"*Alex*," I said with a little more emphasis. "Alex Rivers, Mrs. Edwards. He's my assistant, a fully licensed private investigator, just like me. And no, he didn't give me the message."

"Oh, my." She gave an exaggerated sigh which crackled the air over the phone line. "The help these days! I swear to you, Ms. Jewel, we're all going to drown in a sea of incompetency, and then the *help* will take over the world. God save us then!"

Telling the clients where to shove it wasn't good for business, so I bit my tongue. Not that we lacked clients or money or that I needed to kiss this woman's ass, but if her daughter's handwriting sample could help us solve the other cases, I'd endure just about anything to get it.

"My message," Mrs. Edwards continued, "was that I would like to meet with you in regards to your future."

I paused. The phrase seemed vaguely threatening for some reason. Though I could sometimes pick up subtle hints from my Insight over the phone, this time it was probably just my exhaustion playing tricks on me. Lack of sleep tended to screw with my gifts, and sleep had been an elusive thing the past few months.

I shook my head and said, "Excuse me?"

"Your future, Ms. Jewel. Have you thought much about your retirement? If you come down to my office in the morning, say sevenish, we could discuss your options."

I closed my eyes and rubbed a hand over my forehead. Her daughter had been missing for two days and this lady wanted to talk business? Even if I hadn't been blessed with psychic gifts, her behavior would have seemed fishy to me. It certainly wouldn't be the first case I'd been on where the parents were involved in the crime. Considering the state of the world these days, I was sure it wouldn't be the last.

Mentally moving her name to the top of my suspect list, I said, "Mrs. Edwards, I'm calling about your daughter. Alex and I would like to get a sample of her handwriting."

"My. . . oh, yes, of course. Whatever you need. Have your boy come pick it up tomorrow. Even better," she added quickly, "why not come and pick it up yourself at my office when you come to discuss your retirement options?"

"I'll pick it up at seven," I said, and hung up without waiting for a reply.

I turned to Alex and said, "Retirement? Thirty-three seems a tad young to retire, don't you think?"

Alex snickered and continued straightening his already perfectly-aligned notebooks.

"I suppose you think I deserved that?" I asked.

Alex just grinned, once again avoiding the bait.

"Fine," I said. "Back to business then. What do you think the chances are that this is the Congregation of Truth snatching teens?"

Alex shrugged. "Maybe to trick them into joining?"

I nodded. "Sure. Why not?"

"Or fuel for their. . . activities?"

Again, I nodded. "Could be. We don't know if any of these kids were gifted."

He pondered it a moment, chewing on his lower lip, then said, "Seems like every time there's a group of missing kids, the Congregation has their hands in it in one way or another. It's harder to pin it on them now that they've gone mainstream."

"True."

He shook his head and added, "You'd think a cult like the Congregation would want to stay underground, considering what they actually *do* to gifted people."

I nodded again, absently twirling a curl in my fingers. "They went mainstream so we couldn't hunt them as easily, but I think that's gonna backfire on them. Hey," I looked at Alex and sat up straight. "Maybe Missy Edwards' mother is Congregation. She seemed awfully *blasé* about her kid being gone this long."

"You think?" Alex asked. "She *is* a nasty piece of work. Wouldn't surprise me. But I don't see any obvious connections."

"Yet," I said as I snatched a notebook off the top of Alex's desk. "Would you be offended if I go through your notes here and see if you missed anything?"

Alex shook his head. "Just put it back where it belongs when you're done. In fact," he said as he got up and crossed his small office, "I'll go make some coffee and be right in to help. It's going to be another long night."

FOUR

~~

Over thirty-six hours at work had drained me to near-numbness. Alex and I had combed through every one of his notes *and mine* regarding the missing teens, and still had nothing. I just knew the Congregation was involved, and Alex agreed. They had to be. The whole case reeked of their taint, but so far we had zero evidence to link them. But that was nothing new. The Congregation was good at hiding, and when they couldn't completely hide, they were good at covering their tracks—or flat-out eliminating the people who could blow their cover. When trying to get solid evidence against the Congregation of Truth, tenacity was the key.

I wasn't going to give up. I'd keep going until we had our proof and we took out the Congregation hive responsible. The only reason I wasn't in my office still was the fact I'd made a promise. A promise I'd already broken.

I hadn't intended to stay out this long. In fact, before

I'd left my house, I'd told Justice I'd be back in an hour and we could spend the rest of the evening cuddling on the couch and watching television. But my job didn't take the evenings off, so either could I. The bad guys didn't stop abducting kids just because it was dinner time. And kids didn't stop doing stupid shit just because Mom and Dad expected them to be sleeping or were too self-absorbed to bother checking on their kids once in a while.

The clock in my car flashed nine as I pulled into my front yard. I shut off the engine and cut the lights. Sitting in the sudden quiet of my car, a bad feeling swept over me. My chest grew tight and my skin tingled as I looked across my yard and up at the house. It would be better if I did it fast and got it over with, but I didn't want to move.

A deep, silent darkness surrounded my car, and a prickly chill ran down my arms. I hated being in the dark, but I especially hated being *alone* in the dark. Even though I knew it was irrational and childish, I'd never been able to shake that fear.

But it wasn't just the darkness that had me frozen in place tonight. I was more afraid of what might be waiting for me *inside* my well-lit house than what might be lurking in the dark *outside*. Scared or not, I had to do this. Sleeping in my car wasn't an option. My stomach knotted as I got out of my car, moved quickly across my front yard, and mounted the steps.

It used to be that just walking up these steps meant I was that much closer to my nightly beatings. Or the *other* things my stepfather had in store for me. But time had passed, I'd grown up, and the sadistic bastard had been killed. I'd taken over the house and made it into a sanctuary for myself, spitting in the face of the living nightmare I'd endured here. And for a time it really *had* been a sanctuary. It had been peaceful and safe, and even the memories of my tainted childhood couldn't break that serene spell.

But lately things had changed. Sometimes, if I came home this late, I'd get an earful, like a disobedient child. That was bad enough, but the anxiety over wondering whether I'd get a lecture or a warm welcome was often worse than the actual lectures themselves. Still, not knowing what waited for me made my chest tighten more as I reached for the door. My childhood all over again.

But I'd survived all that my stepfather had thrown at me, so I knew I could survive this, too. One deep breath in, and I opened the door.

Much to my surprise I was met with hugs and smiles from Justice and Timothy both. Relieved, I fell into my recliner and kicked off my shoes as Timothy disappeared into the kitchen. I heard him digging around for a minute or two, then he came out with a sandwich and a glass of chocolate milk, just for me.

I smiled, thanked him, and began eating. I spent the next five minutes enjoying the quiet of my house and the warm feeling of being home and welcome, safe from all the crap I faced every day outside these walls.

But that peace was short-lived.

Justice and I had stopped using Telepathy months ago. We were always tense around each other, too on edge. Having that telepathic link open between us—our emotions mingling, thoughts invading, dreams mixing—just amplified our agitation, so we'd cut it off. No, we didn't use that link anymore, but I didn't need Telepathy to know what he was going to do next.

I felt the air grow thick just before Justice cleared his throat and looked at me from his recliner. "I want you to take a break," he said.

"No way," I replied. "This sandwich is *fantastic!* I'm not stopping until it's all in my belly."

His lips went tight for a moment, then he said, "You know what I'm talking about."

Oh, I knew, but I didn't want to get into it, so I didn't reply. Maybe if I ignored him, he'd stop. After all, how can you argue if you're the only one talking?

He watched me scarf the rest of the sandwich but didn't say another word as he waited for my answer. I took my time picking the crumbs off the plate, doing my best to not look at Justice.

"Mina?"

"Can't," was my only reply before I downed the chocolate milk. Maybe my one-word answer would stop the argument.

Like I'd be so lucky. Even before I'd opened my mouth I'd known it was wasted effort. Justice was raring for a fight, and by golly he was going to get one no matter what I did to prevent it.

"Yes, you can," he said. "You just *choose* not to."

I scowled at Justice. I wanted to say, "Like you *choose* to be a bossy, selfish, ass?" but I didn't. As good as it would make me feel right now, I knew it would just make things worse in the long-run, so I kept my mouth shut.

Part of me did understand his point of view, but the other part wanted *him* to understand *mine*. Sure, I hadn't been home much the last few days, but I had a lot of cases to take care of. A little understanding from my boyfriend shouldn't be too much to ask, should it? I never rode his ass when he came home after midnight at least three times a week. His job was important to him, and I respected that he took it seriously enough to see his projects through to the end. Even if it meant late nights and missed dinners.

But he couldn't seem to give *me* the same respect, even after I'd asked for it a hundred times in a hundred different ways.

The fact of the matter was, I shouldn't *have* to ask for respect. After all, respect is the one thing that should come stock in every relationship. And I certainly didn't feel like I should have to defend myself from his self-righteous and hypocritical onslaught every time I didn't meet his expectations or do exactly as he told me to.

I'd mentioned all of this more times than I cared to remember. He just never listened. Things were his way, and *only* his way.

I was tired of arguing. I was tired of talking and not being heard. I was tired of a lot of things. But I didn't want to fight.

"Justice," I said, "I'm beat. I'll pencil you in for tomorrow night and we can have a nice verbal brawl over it then, okay?"

Timothy piped up then and said, "He's right. You're working yourself into the ground. You're gonna have another breakdown if you keep it up."

I was surprised by Timothy's words. Surprised and hurt. He wasn't usually one to butt in. And really, he had no place to talk.

That's right! The naysayer whispered. *All Timothy ever does is eat your food and spend your money and live in* **your** *house, feeding off of you like a two hundred pound parasite.*

Normally, I'd have ignored that nagging, negative voice in the back of my head, but tonight, we agreed.

And what does he give back? The naysayer asked. *Some mediocre house-keeping? A dry sandwich now and then?*

Yeah. No kidding.

What makes him think he has any right to talk?

Glaring at Timothy, I slammed the empty glass on the coffee table and wiped my mouth on my sleeve. As I stood, I said, "I'm pretty sure I don't need a leech to tell me when I should take a break."

He frowned, but said, "You've just been gone a lot the last week. I'm. . . I'm worried about you, and I think Justice is right."

My face grew hot and my hands shook. "When you get a job," I said, "and you actually contribute something to the household besides your carbon dioxide, then maybe you can make suggestions on how *I* should live. Until then, back the fuck off, Timothy."

Timothy dropped his eyes to his lap and began picking at his thumbnail.

The naysayer laughed in my head, and said, *Why not go kick him in the gut while you're at it? Really drive your point home.*

Mortified with what I'd just said, and pissed at myself for actually listening to that voice in my head, I watched the pain cross Timothy's down-turned face, and my belly knotted up. Regret bubbled through me, but I'd reached my breaking point—tired, overworked, completely stressed, and at a loss for what to do about my caseload. Hell, I was at a loss for what to do about *anything* in my life these days, and coming home to be ganged-up on definitely didn't help.

Justice stared at me with golden eyes, probably expecting an apology for Timothy's sake. Like a coward I stormed out of the living room instead. I turned in to the bathroom and flicked on the light, then slammed the door behind me. Fuming and ashamed, but too stubborn to apologize for my hurtful words, I locked the bathroom door and quietly seethed.

Timothy has no right to tell you what to do when he's nothing but a mooch, the naysayer whispered.

No, he didn't do much to contribute, and I felt like I was raising a big kid most of the time, but I didn't have to be so hard on him either. He cared about me, and he was only trying to be helpful—misguided as he was. I'd been downright mean in response. My anger *should* have been directed at Justice, but Timothy had gotten in the way, and now I'd hurt his feelings.

"Dammit!" I said, slamming an open palm on the edge of the bathroom counter.

The naysayer laughed again, and I ground my teeth together, trying to push the sound out of my head.

"Dammit," I said again, softer.

Yeah, I felt bad for what I'd said to Timothy, but my little outburst wasn't the only reason I was suddenly feeling extra-crappy. Though they could have gone about it in a nicer manner, Timothy and Justice were right this time, and I hated it. I didn't hate that they were right, I hated that their *rightness* proved that I was weak.

I'd had a major breakdown a few months prior. But who could blame me? I'd broken down after contracting Lycanthropy during surveillance on a case, getting pregnant after my first act of consensual sex, then losing the baby because the bad guys tried to kill me. . . Twice.

Anyone would be entitled to an emotional collapse after all that. But because I'm me, my breakdowns can't just be about crying and drowning myself in multiple tubs of ice cream. No, when I have a breakdown, people get hurt. Or end up with a serious case of death. I'd nearly set an entire hospital on fire that day.

On purpose.

My anger bled away as I thought about what I could have done to the innocent people at the hospital. What I'd wanted to do if Justice hadn't been there to stop me.

You mean what you **should** *have done,* the naysayer whispered, *to make them all pay. Somebody should have to pay for the pain you've endured!*

I smacked the counter again and slammed an imaginary wall between my subconscious and my conscious mind. The mental wall and the pain in my hand silenced the words of the naysayer. For the time being, at least.

I leaned in close to the mirror over the sink, taking a long look at my ragged reflection.

The truth of what I'd done that day, and what *could* have happened, left me feeling raw, exhausted, lost. So why didn't I just do it? Why didn't I take some time off and deal with the personal issues I'd been ignoring? Lord knew I had enough of them screaming for attention, and avoiding them wasn't helping matters.

Staring into my own bloodshot eyes, I knew the answer.

If I took a break, who would take the cases nobody else would take? The cases the cops failed to solve because of underfunding and lack of manpower or community support. The cases so quickly forgotten on nightly newscasts in favor of the latest celebrity gossip or political scandal.

I was the last hope for worried parents and so many lost kids. If I wasn't there to take their cases, what would happen?

I knew the answer to that one too, and it was *not* an answer I was willing to accept.

I couldn't take a break because the faces of all those missing kids filled my head every time I closed my eyes. Every night my dreams were filled with their desperate cries for help. All my dreams were scenes of their demise all because I'd failed them.

A knock on the door sent tension across my shoulders and down my arms until I was gripping the sink edge.

"What?" I snapped.

"Can I come in?" Justice asked through the door.

Arms stiff, I dropped my head, watching my auburn curls pile in the empty sink. "Why?"

"Because I want to hold you."

"No."

The last thing I needed was comfort. The intimacy of that act, showing your weakness, depending on someone to care for you while your soul is torn wide open. . . It just left you vulnerable to ridicule and more pain.

No, I didn't *need* comfort and I didn't *want* it.

Besides, this wasn't really something Justice could help with, even if I'd wanted him to. He'd already shown me he didn't understand. Would another argument make him see my point of view, or just waste more of my breath?

The house was silent for a moment, and I thought Justice had actually respected my wish to be alone, until I felt a cool dampness around my ankles. I was immediately angry again. Jerking back from the counter, I stomped my foot through the swirling gray mist collecting along the floor. Backing a few steps next to the tub, I crossed my arms over my chest and glared down.

"You realize no means no, right?" I said, watching the mist churn around the floor, filling in the space my foot had recently occupied.

The mist continued to roll in from under the door, gathering along the floor, covering the white tile in shadows. Then it bubbled upward, growing darker as it rose. Seconds later the mist began to solidify, morphing into a thick black smoke. In a matter of heartbeats I was no longer looking at swirling shadows, instead, I was staring directly at Justice's bare chest.

In the real world, unlike bad fiction, clothes don't shift with you when you change forms. So, Justice stood before me, naked as the day he was born. For once, I was unmoved by the sight of him. I knew then that I was in a dark state of mind, because a naked Justice usually distracted me from whatever was making me angry in the first place. But with Justice being the *source* of my anger, I felt nothing but contempt when I looked at him.

"You can't run away from this," Justice said. As he took a step closer, he added, "Or me."

"I don't want to talk right now, Justice," I said. "Can't you just respect that?"

He'd heard me, but he didn't care. Instead of leaving the bathroom and giving me some time to think, he said, "Remember what Bernie told you?"

Scowling, I mumbled, "How could I forget?"

Bernie, my doctor, friend, and fellow Presence member, had been counseling me since I nearly torched his hospital. He'd warned me of the dangers of overexertion, especially this soon after my own near-death experience. The Fury, my most powerful gift, was dangerous and unpredictable at best, and it was a big part of the reason I'd cracked so bad in the first place.

Rule number one for those with the Fury was also an ominous warning: Each time you used the Fury to kill, no matter how justified, you'll lose a little more control over it.

Period. No ifs, ands, or buts. You'd keep losing control, and eventually the Fury would consume your every thought, control your every action until *you* no longer existed and only your Fury remained.

I didn't want to think about what would happen to me then. Certainly, I couldn't be allowed to roam free, but what Presence decided to do with me. . .

No, I didn't want to think about it.

I'd used my Fury several times to save my own skin, even after I knew the warnings. Unsurprisingly, I was already seeing a frightening change in my anger threshold. These days I was easily set off, mostly for stupid little things. They'd get me mad and Justice would have to knock me out with his mind-control gift. Oh, and you better believe he loved having *that* control over me. No, he never *said* he loved it, but I could tell.

So, to avoid that situation I'd tried to keep my anger in check on my own by holding it all in. But then my repressed anger just fed the Fury and it had begun eating away at me from the inside out. I'd ended up in a coma at one point because of it.

The bottom line for me was that no matter what I did, someone was getting hurt. It was an ugly, painful cycle that I couldn't break.

My job made it worse—the stress of always feeling like I should be working instead of sleeping or eating. But I couldn't abandon the kids. They needed me, and I *would* help them. Even if it meant destroying myself in the process. Maybe then my life would be worth something.

"Take a break, Mina," Justice said, taking another step closer. "Before it's too late."

I shook my head and glared at him.

"Killing yourself won't bring our baby—"

"Shut up," I said, tears already stinging my eyes. "How dare you?"

I gripped my upper arms tight, hugging myself to the point of pain. It wasn't fair to bring that up now. Not in the middle of a fight about something else. Besides, anything he said would just piss me off. I knew he blamed me. I could read it on him, Telepathy or not. The way he'd look at me. The way he'd been treating me lately. He blamed me for letting his baby die.

"Fine," he whispered, his voice harsh with emotion. After a few long moments, he said, "You can't be everybody's heroine."

"Yes, I can."

"Why does it have to be you?"

"Because. . ." I started to say *because it's my job*, but I stopped. It was so much more than that. But how to put it into words? How to make Justice understand why it was so important to me? Why I tried so hard.

"Because," I said at last, "there wasn't anyone there for me when I was little. Nobody came to my rescue no matter how many nights I cried into the pillow." I looked up at Justice, my eyes burning. "Every night I prayed for help before they could come and touch me again, but nobody ever saved me. . . So I prayed for death instead. No child should ever pray for that."

Justice swallowed hard but said nothing, a sad, haunted look in his golden eyes.

"Our—" I choked back the tears, cleared my throat, and said, "Our baby died because of people just like the ones that hurt me." I took a long, shaking breath and looked away, gazing at the small clouded window above the shower. "Those same people are out there right now hurting more kids. I can do something to be sure no other parent has to feel the anguish *I* feel every day. And I can make sure no other children feel the fear and the pain *I* felt for eighteen long years."

"But Presence will always help those children," Justice said.

I looked at him but didn't answer.

"We'll do it together. You don't have to do it by yourself, Mina. We'll help those kids, and we'll take the Congregation down."

I watched his face for a moment, unsure. Something had flashed there. Something unlike anything I'd ever seen on his face before, and I hoped I'd been mistaken.

"Okay, Mina?" he said softly. "We'll help the kids the Congregation is hurting. You, and me, and Presence, all together like we've always done."

And there it was again. A flash. A micro-expression

that sent shivers over my skin and formed a cold stone in my belly. There was no mistaking it.

"You're right," I said. "Presence will always ride to the rescue when gifted kids need help." Tipping my head a little to the side and focusing all my attention on Justice's face, I added, "But what about the ones that don't have gifts?"

He didn't answer, so I stared deep into Justice's eyes and pushed power into my own. I sent a wave of Insight into him and asked, "What about the mundanes? Will *you* risk your life for the kind of people who've shunned you your whole life, Justice?"

Again, he didn't speak, but he didn't need to. My Insight had found a tiny hole in his mental defenses, and I'd found what I needed to know. I watched him struggle to hide it, to patch the hole, but it was too late. I'd seen the truth and I was disgusted by it. Disgusted by *him*.

Justice wasn't willing to help the normal kids, and he didn't think I should either. Sure, he was ashamed. But he wasn't ashamed because he knew he was wrong. He was ashamed because I'd figured him out. He didn't want anyone to know about his prejudice because that would ruin the perfectly benign appearance he'd worked so hard to craft for himself. The gentle, loving appearance everyone had believed was the truth.

Even me.

Hurt and angry, I pushed away from Justice. "You bastard," I said, my voice going rough. "*You* won't help the mundane kids, whether you're man enough to admit it out loud or not. And Presence does what you tell them to, always without question because you made everyone believe you are so benevolent. But it's a lie. How can you—" I shook my head, struggling with the thought. "How can you *be* that way?"

Justice said nothing, and my anger spiked.

"What if our baby had been mundane?"

Again, nothing.

I shook my head again, harder this time, my stomach turning over, my heart breaking. Surely I was mistaken. My emotions were running too high to see things clearly. I'd misunderstood his look, I'd misread the silence, I'd misinterpreted my Insight. If I gave him a chance to explain himself, he'd set me right and I could stop feeling this growing anger toward the man I loved.

"Tell me I'm wrong," I whispered. "Tell me I'm way off base. Tell me you aren't heartless and selfish like your brother was."

Justice shook his head, his brows coming together. "Can't you see the stress you're causing yourself?" he said. "You're not making any sense. You need a break, Mina."

Skirting the issue wasn't going to fly this time. Ignoring my questions wasn't an option.

"I can't take a break. I can't, because if I take a break to appease you, *who* will save the mundane kids?"

Again he said nothing, but that look flashed across his face once more, igniting my anger again.

"Answer me, dammit!" I shouted, smacking his chest with both hands. "Who'll save them if it isn't me?"

He grabbed my wrists to stop the next blow. "I don't know, Mina," he said. "Somebody will."

I shook my head and pulled my arms loose from his grip. I'd heard the words come out of his mouth, but I just couldn't believe them.

Turning away, I said, "That's not good enough. I can't stand around and wait for *somebody* to fix it. It's not just my *job*, it's my reason for living. I didn't survive just so I could sit back and pretend decades of torture never happened." I turned on him and sneered. "Thanks to this little discussion, I know I can't depend on *you* to stick your neck out for the normal children in need, so that means I have to work harder to pick up *your* slack."

My head throbbed and I felt dizzy. My world was crashing down around me again, and there was nothing I could do to stop it.

Justice went quiet. His gaze skittered over my face several times. Finally, his expression softened and he said, "All right, Mina."

I tried to read him, but got nothing. He'd put his mask back on, that caring, understanding mask of lies. And he'd sealed up the mental wall between us so my Insight stayed silent.

Acting like nothing had happened, he nodded and gave a sad smile, reaching to brush the hair back from my face. "I support you in whatever you decide to do."

"Pretty words," I said, drawing away from his touch.

Standing in my bathroom, staring up into his face, I realized Justice wasn't at all the man I'd thought he was. Though he professed understanding and empathy and fairness for all, he truly held hate in his heart for those not like him. He was no different than the mundanes who hated the gifted simply for *being* different.

FIVE

~~

Bottomless tranquility embraced me in beautiful nothingness as I floated. Warmth. Gentle, calming caresses from invisible hands. Only the faint murmur of a man's voice whispered in my head, keeping me company as I drifted. It was the most relaxing, wonderful feeling, until the screech of the phone jerked me back to consciousness.

I was alone in bed, buried under a jumble of disheveled blankets, bright sunlight coming in through the open window. The phone rang a second time, and, still groggy from my interrupted dream, I struggled to free myself from the tangled covers. I shrugged into my bathrobe and looked for the phone as it rang again. Someone had taken it out of the bedroom.

Grumbling, I opened the bedroom door and moved down the hall toward the piercing sound. I didn't want to talk to whoever was calling so early, I just wanted the noise to stop.

Just as I reached for the phone on the coffee table, Justice came around the kitchen corner with the other cordless receiver to his ear. I flopped into my recliner and glanced at the wall clock.

Nine-fifty a.m.

Anger rushed through me like a flash-fire, setting my skin aflame and my heart pounding. *Someone* had turned off my alarm clock, and now I was late for work. Timothy would never do something that stupid, and I knew that *I* hadn't done it. I glared at Justice.

He didn't notice the searing look as he tapped his fingers on the wall and looked out the living room window.

"Well, I think it can wait," Justice said into the phone. He paused, tapped his fingers harder, then said, "Fine, I'll tell her." Then he hung up the phone and looked at me. "Beckett needs to see you. He claims it *cannot* wait."

"I guess *he's* not the one who turned off my alarm clock then," I said, narrowing my eyes.

Justice pursed his lips and glared back. "If *you* won't take care of you, then *I* will."

"Because you know what's best for me, right?"

Justice didn't answer.

"It doesn't matter what's important to *me*, does it, Justice? It only matters what *you* want. What *you* think is best."

Justice looked at me for a few heartbeats, then tossed the receiver onto the couch and walked back into the kitchen. As he turned the corner, he said, "Why are you so upset? It's not like I killed *your* brother or anything."

For a moment I just sat with my mouth agape.

The sheer cruelty of those words drove daggers into my heart. Yes, his twin brother had died by my hand. But Vincent had killed hundreds of innocent people for his own selfish wants. He'd died because he'd been consumed by evil. In fact, Justice himself had been a long-time victim of his brother's greed. Vincent had spent decades draining Justice's energy, his power, his very life just to boost his own. By Justice's own words I'd done the world a favor by ridding it of that infection. And now Justice comes at me, acting as if I'd killed a saint, murdered his best friend?

Minutes passed in stunned silence as his words burned through my brain, leaving an ashy trail of regret, guilt, and pain.

The clock struck ten, and Justice came around the corner, his head lowered and his shoulders drooping.

"I'm sorry, Mina," he muttered. "I didn't mean it."

Tears in my eyes, I shook my head. Sorry didn't cover it. Not this time. It wasn't the first hurtful thing he'd ever said to me, and I suspected it wouldn't be the last.

"You make me so crazy," he said. "You make me say these. . . stupid things."

I made him say stupid things? It was *my* fault that he'd turned into an ass?

Before I could comment, Justice continued. "I'm just frustrated. If I don't try to help you, I feel like I've failed you."

Help me by saying the cruelest thing possible? *Help* me by using guilt to get his way? I thought all that, but all I managed to say was, "Help me?"

"I know you want to work, but I know you need to rest and take some time. And *I* want to see you more. Is it so wrong to want to see you here when I come home each night?"

I gaped at him, once again speechless. He was completely unaware of how his words were coming across. How could he not see how selfish he was being?

"I'm torn," he continued. "Knowing what you want versus what I know is right. It's just hard to make the right decision."

I gave a sharp, unhappy laugh. "Justice," I said, "you don't see me."

He glanced up with a puzzled look. "I see you just fine."

Shaking my head, I said, "You don't *see me*, because I don't fit."

His brows came together and he frowned. "I don't understand."

For a moment I just looked at him, wondering how to explain what I was thinking in a way that wouldn't cause another fight. I'd been doing a lot of that lately, walking on eggshells to try and appease Justice or to avoid making him angry.

It was time to stop. My thoughts and feelings were just as important as his, and if that made him angry, that was *his* issue, not mine. I couldn't be held responsible for his reactions, and I couldn't keep denying my own feelings for the sake of peace in the household.

I said, "You painted a mental picture of your perfect world. But instead of adding *me* to the canvas when we met, you've been trying to squeeze me into the lines you drew all that time ago."

He shook his head, still not getting it.

"I can only be me, Justice. I can't be the person you're trying to force me to be."

"Cant?" he asked. "Or *won't?*"

And he stood there, defiant, unable to see he'd just proven my point for me.

~~

I didn't feel any better after sleeping in, and I knew it wasn't because I'd gotten too much sleep. I'd missed my appointment with Missy Edwards' mother because of that little adventure. It didn't bug me that I looked unprofessional to one of my clients. It bothered me that, thanks to Justice's meddling and the ensuing fight, now I didn't have a writing sample to compare to the note Evan Johansson's mother found in her son's bag.

"Thank you for coming, Mina," Beckett said as I dropped into my chair in the meeting room under Page's Pages. "I'm sorry to bother you, but I thought you might like to hear this in person."

"What's up?" I asked.

"I didn't make it to the antique show yesterday," Beckett began, "so I went early this morning."

I didn't comment, nod, or react in any way as he spoke. If he'd brought me all the way down here to talk about the damn antique show, I was going to be pissed. Just another needless delay in getting my hands on that writing sample. Did these people not understand that time was not our friend? Trails go cold very quickly when kids disappear, and it had already been days since the teens had gone missing. I'd be lucky to find bodies at this rate.

Beckett ignored the seriously unhappy look I shot him, and continued his story. "I was stopped by one of the vendors while browsing his offerings. He was quite. . . miffed. It seems this collector recently sold some items to a Mr. Bragg."

I shrugged and said, "So? What's all this got to do with *me*?"

"The collector asked for you by name."

"Why?" I asked. "I don't even *like* antiques."

"He thinks you can help him."

"Help him how? All these short answers aren't clearing things up for me. What's going on?"

"He believes Mr. Bragg is a threat. That, of course,

piqued my interest. So, once I returned to HQ, I did some research and I uncovered some interesting information on Mr. Bragg. Apparently, he *has* been under suspicion for several murders in recent months."

I rubbed a hand over my face. "I still don't see how this is important to us, Beckett, and I have some really pressing business to take care of."

"Perhaps if you *listened*, it would make sense and you would understand why I called you." His tone hadn't changed at all, and his words weren't terribly harsh, but my brain tingled and my fingertips felt hot. My Insight told me that my attitude might be getting on Beckett's nerves.

Part of me didn't really give a rat's ass if Beckett was annoyed with me. I had every right to be upset about how my day had started and the fact my investigation was being hindered at every turn. But, in all fairness, he *was* right. It wasn't really his fault I was cranky this morning, and Beckett never called me at home unless it was important.

I sighed and slumped down into the seat, giving Beckett all my attention.

Beckett nodded once. "As I was saying, Mr. Bragg has been under suspicion for murder, but the authorities have yet to prove he's done anything wrong. The collector contacted me because he's worried *he* will be blamed, at least in part, should anything else happen."

"How could this collector be blamed unless he had something to do with it?" I asked. "There's no reason to feel guilty unless you've done something wrong."

"I asked the collector that very question. He believes that the items he sold to Mr. Bragg could be considered dangerous weapons."

I squinted my eyes. "Who *is* this collector and what on earth did he sell to Bragg?"

Beckett's face split into a smile that showed straight

white teeth, and his eyes twinkled when he said, "The collector is none other than our dear Mr. Boad."

That name sent an icy shudder through my body. Mr. Boad was the man responsible for my kidnapping and torture on two separate occasions not so long ago. Granted, at the time, he'd been under a kind of spell, being coerced to do someone else's bidding. But the one in control had simply said to get an item from me. The torture had been all Boad's idea. Once the spell had broken and he'd realized how he'd been manipulated, Boad had fled the state, and we hadn't heard from him since. It wasn't entirely his fault how everything had turned out, but he wasn't exactly a good guy either.

"So," I said, trying not to let my hatred for the man leak into my voice. "Boad is back, and he's contacted *us*. To what end, exactly?"

Beckett nodded. "I was surprised myself," he said, then added with a grin, "He did ask that I not let Zia know his location."

Zia was one of our less-friendly operatives, and the one responsible for the spell that coaxed Boad to hurt me in the first place. She'd been searching for Boad ever since he got away from her. Apparently, Zia wanted her puppet back, but Boad wanted to be as far from the woman as he could get.

I didn't blame him. *I* certainly didn't like being around Zia. But I liked being around Boad even less. As far as I was concerned, putting those two in a room together and letting them fight it out sounded like a great way to get a little payback for the shit I had taken from both of them.

A smile curled my lips and I asked, "You gonna tell her where Boad is?"

"It has crossed my mind," Beckett said. "If Zia asks me directly, I will not be able to lie to her. You know how she can be. However, I will do my best to avoid her until we get this sorted out for Mr. Boad."

"*For* Mr. Boad?" Sitting back in the chair, I folded one leg up and put my foot under me. "Why should we do anything *for* him?"

"I thought you might balk at the idea."

"So you came up with a story to convince me?"

Beckett rubbed his smooth chin and smiled. "If you choose to see it that way. . . Things *did* happen as I described, but really, this is not about how it all started. It is not about Boad or Bragg or even *you*. I believe by helping Boad, we'll be helping society as well."

I rolled my eyes and said, "How so?"

"If Jeff Bragg is responsible for these murders, catching him will be doing a service to the general public by removing a threat. If Bragg is behind bars, he can't hurt anyone else."

I narrowed my eyes for a heartbeat, then shook my head with a small smile. "Well played, sir," I said with a tip of my head. "Fine. We'll look into it. I'd rather remove a threat before it escalates. But not *for* Boad."

Beckett smiled. He'd won, and he knew it, but he was too much of a gentleman to rub that in my face. Points for Beckett. *I'd* have rubbed it in *his* face if the roles had been reversed.

"So what items did Boad sell to this guy?" I asked.

"A small trinket box, supposedly cursed by its former owner to bring death to whomever opens it; a mirror said to show the viewer a glimpse of the future at the price of one year of his life; a locket said to have an angry spirit attached to it; and a book of questionable origin. All have a loose, unfounded history as far as I can tell."

I laughed. "It sounds like Boad has gotten paranoid since dealing with Zia. None of the items sound like anything we have documented. Sounds more like superstitious crap or sideshow gaff to me."

Beckett nodded once. "Perhaps, but I think we should find Mr. Bragg and speak with him ourselves."

"When you say, *we*," I said, "I assume you mean *me?*"

Beckett smiled again. "You *are* the private eye."

~ ~

Bragg didn't seem to be hiding at all. Usually, if one is guilty of murder, they do their best to blend in or disappear completely. But Bragg hadn't even used an alias when he'd applied to rent the tiny apartment on the far east side of downtown Port Orchard. His building was nearest the road, and his bedroom window overlooked Bay Street and all the shops along the water.

Movies often make a private investigator's job look exciting and sometimes even glamorous. But the reality of my job was that I got to hide in cramped places and watch people from afar for hours on end before I got a shred of useful information. This wasn't the first time I'd been crouched behind a bush all morning.

It hadn't occurred to me when I'd first picked this spot between the stone bench and the prickly False Cypress that I could have just planted my ass on the bench and pretended to read a book. Of course, my back would have been to Bragg's apartment and I'd have to turn around frequently to hopefully catch a glimpse of him—which would then look suspicious and not very detective-like. But at this moment my burning thigh muscles weren't listening to reason, and my hunched and aching spine agreed with my legs.

A steady flow of pedestrian traffic had prevented me from getting out of the bush for the last hour, and when I finally saw a break in the action, it was too late. Before I could take advantage of the lull in foot traffic and get out of the bush without being seen, Bragg emerged from his apartment building.

There were no clear pictures of Jeff Bragg from what Beckett had found during his limited research, but I suspected it was Bragg who stuck his head over the banister and gazed down the street. His small eyes darted back and forth as he cautiously descended his stairs. The further down the stairs he came, the more I realized how unsteady he looked with limbs too long and spidery for his tall frame. And when the cloud-filtered sunlight hit him at the bottom of the stairs, I saw he was almost sickly pale, though the center of each cheek had a faint blush. Sandy blond hair topped his head, and a thin, hooked nose was his most prominent feature. Not ugly, but nothing you'd turn to watch walk away either. Jeff Bragg was utterly average.

Bragg stepped into the parking lot next to his apartment building, looking side to side and intently watching passers-by if they so much as glanced his direction. He inched his way to a rusted blue hatchback and inspected the inside through the windows. Then he squatted and looked under the car. A moment later he stood and unlocked the driver's side door, got in, and drove away from town.

I frowned from my place behind the bush, looking through the branches at the spot his car had been parked in. Maybe he *was* guilty of something. His behavior certainly wasn't normal. Then again, maybe he was just naturally paranoid. I'd been wrongly accused of murdering my abusive stepfather more than a decade earlier. I was innocent, but sometimes I still felt like the blaming eyes followed me down the street. Could I blame Bragg for being cautious when I often felt the same anxiety? But even with my own deep paranoia, I didn't expect an ambush whenever I walked out my front door, or *paparazzi* hiding in the backseat of my car.

Guilty or innocent? The jury was still out on Jeff Bragg as far as I was concerned, and I didn't think I'd get a verdict by watching his empty apartment all day.

I stayed in my position across the street for half an hour more thanks to a new wave of window shoppers. Just as I was beginning to think I'd never walk upright again, Bragg returned. He got out of the car looking rather disheveled, a package under his arm. His clothes were rumpled, his hair an unkempt mop, and his eyes were wide like he'd been surprised earlier and was still shaking off the effects. He went up the stairs to his apartment and shut the door with a loud *bang*.

A moment later someone walked by with a cheeseburger in hand. My stomach growled as the smell wafted past me, and I fought an urge to tackle the man for his tasty prize.

Just as I was about to climb out of the bush and face the questioning glances of the lunchtime walkers, Bragg came back out of his apartment, clothes straightened, hair combed, and a book in one hand. He went through his paranoid routine with the car, then walked across the street toward me.

I ducked further behind the bush as Bragg walked past. He paused, and I thought I'd been caught. But all he did was turn slightly to the right so I could see his profile partially blocked by one thin shoulder. He put the book under his arm and then continue to walk to the deli on the corner.

I gave him a good ten minutes to settle in, then I stood and stretched, ignoring the startled looks of the Bay Street shoppers. My cramped legs screamed in protest, but it felt damn good to be standing again. After loosening my muscles as best I could, I strolled toward the sandwich shop, acting as if it wasn't strange at all to emerge from behind a bush in the middle of a busy sidewalk.

Jeff Bragg sat in the booth farthest from the door, his book and half a sandwich on the table in front of him. I kept my eye on him as I ordered my sandwich and a small soup to go. He didn't look up at anyone as they passed, and he didn't look out the window. He just stared at his sandwich as if it were his only link to reality.

Maybe it was.

He jumped and almost choked on his sandwich when I sat across from him in the booth. His mouth opened in a little O of surprise when he finally focused his pale eyes on me. He studied my face for a few heartbeats and then swallowed.

"Hi, I'm Mina." I offered my hand across the table.

He blinked at my hand, dropped the half of his sandwich he'd been holding, wiped his hands on his pants, and then shook my hand.

"I'm. . . Jeffrey."

His palm was warm and sticky, and a nervous tremble vibrated his whole arm. I could feel the frail bones of his hand under mine, and I wondered if he realized how easily I could crush them. Did he sense my energy? Was he sensitive or gifted and could tell I wasn't a normal human?

I looked hard at his light blue-green eyes, searching for some spark of recognition, some hint of fear. But I saw nothing to indicate he was anything special at all.

"Nice to meet you, Jeff," I said.

His cheeks went red and he said, "Jeffrey, please."

"All right, *Jeffrey*. I noticed you're new in town," I said. "Thought I'd introduce myself and give a nice warm welcome to Poor Tortured."

"Poor. . . *Tortured?*" he asked, his head cocked to one side and brows drawn together in worry.

I laughed and said, "Yeah, that's just my pet name for Port Orchard."

Jeffrey eyed me suspiciously. Was it because he didn't like me or that he had no sense of humor? Or did he sense something now? What should I say next? I was never very good with people, especially people suspected of murder.

Jeffrey's social skills were worse than mine. Without another word, he looked down at his plate and started eating again like I wasn't even there. I watched him eat for several minutes. He didn't look up once.

"Well, I won't annoy you any longer," I said, collecting my lunch and preparing to leave. "I just wanted to welcome you to town."

His head snapped up then. His eyes looked hollow. His sudden change in demeanor surprised me, and I froze in place, tightening the grip on my lunch sack.

"Don't you want to stay?" he asked quietly.

At his words I felt a warmth touch my finger tips. A moment later the warmth began to creep up my hands like hot rolling honey, moving up my arms, slow, sticky, and thick. Jeffrey's haunted, pale eyes stayed on my face, and I was stuck, as if the warm honey-feeling somehow held me in place.

"I—" I had to swallow before I could speak again. "I guess I could stay for a little while."

And suddenly I was just sitting. I didn't remember doing it, and I didn't even really *want* to, but there I was, sitting across from that pallid, thin man.

Bragg smiled and it didn't look right. It didn't look natural, like something was sitting just under his skin, pulling the strings to make that crooked, eerie grin. He ate his sandwich, sipped his drink, and watched me with that twitchy, almost joyous expression.

All I could do was watch him back. It was like my whole world stopped and only Jeffrey Bragg remained. Only Jeffrey Bragg was moving and important and real.

The thick, creeping honey moved slowly along my skin. It reached my elbows and I shuddered, but not from fear or worry. Creepy as my lunch companion was, the sensation on my arms wasn't entirely bad. Bragg smiled and took another drink. The warmth crept up to my shoulders and an involuntary sigh escaped my lips. No, definitely not bad. The warmth went deeper than just my skin, deeper than my muscles. The heat moved into me, straight to my core, relaxing and warming me. But when the hot, invisible ooze began moving up my neck, tightening around my throat, I panicked.

It was that panic that helped me snap out of the trance, or whatever it was. I stood up and forced a smile back in place. I welcomed him to town again, and then almost ran out of the deli. As I scrambled by the shop, I glanced in the window, only to find Bragg looking right at me, smiling.

SIX

~~

The numbers on the microwave counted down, and I watched my container of soup turn round and round, the receiver of my phone pressed against my ear. It had taken me ten minutes on foot to get to my office from the sandwich shop. Normally it took me twenty.

"Detective Richards; speak," came the voice on the other end of the line.

"I know this is gonna sound crazy," I said.

"Everything coming out of your mouth sounds crazy to me, Ms. Jewel."

I ignored the jab and cleared my throat. "Jeffrey Bragg came into town a couple nights before Walter Garrot's heart blew up."

"And you think Mr. Bragg had something to do with Garrot?"

"I'm pretty sure he did."

"And how did you come to this conclusion?"

Detective Richards sounded suspicious, and for good reason. Most of the time I had concrete proof before I called him, but I wasn't willing to get any closer to Bragg in order to get it this time.

"He bought some items from a collector I know," I said. "The guy got spooked after he found out Bragg was in some trouble, so he called me and asked if I could look into it for him."

"What does Bragg's history have to do with your collector friend?"

I paused, knowing the reaction I'd likely get. There wasn't really any other way to say what I was thinking though, so I just blurted out, "The collector thinks the items are cursed."

"Uh-huh. . ." Detective Richards said, and I heard his interest begin to slip away.

"But there isn't any proof," I continued. "Really, it's a long story you'd never believe, and it isn't important anyway. What's important is that I was checking Bragg out to make sure he wasn't up to anything."

"And?"

"He gives me the creeps."

There was a pause, and then, "You're basing your allegations on the fact this guy gave you *the creeps*?"

"Fine," I said, my cheeks going hot. "That sounds really lame when you say it that way. How about, I'm basing it on the fact he was able to make me do something against my will?"

Detective Richards went quiet again. I heard his breathing shift before he asked, "He forced you to do something? Was he armed?" Then he added softly, "Are you okay?"

"No," I said, shaking my head even though I knew the detective couldn't see me through the phone. "I mean, yes," I added quickly. "Yes, I'm fine. No, he wasn't armed. But he didn't need to be armed. All he had to do was tell me to sit down, and I did it. It was like. . ." I shrugged, staring at the soup still spinning in my microwave. "It was like Dr. Goodson described in her statement. Only this wasn't a bad feeling, and that's the part that creeped me out. It was crawling, whatever it was, but it wasn't bad."

"Dr. Goodson didn't like what she felt. How can you say Mr. Bragg is responsible for this when what you felt was pleasant and what Goodson felt was. . . unsavory?"

"I never said it was pleasant. I said it wasn't bad."

He paused again, and I could hear a pencil scratching on paper. "All right," he said after a few moments, "lets say I believe you. Bragg had something to do with Walter Garrot's murder. . ."

I turned away from the microwave, glad he wasn't pushing the whole pleasant versus not bad issue. I pressed my back against the counter, folding my arms across my stomach. With the phone cradled between my cheek and shoulder, I said, "Yeah?"

"What does he get out of murdering Garrot?"

"What do you mean, Richards?"

"What's the connection?" he asked. "What's his motive?"

"Motive?"

"There *has* to be a motive, Ms. Jewel."

It was too ridiculous. I chuffed into the phone. "You're asking about motive when the method of murder is so far out of the norm?"

"With the method of murder so far out there, we need to find some solid, *normal* link to help the case gain credibility. Without motive, this is going to be a nightmare to prosecute."

A loud *bang* sounded in the room. Reflexes made me

hit the floor, arms going over my head protectively. After a period of lung-bursting breath-holding, I heard a tinny voice above my head.

"Ms. Jewel? Ms. Jewel!"

I still had the receiver in my hand squeezing it above my head as if to use it to protect me from the blast.

I stood up and put the phone to my ear. "Yeah, I'm here." I popped the microwave door open. "Damn."

"What? What happened? Is everything okay? What was that noise? Talk to me."

"I forgot to take the lid off. Just a sec."

I placed the phone on the counter by the microwave and grabbed a paper towel. My unattended soup had boiled too long. The steam had collected and finally blown the air-tight lid right off when I wasn't looking. Bits of noodles and shreds of chicken dropped from the ceiling of the microwave and plopped into the shallow pool of broth oozing out the door. Little bits of carrot stuck to the door like bright bits of raw flesh.

I frowned and stared at the carrots. A second later I snatched up the phone.

"Get someone down to the morgue and look for any signs of heating in Walter Garrot's chest," I said.

"That's a little out of left field, don't you think? Even for *you?*" Richards replied.

"Just do it," I said, and hung up the phone before he could protest.

~~

Oliver Page tottered about the meeting room, placing a plate of cookies and a cup of something steamy in front of each of us gathered there. His shiny bald spot reflected the dim light of the room, and his thinning, rust-colored hair looked especially wild, as if he'd scratched his head and forgotten to pat the fuzz back down. He smiled as he squinted over his round, wire-framed glasses. Stress and worry never seemed to touch Oliver. His appearance and demeanor reminded me of a kindly grandpa handing out after-school snacks. Of course, I'd never known any of my grandparents, so maybe it was just wishful thinking that they all acted this way.

"So," Justice said, "you believe we've got some kind of gifted murderer?"

I nodded, took a bite of sugar cookie, and leaned back in my chair. "Yeah, looks that way. Only problem is, I can't prove it. Not without spilling the secret of Presence, that is."

"Well, we don't want to do that," Timothy said. He'd already eaten four of his cookies and was shoving the fifth in his mouth by the time Oliver had finished serving the treats to everyone else.

"I'm certain there's a way to get information without exposing ourselves," Beckett offered. His cookies remained untouched on the table in front of him. "Perhaps Mr. Bragg just needs to feel secure, safe. Maybe one of us should become his *friend*."

"Why?" Timothy asked, as he reached across the table and snatched a cookie off Beckett's plate.

"Friendship opens the door for trust," Beckett said, pushing his plate closer to the grinning werewolf. "And trust often makes people want to confide in you."

"He's got some kind of connection with you already, Mina," Justice said. "Are you willing to go in closer and get more information for us?"

I scowled at Justice. I'd already told him in private that I didn't want anything else to do with Bragg. I'd told him the guy made me uncomfortable, and I didn't want to risk a repeat of that warm, sticky, suffocating power. That wasn't enough, apparently.

Justice made it look like he was just doing his job as our leader, delegating tasks and all that, but I knew better. This was his way of being controlling without actually appearing that way to others. He'd been doing it all along, subtly, and until recently I hadn't noticed. I saw it now, but I was the only one who'd caught on to his games. I also knew that if I said anything to anyone else they'd simply dismiss it. Worst case, they'd accuse me of imagining things or overreacting. I'd already spent more than half my life doubting what I was seeing or feeling. I didn't need to start that crap again.

"Yes, I think that is the best plan," Justice added without my input. "If we could get enough to pin the murder on Bragg, Presence wouldn't have to risk detection."

It would be easier just to kill him, the naysayer whispered.

"Can't we just get rid of Bragg and leave the cops out of it?" I asked.

"That's very unlike you, Mina," Oliver said, and it sounded almost scolding.

I was instantly ashamed of myself. I shot Oliver a dirty look, found I couldn't stay mad at him, then sighed.

"Leave the cops out of it?" Justice asked. "Or leave *you* out of it?"

Narrowing my eyes at Justice, I said, "I really don't want to get near that guy again. He's fucking creepy."

"Just block him out, Mina. We know you're good at blocking things out."

Bringing our personal issues to a business meeting wasn't very mature, and I wasn't going to be the one to look like a child in front of our co-workers. Besides, it wasn't any of their business. It was bad enough that Timothy knew what was going on at home, I didn't need all of Presence butting in, too.

"Whatever Bragg does," I said, "it doesn't feel like regular gifts. There's something wrong with him." Goosebumps tingled on my arms and neck at the thought of that warm, smothering energy.

Justice stared at me, his golden eyes cold.

Oliver looked from me to Justice, a curious expression on his face. Instead of commenting on our behavior and Justice's snippy remarks he said, "What if I came with you, Mina? I could stay close and use my Insight to get a look at Mr. Bragg's inner workings." He smiled kindly, then added, "You wouldn't have to be alone then. Perhaps that might ease some of your anxiety, knowing a friend is nearby."

It was a good idea, but the thought of getting near Jeffrey Bragg again made my nose wrinkle. It wasn't just that odd energy he let off, it was the way he almost seemed like two different people sharing one body.

Everyone watched me, waiting for an answer. No pressure, right?

I sighed. "Fine, I'll do it."

~~

As it turned out, I didn't have to approach Bragg at all. The next morning he walked right into Oliver's shop. I happened to be there dropping off a borrowed journal when Bragg came in. He glanced around the shop, saw me, gave a nervous smile, then walked toward Oliver's desk. I tried not to look surprised to see him and instead made myself look busy flipping through books at a nearby table.

"Are you Oliver Page?" Bragg asked quietly.

"Yes," Oliver said in his usual cheerful tone. "How

may I help you?"

Even with my back to them, I knew Oliver was giving his most innocent smile. Nobody ever suspected Oliver and his dusty little shop were the cover for a clandestine psychic organization. Damn, he was good.

"I've got a book here," Bragg said. "Kinda weird, and I really don't think. . . I mean to say, I don't. . ." Bragg cleared his throat and said quickly, "I shouldn't even be here."

"Did you want me to look at your book, sir?" Oliver asked.

Slowly, I made my way around to the far side of the table so I could see Oliver and Jeffrey out of the corner of my eye. Jeffrey's eyes were constantly moving, glancing at the front door and then to the back of the shop.

"Yeah, can you look at it for me? Tell me something about it?" More rapid glances around the room, a nervous hand playing along his smooth cheek.

"I'd be happy to," Oliver said brightly.

Jeffrey held the book out. When Oliver tried to take it, Jeffrey fixed him with a steady, intense gaze, like he was testing Oliver's will or strength or both. Oliver smiled and let go of the book. He folded his chubby hands in front of him on the desk and looked up at Jeffrey, who stood motionless, still holding the book out.

"My friend," Oliver said, "if you do not release the book, I cannot look at it. If I cannot look at it, it will be difficult to tell you anything about it."

Jeffrey seemed to shake himself awake. He shuddered once and rubbed his eyes with his right hand. Gritting his teeth, Jeffrey dropped the book on Oliver's desk and snatched his hand back, a light sweat shimmering on his forehead. His eyes never moved from the book even as Oliver reached for it, picked it up, and flipped it open.

While I busied myself with one of the journals on the table, I kept my eye on Jeffrey's face. I wanted to know what was in the book, but the way Jeffrey looked had me captivated. Why was he sweating? Why had it been so hard for him to let the book go? He wore the same crazed, frantic expression as when he'd been inspecting the backseat and underneath his car, and his clenched hands seemed to tremble with the effort not to pluck the book from Oliver's hands.

Oliver flipped through Jeffrey's book, an almost wistful smile on his face as his eyes scanned the pages. But I knew he wasn't paying attention to what he was reading. I knew he was taking a deeper look not at the stiff yellowed pages in front of him, but at Jeffrey himself. And if we were lucky, Jeffrey would remain clueless.

The soft hands of Oliver's Insight explored the shop, touching every corner, every inch of space in the room. He filled the room slowly so as not to spook Jeffrey with those gentle, invisible hands. Oliver's Insight was like the memory of warm water lapping around your ankles, then your thighs, then up higher and higher until it covered you, and washed gently through your mind.

Jeffrey didn't flinch or look more frightened than he had to begin with. He didn't gaze around the shop or startle and look down at his feet to see if there really was tepid water flowing into the room. He kept his attention completely on Oliver and that book.

After a few quiet moments Oliver's power receded gently, leaving my skin tingling like the clean feeling after a hot shower. It was a good sign that Oliver didn't yank the power back. It meant he'd gone in and out of Jeffrey's head without incident, hopefully coming out with some answers for us.

Oliver continued to page through the book,

unchanging. To an outsider it would have appeared that the little old man had been reading the book the whole time, and nothing odd had happened at all. Well, except for the thin, frightened-looking man now chewing his finger nails and staring holes into the bald top of Oliver's head.

I made my way to the side of the table closest to Jeffrey, maybe five feet away. He didn't even glance up. All the better for me. I didn't want to talk to him. I just wanted to get a closer look. My own Insight was clumsy at best; I wasn't about to attempt what Oliver had done. Mine would have been more like a truck clattering around inside Jeffrey's skull. In my defense, I'd only been using Insight for three years compared to Oliver's fifty-plus. I definitely wasn't ready to sneak inside someone's head.

This close to Oliver's desk, I could hear the pages in Jeffrey's book as they turned, a whisper-soft scraping sound, like leaves in the fall brushing against one another as they drifted to the ground. I glanced at the book and was surprised at the position of Oliver's hand. Normally he would rest one palm on the open book, and fondle a page with his other hand, absently stroking the book as he read. But today he handled each page of Jeffrey's book gingerly as he turned it, held only between his thumb and forefinger, and his other hand rested on the table instead of the unread portion of the book.

Whisper-scrape. Another page turned, and I saw the material was stiff and strangely patterned. Light from the shop window passed through the aged material, making the page almost glow with a sallow light.

I shuddered, fighting a sudden urge to step away from Jeffrey and his strange book.

"It appears you've found yourself a treasure, Mr. . ."

Jeffrey snapped his eyes from the book to Oliver's face. "Bragg. Jeffrey Bragg," he said without taking his finger from his mouth. "What do you mean a treasure?"

Oliver smiled and closed the book carefully, handed it across the desk to Jeffrey, then folded his hands in front of him. "This is a very old book, Mr. Bragg. It contains myth versus truth on the Djinn."

"The what?" Jeffrey stopped chewing his nail and slowly lowered his hand to his side.

"The Djinn. More commonly known as 'the genie' to us Americans."

A glimmer of sweat appeared on Jeffrey's upper lip, and he wiped it away with the back of one hand. "Really?"

Oliver nodded pleasantly, completely ignoring the bead of sweat sliding down Jeffrey's temple and dropping onto the shoulder of his blue cotton shirt.

Page's Pages was always a nice comfortable temperature. Too much heat was bad for the ancient Presence journals, so Oliver always kept the shop cool. But now that I was thinking about it, the room did seem to be getting warmer, and there was no hint of that constant light breeze that usually blew in from the basement door leading down to Presence HQ. I looked at Oliver and frowned.

"Does it say. . . how to get rid of them?" Jeffrey asked. "I mean if they were real, which of course they aren't, I just mean for curiosity's sake. Did it mention how to. . . stop them?"

Before Oliver could answer, a hot breeze scrubbed against my skin, instantly drying my face and bare arms. The hairs on the back of my neck stood up, and the hairs on my forearms prickled, as if they all knew something awful was about to happen and they were going to get the hell out, with or without the rest of me.

Jeffrey turned toward me, his head moving painfully slow and jerky, like he was fighting it. His shoulders jolted violently and then his head snapped in my direction. He just looked at me, his expression blank. Another gust of hot air blew across my face, scorching hellfire straight into my lungs. I squinted against the wind, my face burning. Jeffrey's lips twisted into a sinister grin, and I knew in that instant that the burning wind was somehow coming from Jeffrey.

I swallowed, dropped the book I'd been thumbing through, and stared back. I wanted to run, my brain even *screamed* for me to run, but my legs wouldn't listen. Hot, sticky, invisible goo cemented my feet to the ground, rolled between my toes and up my ankles. Warm molasses moved up my legs, penetrating deep into my thigh muscles, relaxing and weakening them. I was powerless to move away. Up my belly, warming my stomach. Up my chest and enveloping my breasts, constricting my breathing, and I felt panic grip me once more. It would creep higher and higher like it had in the sandwich shop, holding me in place, preventing me from moving. And then it would creep up my neck, squeeze my throat, cover my face.

The naysayer screamed in my head, *You'll suffocate, you fool! Turn away, now!*

The panic in the naysayer's voice pulled me back into the moment. With hands over my eyes I spun away from Jeffrey. It didn't matter how weird it looked or even if I gave away the fact I knew he was up to something not natural, the naysayer was right. I *had* to look away. Something about Jeffrey's eyes. . . If I kept looking I'd be doomed.

The bell above the door jingled and I turned in time to see the back of Jeffrey's shirt as he turned left and jogged away from the shop.

With Jeffrey gone, the stickiness had left the room, and I could move my feet freely again. And though the air was starting to cool, my skin had turned a bright red and felt tender to the touch. I looked closely, only to find small blisters beginning to form on the backs of my hands.

Breathless, heart pounding, and scared half to death, I whispered, "What was that?"

Oliver rubbed his arms momentarily, then took off his glasses and rubbed his eyes with his fingertips. After he slipped the wire frames back on his nose, he looked up at me, his face as red as my arms, and said, "Mina, my dear, we have a problem."

SEVEN

~~

"The book Mr. Bragg brought in this afternoon is one I've never seen," Oliver said as he paced the meeting room. "Not in person, at least."

Justice, Timothy, Beckett and I sat around the table watching Oliver totter by, his red, chubby hands behind his back, wringing themselves into knots. I'd never seen Oliver this agitated. He'd always been the pillar of calm, even in our highest stress situations. Seeing Oliver this twitchy and uncomfortable added to my own bubbling anxiety.

I rubbed my arms and winced. Though I'd attempted to heal us both of the blistering from Jeffrey's wind, some of the redness and tenderness still remained. There would always be some kind of minor remnants of psychic healing —stiff joints, itchy skin, minor aches for a day or two—but to still feel pain of this level and have an obvious visible mark remaining? Something was definitely odd about Jeffrey Bragg and his powers.

"So what is this book, exactly?" Justice asked.

Oliver put a chubby hand to his red-mottled forehead. "It's a detailed account of myths and facts about the Djinn, just as I told Mr. Bragg. What I *didn't* tell him is it's written in something other than standard ink on paper that I'm almost afraid to guess its origin."

The sound of the whisper-scraping pages flitted through my memory and I shuddered. The question of the book's origin was at the forefront of my brain and my curiosity tried to prod me into asking, but this was one secret I really didn't need to know. I wrinkled my nose and grimaced.

Oliver nodded once at me and added, "I can safely say it contains power that a normal book should not."

"What does this mean for Presence?" Justice said.

Oliver continued his circuit around the table as he spoke. "It means we're going to have a mess to clean up. That book is primeval, ancient beyond anything I can even guess. And even more alarming is what I found inside Mr. Bragg's head."

The room was silent. The question was in the air, but none of us wanted to ask it. When none of us spoke up, Oliver said, "I do believe Mr. Bragg has been possessed by a Djinn."

I blinked once, slow and deliberate. "But they aren't real," I said, shaking my head. "They can't be real."

Justice raised his eyebrows. "The werewolf says the Djinn can't be real?" And he chuckled, though I didn't sense any humor from him.

"Fuck off, Justice," I snapped.

"Testy, testy, Mina," Beckett said.

His expression leaked concern, and I felt a tad guilty for my outburst, but I continued to scowl anyway.

Oliver looked from me to Justice, his brows coming

together in a little frown.

If nobody had known Justice and I weren't getting along before, they sure did now. Thankfully, nobody tried to pry.

"So does Mr. Bragg know he's possessed?" Beckett asked.

"Oh, yes," Oliver said as he nodded and tucked his hands inside the tiny pockets of his brown vest. "He knows, and he's not happy about it, but he feels powerless. I felt a strong presence of the Djinn and very little from Mr. Bragg."

"What does that mean?" I asked.

"That means, if I am correct, that Mr. Bragg is growing weaker as each day passes, and soon the Djinn is going to own his body."

"What happens to his. . ." I stumbled around for the right word, my hands flopping in front of me. "What happens to his *soul* if the Djinn takes over completely?"

"I'm afraid we lose Mr. Bragg. As for what happens to his soul, that depends on what you believe. Certainly now is not the time for a theological discussion."

"So basically, this Djinn is going to kill Bragg and steal his body?"

Oliver nodded. "In simple terms, yes."

"How do we get rid of it?" I said. "I mean, *can* we get rid of it without hurting Bragg?"

Oliver creased his brows and scratched his bald spot. "This is not something I'm terribly familiar with, Mina. I'm not at all certain what we *can* do."

"Well, shit."

"But all is not lost!" Oliver said, one finger raised. "I have a friend in Riyadh who can probably help us. I'll make the call after our meeting. In the mean time, I suggest we keep a close eye on Mr. Bragg, befriend him if we can."

"What good would that do?" I asked. "We already know he's possessed by a Djinn. How would befriending him help us now?" The thought of palling around with Bragg and his Djinn made me shudder.

"It would keep the Djinn close-by," Oliver said.

Rubbing my tingling arms I asked, "And that's a good thing, *how*?"

~~

Five p.m. found me climbing the worn concrete steps to Jeffrey's apartment. I wore a long, gauzy skirt, blue tank top, and a light-weight sweater. Oliver had chosen my clothes for me, saying the faded blue jeans and the black t-shirt with the flaming skull didn't look very inviting or friendly. Funny, that had been the point when I'd put them on before this little visit.

A stiff wind blew in from the Puget Sound making my hair flow around my shoulders and waist. It brought with it the crisp, tangy scent of the ocean, and I paused on the landing to breathe deep, clear my head, and center myself. I was supposed to be friendly and open. That was *so* not me, especially after Bragg's attempt to broil us alive in the shop today.

Jeffrey answered his door on the first knock, almost like he'd been waiting for me. Creepy. He popped his head and shoulders around the door and stared down at me with dull, disinterested eyes. I took a step back, out of arm's reach, just in case. He seemed to look me over for a heartbeat, then he stepped into his doorway and gave a nervous smile, his eyes suddenly bursting to life.

"Hi," Jeffrey said. Though he sounded nervous, he also gave off the excited, happy vibe of a little puppy waiting for a pat on the head.

He wiped his palms on his slacks and then extended his hand to me. I wanted to reject the handshake, but figured I'd better play nice or I'd screw this up for everyone. I shook his hand with as little skin-to-skin contact as I could manage, then I forced a smile.

"I was wondering if you'd like to join me for dinner?" I asked.

Jeffrey blinked once, glanced over his shoulder into his apartment, then looked down at me again. He swallowed hard and gave a crooked, faltering smile. "Me?"

"Who else you got hiding in there?"

He frowned, all the happy-puppy vibes suddenly gone. "What do you mean by that? There's nobody else here."

He reached behind him and pulled the door closed as he stepped out onto the narrow landing. His movement made us a little too close for comfort, so I took another step back.

My foot slipped, and I had enough time to think, *Oh shit,* before I tipped backwards.

In that split second before I really hurt myself, I can always see the event play out in my head like I've got all the time in the world. This time, I'd fall back and hit the second or third step, probably cracking my skull on the first impact. Then I'd tumble down and down, breaking different bones as I bounced off each step. Finally, I'd land in a crumpled heap at the bottom of the stairs, and they'd have to scoop me up with a shovel and carry me away in little plastic bags.

I was just starting to close my eyes and brace for the fall when I saw something that couldn't have been.

Jeffrey stepped forward, reaching out lightning quick to snatch my wrist. As he did so, a faint outline of himself stayed by his apartment door. It looked like it was scowling at me, arms crossed over its chest defiantly, eyes ablaze with contempt. Before I could blink, it was gone and Jeffrey was yanking me forward. He held my wrist until I was steady on my feet again, and I didn't pull away.

Breathless, speechless, and pretty damn shaken, I just blinked up into Jeffrey's pale eyes. He let go of my wrist and wiped his hand on his slacks again.

"You okay?" he asked.

I nodded. My heart thudded in my throat, and my mouth had gone dry. I searched his face for any sign of that second self, but there was nothing. Just plain old Jeffrey Bragg, complete with sandy tussled hair, rumpled clothes, and nervous, darting eyes.

He scratched his head and licked his lips. "So, uh. . . is that offer for dinner still on the table?"

~~

Dinner with Jeffrey had been blessedly uneventful. He only spoke to answer my questions or comment on the weather; we'd discussed springtime in Washington at least a dozen times. Even though I got the impression that Jeffrey *wanted* to be friendly I had to pry information out of him. It felt more like an interrogation than a relaxed conversation. I didn't even ask anything scary; it was all easy stuff like where he'd moved from—which I already knew was California since I'd researched him to begin with—or what kind of music he liked—Country and R&B.

All in all it had been a huge waste of my time, but Oliver was proud of me for trying, and Justice seemed pleased that I'd kept my smart-ass comments to myself. For the most part, at least. I made sure to tell Justice about the odd vision I had at the top of the stairs. Despite his dismissal of the whole thing and telling me it was nothing to worry about, it was still bothering me when I went to my office the next morning.

"Hey, Mina," Angie, my secretary and fellow Presence member said. "Alex needs to speak with you. He's all buzzy and hyped up about something."

"So, normal Alex?" I asked with a grin.

Angie smiled and nodded.

"All right, give me five minutes alone with my mug and then send him in."

I grabbed a cup of coffee from the pot in the lobby before I slipped through the door to my private office. I'd need a gallon of this stuff to handle Alex today. Not that his exaggerated and often jerky movements were truly annoying, it's just that I was still on edge from the previous day's events.

You'd think after being nearly killed so many times you'd get used to it, but you never really do. It wasn't just the close call that had me unraveled though. I was shaken from the vision. I'd never been one to see things like that. Could it be a new gift to add to my list? I hadn't had a new gift pop up in months. I'd even begun to think—hopefully —that I was done adding to my repertoire. But if it *was* a new gift, then what did it mean? How was I supposed to control it? How was I supposed to interpret it?

All those questions and one big fat concern. A gift like that didn't fit. All my gifts were somehow related. They all fit together into a neat little puzzle, one helping the others. Visions didn't fit any of the things I could already do. So what was going on?

Coffee steaming in front of me and a pile of files waiting to be read, I stared out the window in my office, pondering all of it, and finding myself nowhere near a suitable answer.

Alex knocked once then opened my office door and peeked in.

"Is it safe?" he asked, eyeballing my full coffee cup.

"I haven't even had a sip yet," I said. "If you enter, you do so at your own risk."

Alex came in and closed the door. He carried a green folder and his own cup of coffee. He sat across from me, set his mug down, and began pulling papers from the folder, setting them in a neat, straight line on my desk.

"These are all photocopies of notes for the party," Alex said with a single, heavy nod.

"I thought they all got texts?"

Alex shrugged. "I guess not."

"Huh," I breathed. "Well, whoever sent the notes maybe didn't want to be traced by using a cell phone?"

Alex nodded, his long bangs bouncing with the movement. "Makes sense."

"I'm not real great with math," I said as I eyeballed the line of notes, "but I do know there's more notes than missing kids."

"Yeah," he said. "Only six missing kids out of fifteen notes recovered. These other notes were taken from the kids who didn't go to the party."

"Why didn't they go to the party, and why didn't they come forward before?"

"Scared, I guess."

I glanced at the photocopies. "Where are the originals, Alex?"

"I gave them to the police." Alex looked up and shrugged. "I touched them all first and got as much as I could from them."

I cocked an eyebrow.

Alex sighed and rolled his eyes up. "And I didn't like trying to line up the crumpled papers. I photocopied them so they'd fit nicer in the folder." His pale skin went a deep red and he looked away.

I gave up the perfect opportunity to tease Alex in favor of getting the meeting over with. "All right, so we have a bunch of notes here for the party. They look like they all say the same thing, same crappy almost-English, same vague instructions."

Alex nodded.

"And because they all have the same vague instructions, that means these kids already knew where to meet. We can assume they'd been there before and just needed to know when to show up."

Alex nodded again.

"And let me guess," I said with a frown, "the kids who didn't go to the party are playing innocent and not telling the location?"

"Yeah."

"Did you ask around the neighborhoods where the kids live? See if anyone saw a group of teens walking around?"

"Do I look new to you?" Alex frowned. "Yes, I asked around, and nobody saw anything."

"Of course they didn't," I muttered. "Because that would make our lives that much easier."

I drained my coffee cup and wiped my mouth on the back of my hand. "Okay, what did you pick up off the notes?"

Alex straightened in his chair and began to bounce his left knee. "They were written by the same person. You're right that it was a female who wrote them, but she wasn't a student. I got the impression she was at least your age, mid-thirties—"

"Hey!" I reached across the desk and smacked Alex lightly on the forehead. "Thirty-three is not *mid-thirties*, thank you very much."

Scowling, he rubbed his forehead and said, "Fine,

early thirties then. Anyway, she isn't a kid and as far as I can tell she isn't an employee of the school either."

I waited, watching Alex. When seconds ticked by and he stayed quiet, I asked, "That's it?"

Alex put his hands out to his sides, palms up, and shrugged. "What else did you expect?"

"Usually, you give me a detailed description of our perp, right down to a mole on the inside of their left ass cheek. This is pretty flimsy stuff today. What gives, Alex?"

Alex blushed again and shook his head. "This one's weird. I can't get more than a hazy impression of who they are. I can't even see her face this time. I know each note was written by the same woman, but they were delivered by several other people. Then the notes kind of passed around to different kids, and then the impressions of their parents are there as well. That's a lot of stuff to sift through."

"Interesting," I said. "Well, leave the file here and I'll look through it later. I've got a client in twenty minutes and I haven't even started on her case yet."

So much for a our big breakthrough on the case. Once again we were stalled, and it didn't look like there was any way out of it.

Alex nodded, slid the notes back into the folder, placed the file on top of my pile, and left the room. When the door clicked shut I turned my head and put my still burning cheek on the cold desktop.

~~

At noon I was on my way out the door when the phone rang. I ran back to my desk and picked it up.

"Yeah?" I said.

"What are your plans for lunch?" Justice said brightly on the other end.

Apparently, he wasn't being an ass anymore. But that didn't make me feel any better because I knew it wouldn't last. I knew this pattern all too well because I'd been living it for so long.

We'd moved quietly into the honeymoon phase. Justice would be nice to me for a while, giving me gifts and doing nice things for me. Sometimes it lasted for weeks, sometimes just hours. But even while he was sweeping me off my feet with love and kindness, I knew that at any time he could surprise me with the exact opposite. He'd often claim it was my fault for setting him off or that it was for my own good and I should just do what he said to avoid his ire in the first place.

I never knew when the change would happen, and the anticipation ate me up. It was only recently that I'd realized this emotional turmoil was a lot like the abuse I'd endured when I was a child. Only this time, there were no visible scars to prove to the world that I wasn't crazy or making it up.

But now wasn't the time to think about any of that. Now wasn't the time to try and fix whatever had broken between us. And it definitely wasn't the time to tell Justice he was behaving like my stepfather used to.

"Well," I said, "I'm having lunch with Jeffrey, why?"

"Oh."

"What's wrong?"

"Nothing. I was just hoping we could have lunch together today."

It looked like he was playing Sad-Justice this time— his passive-aggressive way of trying to make me feel like I'd done something wrong. As much as I hated that act, it was better than Self-Righteous-Justice who blamed his every nasty comment or action on something *I'd* done.

Rather than risk starting another argument so soon

after the last, I decided to play his game once more. I'd pretend the fight never happened and that Justice was truly the nice guy he wanted everyone to believe he was. Sometimes it was just easier to pretend.

"I'd love to, but you and Oliver are making me get all friendly with the freak. . . I can cancel if you want."

"No, you're right. You need to stay close to him. I'll just see you tonight after work." He paused, then added, "Will you be on time tonight?"

I was tempted to say something nasty but quickly swallowed that urge. A snide remark would definitely set him off, and I wanted to avoid that if at all possible.

"I'm planning on it," I said instead. "But you know how it goes." There, nice and vague.

"Yeah." Justice paused again.

I half expected him to accuse me of being stubborn, or of not caring for myself, or even not caring for him. But he stayed quiet, and tension moved between us over the phone line.

After what seemed like minutes, he said, "I love you, Mina."

Relief ran through me at his words, and I took in a deep breath. No fights today. At least not right now. But I was tired of wondering when the next big fight would happen. And I was tired of tiptoeing around him in hopes of staving off the comments. But I didn't say any of that. "I love you, too, Justice," I said instead.

We hung up and I was immediately thankful the call was over. Nothing had changed and nothing was fixed, but I'd made it through a conversation with Justice without screaming or crying or feeling guilty for some imagined offense.

I moved through my private office once more and left through the lobby door, trying not to dwell too deeply on my screwed up love life. I had other concerns to worry about. My plate was overflowing, and all this bullshit with Justice seemed to take up more time than I had to give.

Timothy wanted me to hang out with him more like we used to do. I might have actually obliged him, but knowing he was siding with Justice made me want to avoid him at all costs. Timothy was too malleable, like a small, attention-starved child. It wasn't his fault. He was just easy to sway if you pushed hard enough. He'd either tell me he understood where I was coming from, and then turn around and tell Justice everything I said, or he'd go on and on about how right Justice was and how I should just do what he told me to do. For my own good, of course.

Latrator, my werewolf pack leader, wanted me to spend more time with the Lycans. I'd been ignoring them for months. Part of that had to do with spending so much time trying to appease Justice, but some of it was my animosity over *being* a Lycan at all. If I hadn't been a Lycan, my baby probably would have been alive today.

Then there were the PI cases piling up and going nowhere. And the local police needing my help with the Garrot case. Add to all that my new assignment for Presence—which I thought was a big pain in the ass. With all the drama in my life, I really didn't have the patience to deal with Jeffrey Bragg and his Djinn.

If you want to get rid of a Djinn, the naysayer offered, *just kill the host and be done with it.*

"Shush," I said under my breath.

Just the thought of it made me feel bad. I didn't *really* want to kill Jeffrey, even if it would make that problem go away. It wasn't his fault that the Djinn had possessed him. At least, I hoped it wasn't his fault. And it was unfair of me to think of killing him just to make *my* life easier. Besides, what if killing the host released the Djinn to go and possess someone else? We'd be right back at square one, and maybe the next guy would be even weirder than Jeffrey Bragg.

So, kill him, too!

"Shut up," I snapped, as I walked down the sidewalk toward my destination. "I'm *not* killing anyone."

By the time I reached Myhres my head was throbbing, but I'd managed to silence the naysayer once again and put on my happy face. I moved down the row of booths to where Jeffrey was waiting. As he stood, he dropped his napkin and fork on the floor.

"Sorry I'm late," I said and slipped into the booth.

Jeffrey picked up his napkin and fork, placed them on the table, and slid into his seat across from me. "That's okay. I just got here myself."

And then the silence.

Sitting here with Jeffrey wouldn't be so bad if he'd actually speak or make some kind of an effort to interact with me. He gave off that uneasy teenaged boy vibe and wouldn't even look at me. Couple that with my own social awkwardness and we were doomed to sit in silence unless one of us grew a spine.

After we'd ordered our lunches I looked across the table at Jeffrey. He glanced up and grinned as he tore his napkin into little pieces.

I'd known a man not long ago with some of the same mannerisms. I'd thought that man had been kind and innocent and sweet. I'd thought wrong. Come to think of it, it sure seemed like I had a knack for getting involved with all the assholes in nice-guy clothing. But I'd try not to hold that against Jeffrey.

I tapped the table with my fingertips and asked, "Why are you so nervous?"

He dropped the napkin and covered it with his spidery hand. "I'm not nervous."

I smirked. "Really?"

I'm not sure what made me do it, but I slipped off my shoe and nudged Jeffrey's leg under the table. He just about jumped out of the seat, eyes wide and face contorted in near-terror.

"You look pretty nervous to me," I said with a grin.

He chuckled and looked around the room as he settled back into his seat. "Okay, I'm nervous." He shrugged and looked at the pile of napkin shreds on the table.

"Why?" I asked.

"I dunno. I guess I'm not used to being pursued by women."

"*Pursued?*" I laughed before I could stop myself. "I mean, I wouldn't say I'm pursuing you. I'm just trying to—"

Jeffrey's face went serious when he said, "Stay close so you can find out about the Djinn?"

To say I was surprised would have been an understatement. All I could do was blink at him for a few seconds. So much for Mina the sneaky private eye.

Since the gig was obviously up, I asked, "How did you know?"

He snorted. "How do you *think* I know?"

And then I felt like a big meanie. Sometimes my Insight would fire off a quick hint about the situation without me having to purposefully crawl inside someone's head. It did so now, and I knew he'd been hoping I was romantically interested in him. He'd been hoping the Djinn had been wrong for once and that I was following him because I liked him. Instead, I'd just proved the Djinn right, and in the process, I'd crushed Jeffrey's hopes.

Though I felt bad and part of me wanted to try to comfort him—even though comforting wasn't really a strong point for me—there was no time to think of his tender feelings. I had a job to do, and getting to the bottom of the Djinn problem would mean I'd have more time to work on all the other crap in my life.

Get in. Fix it. Move on. Quick and clean.

Maybe that was a cold way to think about another human being's suffering, but I couldn't fix whatever emotional scars Jeffrey had. I was just hoping I could put an end to the Djinn's control over him. With the Djinn gone Jeffrey could fix himself, and *I* didn't have to be involved in that.

"So does it talk to you then?" I asked.

Jeffrey nodded, suddenly looking weary. He rubbed one big hand over his face a couple of times as if wiping away sleep. "Yeah, it talks to me. . . a lot. I wish it wouldn't."

"What does it say?"

"It says a lot of things."

Insight or not it was obvious this conversation was making Jeffrey uncomfortable. Regardless, I had a job to do. "You know," I said, "the more detail you give me, the better I can understand."

He took a deep breath and looked to the ceiling for a moment. I thought he wasn't going to elaborate, and I was getting ready to push him for more, but then he said, "Most of the time it just babbles. To drive me nuts, I think. Other times I get. . . hints."

I frowned. "Hints? What kind of hints?"

Jeffrey wouldn't look at me when he said, "Like when to run and when to hide and when it's safe to act somewhat normal for a change. It tells me when it thinks someone is on to me." He shook his head. "But it always thinks everyone is on to me. I never get a chance to—"

He rubbed his face again, and when he dropped his hands to the table and looked at me, his features were pinched, pained. He seemed uneasy. But not like he'd been before, not nervous and ready to run at any second. He seemed more than uncomfortable. More than upset. Jeffrey was sad.

When he dropped his gaze to the table, I asked softly, "How did it happen?"

"How did I get stuck with the Djinn?"

"Yeah."

"I'm not really sure. I thought I was just unlucky for a while. Weird stuff always happened around me."

"What kind of weird stuff?"

He shrugged, looking up again. "Animals freaking out, people getting hurt, stuff breaking for no reason."

He flicked a napkin shred across the table. It landed in front of me. I poked it with one finger and pushed it back across the table into Jeffrey's pile.

He glanced up at me and smiled, then quickly looked down again as he said, "Women never wanted anything to do with me. I thought it was me for the longest time."

"What happened to change your mind?"

"Who says I've changed my mind?" Jeffrey said and gave a sharp, humorless laugh. "I still think there's something wrong with me, but the Djinn is a bonus."

I smiled at him. Not laughing or mocking. Just an understanding smile and nod of the head. I knew all about feeling abnormal. Jeffrey glanced up again and caught that understanding. I could see him relax his shoulders, the tightness in his face releasing a little, giving a hint of the real Jeffrey Bragg under all that sadness and stress.

"My family used to have some pretty cool old stuff hanging around when I was a kid," he said quietly. "I thought it'd be fun to collect some of my own. Nothing expensive. Just odds and ends, anything that caught my eye. It gave me something to focus on so I didn't dwell on my misery. Then last year I bought these pieces from some old guy at a traveling antique show. He said they were special, haunted or something." Jeffrey's cheeks went pink and he added quickly, "Not that I believed it for real, but I couldn't say no. So I brought them home and set them out. Next thing I know the Djinn is babbling in my head."

"That was the first time you'd heard it?"

"Yeah, it freaked me out. I thought I'd finally lost it. You know, hearing voices and stuff?"

The waitress brought our food. We sat in silence as she placed our plates on the table and refilled our water. As soon as she was gone I asked, "What was it saying to you in the beginning?"

"It wanted me to read the book so I'd understand. I looked at it, but I didn't understand any of it. That's when I searched for help on the internet. I did some research on people who might know something about weird old books, and I found Page's Pages. I came out here to talk to Mr. Page, and you know the rest."

"Did you know I was following you?"

Jeffrey frowned and shook his head. "I didn't, but *it* did. It told me you were watching me. It said you were hiding somewhere and I should be careful. It said you'd try and kill me." He fixed me with tired eyes. "Are you going to kill me, Mina?"

Oddly enough, I'd been asked that before, but I didn't tell Jeffrey that. Instead, I said, "Do I look like I'm capable of killing you?"

He smiled and shook his head. "The Djinn said you'd say that."

I shrugged. "Well, I didn't *plan* on killing you, if that makes you feel any better."

"But you want to kill the Djinn?"

What was I supposed to say? The truth. I nodded and said, "Yup."

Jeffrey closed his eyes and leaned back in the booth.

As he did so, the dark cloud of worry that had been surrounding him melted away.

"Thank you," he whispered.

EIGHT

~~

By the time I'd returned to my office after lunch, I was feeling much better. Not that I'd forgotten about my other problems, but just the knowledge that Jeffrey wasn't such a bad guy after all helped ease some of that anxiety I'd been carrying around for so long. Of course, I wasn't always the best judge of character, and I hadn't even tried using my full Insight on him yet. Maybe I'd change my mind later, but right now, Jeffrey seemed like a lost, sad puppy who just needed some help avoiding all the boots trying to kick him.

There was still a lot about Jeffrey I didn't know, and not knowing things could be very dangerous, as my history proved. But we did know that he wanted to get rid of the Djinn. *That* was good news, at least. I wasn't going to let myself get too optimistic though. Was it the Djinn trying to trick us, or was that really Jeffrey I'd been talking to? And what about the deaths that Jeffrey was being blamed for? It was entirely possible that he was, in fact, a murderer, but just happened to have a Djinn possession, too. The two were possibly unrelated, but the Djinn was definitely complicating matters.

Lots to sort out, for sure, but at least I had somewhere to go now. With Presence backing me up, I'd keep following Jeffrey's case, and keep following the clues, and we'd get at least one thing solved.

"Mina, you've got a walk-in client," Angie's voice crackled over the intercom. "Shall I send him in?"

I pressed the button and said, "Yes, thank you, Angie."

A moment later the door opened, and I nearly fell out of my chair as my heart seized up and my veins turned to ice.

Mr. Boad closed the door, took four long steps, and stopped in front of my desk, his manicured hands folded in front of him. He was wearing a dark pinstripe suit and a crisp, dark blue fedora. A thin black tie made a straight line down his chest and disappeared under his buttoned jacket.

"Ms. Jewel, a pleasure to see you again."

"Fuck off, Boad."

"I understand your reluctance to see me. I would feel the same way, were I in your position."

"Good, then you'll understand why I'm telling you to get the hell out."

"I do." He nodded once. "However, I won't be going anywhere." Boad sat in my client chair and smiled, a smug look that begged for a good punching right in the center of his face.

Refraining from attacking the old man, I said, "What do you want?" as I scooted my chair as far from my desk, and Mr. Boad, as I could get.

Boad wasn't a physical threat. It was his goons that

were the problem. He had a whole army of big, dumb muscle-heads just waiting for his word, and they'd move in to do whatever Boad told them to. No questions asked. No remorse. Were they out in my waiting room right now giving Angie the stink-eye?

"I believe your friend, Mr. Beckett, told you of my little predicament?" Boad said.

"Yeah? So? Why's your predicament *my* problem?"

It was an interesting twist of fate that Boad would be coming to me, his former victim, for help. Desperate times call for desperate measures. Never before had an old adage made more sense to me.

"It's your problem because you have a conscience," he said.

"But you don't," I spat back.

He nodded, a slow, single tip of his head. "Fair enough, Ms. Jewel. I am looking after my own skin. I care nothing for the general public's safety." He waved one hand in the air, dismissing the thought. "If our little problem persists, I could end up in prison."

"I think that's where you belong."

"That may very well be true. However, I know that you don't want any additional deaths. You and yours have the power to stop this. . . *thing* before it strikes again."

"And in the process you sit safe and sound, and nobody will ever point the finger at you."

"That is the idea."

Tapping my fingers on my thigh, I looked over the desk at Boad. His salt and pepper hair had gained a little more salt, as far as I could see under the hat, and the lines around his mouth and eyes were a bit deeper. Otherwise he hadn't changed much. Zia's spell hadn't permanently damaged him. Unfortunately.

"Tell me what you know about the Djinn," I finally

said.

Boad smiled and a thread of tension left his face. It surprised me to realize he'd actually been worried. Surprised me, and empowered me.

"I know that a Djinn can be bound to an object, much like the story of Aladdin's lamp."

"And you think something you sold to Jeffrey Bragg had a Djinn stuck to it?"

That idea didn't match up to the time frame Jeffrey described, but I didn't tell Boad that. If he felt guilt over this, or fear, then all the better for us. We could use that against him. That, and anything that caused Boad discomfort made me a little happier.

"That is my guess. It wasn't until quite some time after I sold him the items that I heard about his unfortunate circumstances."

"What circumstances?"

"Mr. Bragg is a fugitive from the law, Ms. Jewel. Did you not know this already?"

Jeffrey wasn't technically a fugitive, but Boad didn't need to know those details either. My goal was not to fill in the blanks for Boad, but to use Boad's information to fill in *my* blanks. I could play dumb if it got me answers and kept Boad in the dark.

"How the hell am I supposed to know that?" I said.

Boad shrugged slowly, casually. "No matter. You know it now. The question is, what will you *do* about it? Hopefully, sooner rather than later."

"You know something, Boad?" I moved my chair forward and scooted my legs under my desk, folding my hands on top. "I'm sick of your tone. I'm sick of your attitude. I'm sick of watching you think everyone is here to clean up *your* mess."

Boad gave an amused smile and straightened his tie.

Smirking, I picked up my phone and punched a speed dial button. While I waited, I watched Boad.

"Hey, Zia," I said into the phone.

The color instantly drained from Boad's face and his eyes went wide, his smug expression turning to fear in a heartbeat. He stiffened in his chair, then held perfectly still, frozen like a possum on the freeway.

"Boad is at my office," I said, grinning at the frightened man across from me. "You might wanna hurry on over." Then I hung up.

Mr. Boad jumped from his chair and started toward the door.

I wasn't going to let him get away that easy. I used my Lycan speed and zipped around the desk, slipped between Boad and my office door, and pressed my back against the door. Boad stood in front of me, breath coming ragged, eyes wide with a level of terror I'd never seen in him before. Sweat shimmered on his face, and a light tremble moved over his chin.

Grinning wider, I leaned in close. "How's it feel, Boad?" I whispered, just a breath between us. "How's it feel to be powerless for a change?"

He dug in his jacket pocket.

I didn't flinch. He wouldn't hurt me. Boad didn't do his own dirty work.

He pulled a clean, neatly folded hankie from the pocket, took off his hat, and dabbed his forehead. It was the first time I'd seen him without the hat. His thinning hair was damp, pressed down around his head where the ever-present fedora had been.

"She—" his voice cracked and he had to stop to swallow. "*She'll* be here soon, won't she?"

I paused for a heartbeat, grinned, and then shook my head slowly. "She's not coming, Boad."

"But—"

"I called my own house. There's nobody there but my boyfriend, who is probably really confused right now." I grinned wider and narrowed my eyes. "I just wanted you to know that you're *not* the only one who has power. I wanted you to see that I'm not easily pushed around anymore. You'll sit down, you'll tell me everything I want to know, and if I feel like it, I'll help you hide from Zia again when this is all over."

Boad's face was still pale, but he'd stopped sweating. I watched mixed emotions play across his face for a few more seconds. Then, without a word, Boad turned and went back to the chair. He placed the fedora back on his head and folded his trembling hands in his lap.

"I'd like to make one thing clear, Ms. Jewel," Boad said, his voice almost normal. "You were *never* easy to push around."

NINE

~~

By eight o'clock I was on my couch leaning against Justice, with Timothy laying on the couch next to me, his head resting in my lap. The three of us had eaten our dinner in silence, then curled up on the couch, and we hadn't moved since.

Much to my surprise, Justice hadn't yelled at me or made any comments about my late arrival at home, so I took the cue and kept my mouth shut, too. Even with all the fighting we'd been doing, and my recent epiphany about Justice's true self and his prejudices, I could still enjoy these quiet moments. The anxiety was still there, burning a hole in my stomach, but I'd take these peaceful times any chance I could get them. I needed the comfort of touch, even if I couldn't ask for it out loud.

Since contracting Lycanthropy I'd had a strong urge to be close to others. Being near other people seemed to pull away the tension and the pain and the sadness. Ideally, I would just flop into the puppy pile with Latrator and the rest of my Lycan pack and get all the wordless, non-judging, and non-sexual comfort I needed so desperately. But I hadn't visited my pack in months, and I was definitely suffering for it.

I kept telling myself I wasn't ready to face them yet. In reality, I knew I just wasn't ready to stop blaming the loss of my unborn child on my Lycanthropy. Seeing the faces of my fellow Lycans and feeling their unquestioning love would mean I'd have to truly explore my anger and my resentment, and I'd have to place it all where it really belonged.

Timothy sighed and snuggled deeper into my lap. I responded by stroking his hair and snuggling closer to Justice, too. Justice kissed the top of my head.

"This is better," Timothy said. "This is what I needed. I've missed you, Mina."

Justice pulled me closer. "We've *both* missed you."

Even with the chasm that had grown between us, Justice's words and soft touch made me feel good. I knew it was just the quiet, loving phase of his cycle. I knew that soon he'd be angry again. But I clung to the words and the kindness he offered me, because, like Timothy, that's what I needed most right now.

Despite the knowledge that the peace wouldn't last, I snuggled down into it and absorbed as much of it as I could. The longer I basked in it the more positive I felt. Maybe we'd get past all the anger and the blame. Maybe Justice would stop trying to control me with guilt. Maybe all I had to do was endure one more cycle, and then he'd see what he'd been doing to me and everything would start to get better.

I'd just started to drift off to sleep when the phone rang. I did my best to ignore it, but after six rings it stopped and then started right back up again.

"Jeeze," I said under my breath as I extracted myself from Timothy's grip. I stomped over to the phone, snatched it off the charger, and shouted into the receiver. "What?"

"Hello, to you, too, Mina," Oliver said with a chuckle in his voice.

I relaxed, but just barely. "Sorry, Oliver."

"No harm done, my dear. I'm calling to let you know my friend from Riyadh has arrived safely and awaits us in the meeting room."

I'd forgotten all about Oliver's friend. In fact, I'd forgotten all about Jeffrey and his Djinn, too. Once again, my problems with Justice were overshadowing everything else in my life. My efforts to keep the peace were taking up all my energy, leaving nothing for work, Presence, or even myself. Though I'd never had a relationship before, I knew in my heart that this wasn't how it was supposed to be. Something had to be done.

I closed my eyes and took a deep breath. Personal problems later. Right now, I had a Djinn to catch.

"Okay," I said. "I'm on my way."

I hung up and turned to look at Timothy and Justice. They were right where I'd left them, watching me, an empty space between them on the couch.

~~

She was a stunning woman. An ageless beauty with dark skin and darker eyes. Light glinted off her straight, black hair as it brushed the backs of her knees. She wore a red silk *Abaya* that touched the top of her dainty black shoes, and a gold sash draped across her body. She was at least an inch shorter than me, which made her under five four. The room smelled like nothing I'd ever experienced before. Exotic spices, something sweet and a little tangy with an underlying musk. It wasn't unpleasant, but my sensitive nose wasn't used to so many new smells at once.

Oliver beamed and bounced up and down on his toes like an excited little boy, his hands clasped behind his back. "Mina, this is my dear friend, Nafeeza," Oliver said.

Nafeeza smiled and the whole room lit up. She offered a hand and I shook it. She had a nice firm grip. Nafeeza looked genteel and frail, but she definitely had some fire in her. Like me, her looks were deceiving. Maybe we could be friends.

"Thank you for coming out on such short notice," I said.

"When Oliver calls, I come," she said with a heavy Middle Eastern accent.

"Come, sit down, Nafeeza," Oliver said. "I know you must be weary from your travels, but we have much to discuss."

Nafeeza nodded once, followed him to a chair by the meeting table, and sat down gracefully, smoothing her dress under her legs as she sat. Folding her hands in her lap, she said, "Tell me of your Djinn."

I sat across the table from our guest and leaned back in the chair. "Well, Jeffrey doesn't know how long he's had the Djinn. He knows it's been a long time, most of his life maybe. But it was just the past year or so that he's been able to hear it talking to him."

"I see," Nafeeza said. She nodded once. "Continue please."

"He said he's always been unlucky, people and animals around him getting hurt or acting weird. He stays to himself because of it. That's all I've got. I'm sorry it isn't much to go on. This isn't an area we're used to dealing with."

"It is fine," she said with a small nod. "Before we remove the Djinn, first we must decide which class we are dealing with."

"There's classes?" I raised an eyebrow.

Nafeeza nodded. "The *Ghul*, *Sila*, and *Ifrit* tend to cause the most trouble. I do not think we are dealing with a *Ghul*, as you have not mentioned anything about a graveyard or corpses."

I cringed. "Corpses?" There was at least one corpse I thought Jeffrey's Djinn had something to do with, but I didn't say that out loud. Though Nafeeza was on our side, I didn't think she needed to know every tiny detail. Not yet. Friend of Oliver or not, I didn't just give my trust away.

"The *Ghul* stay close to graveyards and deal mostly in death magic. They are the lowest of the classes, and thought unable to travel outside of our homeland."

"That's good," I said. "But, I didn't realize there were rules."

Nafeeza smiled and looked around the room. "There are rules for everything."

Justice nodded once toward Nafeeza and said, "Agreed. However, Mina does like to bend rules occasionally."

I shot an annoyed look at Justice and he shrugged.

"We are most likely dealing with a *Sila* or *Ifrit*," Nafeeza said. "Both of which are considered neutral. They are capable of choosing good or evil."

"Like people," I said.

"No," Nafeeza said with a shake of the head. "They are not like people at all!"

"I'm sorry. I didn't mean to offend you."

Nafeeza nodded toward me.

"So how did this Djinn come to be with Mr. Bragg?"

Justice asked.

"The Djinn are beings of fire, magic, and free will, said to live among us, though on a separate plane of existence. Sometimes those planes meet and the Djinn can come through and cause. . . mischief. Sometimes the visiting Djinn is captured and bound to an item. Very rarely the Djinn will find a host and possess him or her, then do its own bidding through that host."

"And Jeffrey was just unlucky enough to get possessed," I said.

"I have heard of good Djinn possessing evil men and making them do good things. A kind of punishment for their evil ways, involuntary atonement for their wicked acts."

Shaking my head, I said, "I don't think Jeffrey is evil or that his Djinn is good."

Nafeeza shook her head as well. "I do not think this is a good Djinn either. I believe your friend is suffering. That is why I agreed to help. Do you think he will see me, this friend of yours?"

I shrugged. "I don't see why not. He wants the Djinn gone, probably more than we do."

"If the Djinn is as strongly bound to your friend as Oliver fears, then it is possible he will be unable to control it for much longer."

"That's not good. What can we do?"

"We must be careful. The spirit will recognize me as someone who would pose a threat to its existence. It will try to avoid me. If we corner it, it will fight back, and that is what I would like to avoid."

"But," Oliver said, "can the Djinn see and hear everything that Mr. Bragg does, even if Mr. Bragg is in control at the time?"

That sure would put a damper on any plans. If it

could see us and hear us even with Jeffrey in control, that would mean it knew Jeffrey had been trying to get rid of it. That would mean it already knew about me and Oliver. This could get ugly. At least I hadn't mentioned anything about Presence. We might still be able to sneak up on it.

"I am afraid so," Nafeeza said. "If the Djinn has been in your friend's body as long as he says, then it has surely discovered a way to experience everything going on around it. We will need to be careful and always on our guard."

"You know," I said, "I saw this weird kind of double image the other day. It was like Jeffrey stepped away from his door, but this second self stayed there with his arms crossed, just scowling down at me."

"Ah," Nafeeza said. "The Djinn and your friend had a disagreement. What was happening when you saw the Djinn?"

My cheeks went warm, and I mumbled, "I was falling down the stairs."

"And your friend was trying to help you, I assume?"

"Yeah, he reached out and caught me before I fell back."

Nafeeza nodded and smiled. "This is a good sign. This means your friend still has some control, and the Djinn does not always win."

"For now at least," I said. "Oliver thinks Jeffrey is losing control pretty quickly."

Oliver nodded and said, "I'm afraid there isn't much of Mr. Bragg left as it is, Nafeeza."

"Then we must act soon," Nafeeza said as she stood.

~ ~

Nafeeza and I were standing on the long dock at the waterfront on Bay Street when Jeffrey came up to us the next morning. He'd agreed to meet us to discuss the plan. Over the phone he'd sounded eager to get things started, but now he didn't look too happy. His gaze darted from me to Nafeeza and then out to the ocean, his brow creased in worry.

"Why are *you* here?" Jeffrey said, as he leaned his forearms against the dock's splintered white railing.

Nafeeza touched his hand with her dainty fingertips. Jeffrey jerked away and stumbled back two steps, his eyes narrowing.

The harsh whisper that scratched from Jeffrey's mouth sent a tingle over my arms when it warned, "Do not touch me."

"I wish to touch your host, not you," Nafeeza said.

If she was ruffled by his reaction or that strange voice, I couldn't tell. She stood with her shoulders straight and her feet firmly in place as she gave Jeffrey intense eye contact.

Jeffrey's lip curled.

"If you do not wish to be touched by me," she said, "then I suggest you go away so I may touch your host freely." She took a challenging step toward Jeffrey.

Jeffrey's eyes narrowed further, just two thin slits in his pale face as he looked down at Nafeeza.

He looked so angry and ready to pounce, I was surprised when he said, "I will go, but be warned: I know why you have come. You will not win your prize so easily."

Jeffrey's eyes shut and his head snapped back. Then his shoulders jerked forward as if someone had struck him between the shoulder blades. A visible shiver ran down his body from head toe. He gasped and opened his eyes wide, staring down at me.

"It's getting stronger, isn't it?" Jeffrey wiped a trembling hand down his face, then leaned his forearms against the railing again. He stared down into the deep green water lapping at the pier. "You've got to help me, Mina."

"I'm trying, Jeffrey," I said, because I wasn't sure what else *to* say.

His shoulders drooped and his head hung low, his mussed hair falling forward to cover his eyes. Desperation rolled off of him in cold wisps that prickled my skin. His posture cried, "I give up!" though he didn't speak a word. My heart broke for him, and I felt powerless.

I stepped next to Jeffrey and slowly reached one hand out toward him. What if he didn't want me to touch him either? But he looked so lost, so hurt, I couldn't stand there and do nothing. After a moment of hesitation, I laid my hand against his back and rubbed in slow, soft circles. Honestly, I wasn't sure how much good that gesture would do, but the touch did seem to bring him a bit of relief as he melted against my hand. His head sagged further but his body leaned ever so slightly toward me, so I kept rubbing.

"Nafeeza has some ideas for us if you're willing to trust her," I said softly, bending to see his face.

Jeffrey raised his red-rimmed eyes and looked past me to study Nafeeza for a moment. He dropped his gaze back to the water and nodded. "I trust *you*, Mina. I have to. Anything is better than what it did last night."

My hand stopped, and I stared at the side of Jeffrey's face. He wouldn't turn to look at me.

"What did it do last night?" I asked, but I didn't want to know. Not really.

Jeffrey turned away so I couldn't see his expression, and a tremble went through his body.

I pulled my hand away and asked, "What happened last night, Jeffrey?"

My cell phone rang, high and piercing, echoing over

the water. I snatched it out of my pocket and jabbed at the call button.

"This is Mina."

"Detective Richards, Ms. Jewel. I need you to come down to the station as soon as possible."

"Why?"

Richards was quiet for a breath, then said, "There's been an incident."

TEN

~~

After I dropped Nafeeza at Page's Pages I drove a few blocks to the police station on the corner of Bay Street and Division. Detective Richards was outside smoking a cigarette when I pulled up to the ornate building. He didn't wave or say hello when I got out of my car. Not that his lack of immediate acknowledgment was unusual; he was a thinker before he was a talker. Even so, my gut wrenched with all the imagined horrors running through my brain.

Richards snuffed out his cigarette in the ashtray by the large double doors. Again, he didn't acknowledge me as I approached, he just walked into the building. I assumed I was to follow, so I did.

His office was clean and organized, almost sterile with the shining metal shelves and desk and perfectly aligned file cabinets. I'd never be able to get a lick of work done in a room like this. I'd be too afraid to touch anything and then spend the rest of the day wiping my fingerprints off it all.

Richards sat behind his desk and motioned for me to take the seat across from him. Then he just looked at me, rubbing his upper lip with the knuckle of one finger, over and over.

"Okay, I give," I said after a moment of silent staring. "Why'd you call me down here? It's gotta be weird if I've been called."

I'd been trying for lighthearted, something to help break up that awful nervousness tightening my muscles, but my comment fell flat and I only felt worse after saying it. His reply didn't make things any better either.

"Yeah." Detective Richards took a slow, deep breath. "It's pretty weird." He paused and his brows furrowed, tension tugging them close together. "Early this morning the assistant medical examiner sent his official report on Walter Garrot's autopsy."

"Why does this sound so ominous?"

"I don't know how you knew, Ms. Jewel, but there was definitely signs of heating in his chest, just like you said. It wasn't obvious when we first found Garrot. It took the M.E. a lot of time staring into his microscope, but he found it. I don't understand all the medical jargon he used, but he said down on a cellular level there was some kind of heat involved in Garrot's case."

Nodding, I tugged on one of my long curls. "Okay, but there must be more, because that sounds like something you could have said to me over the phone."

"You're right. Again." Then he shook his head, almost as if trying to convince himself he didn't need to say the rest.

And though I didn't really want to hear the rest either, I said, "What's going on?"

"I know you've been working on a round of missing

teen cases."

"Yeah," I said as my heart seized up. Not like I should be surprised by his comment. I'd had a bad feeling the moment he'd called me, but I'd been wishing it was something else. *Anything* else but my kids. "You got something for me?"

"We found five bodies early this morning, all with their hearts ripped out of their chests."

"Ripped?" I stiffened in the chair. "Or blown out like Walter Garrot's? And are they my kids?"

"That's what we want to know."

My stomach flipped and tightened. "No, no, no," I said, shaking my head. "I am not looking at more pictures, especially if you think these could be *my* kids."

"Ms. Jewel, you're the last person I came to. Nobody else can figure this out. Nobody else can make any sense of it. Do you know how much crap I had to go through to get the okay to pull you in on this one?"

"I don't really care, Detective." A surge of adrenalin rushed through me, and I had an urge to bolt out of the chair and flee the office. But I stayed in my seat and said, "I'm *not* looking at pictures of blown out hearts and dead kids. I've had nightmares about Walter Garrot. Can you imagine what the dreams will be like with *kids*?"

"I don't think you understand," he said. "We've gotten calls from anxious parents all morning. Someone leaked to the press that we found bodies. We *need* answers."

"God, why do I do this?" I whispered and covered my face in my hands for a moment.

What if it *was* my missing teens? What if I looked at the pictures and I recognized those innocent faces? Could I refuse to look just to save myself from some nightmares?

No. Doing nothing would make me just as guilty as the person who'd hurt them. If I couldn't bring the kids back home safely, the least I could do was help find their killer.

"Okay, show me," I said as I dropped my hands to my lap and held my breath.

Detective Richards reached for the top folder on his desk. He opened it, paused, then pulled out a stack of black and white photos. After he spread them out for me I glanced down.

"Oh, God," I said and had to swallow the sickness down. My throat was suddenly thick and tight, the acid burn working its way up.

In the blink of an eye, the expensive shiny desk had been transformed into a macabre gallery of dead kids. Each body had been laid out on the ground, completely nude, arms and legs spread wide. They were positioned in a semi-circle, each left ankle touching the right ankle of the next kid. Each one had a gaping hole in their chest where the heart should have been. The ribs were shattered, the skin blown apart. They looked like shotgun victims, but they couldn't have been or I wouldn't have been called.

I had to look away. I stared out the window at the day just starting to get sunny and warm. There would be kids playing on the rocky beach, and couples going out for picnics, and people strolling along Bay Street looking in shop windows at things they'd never buy. But five families were going to be getting a call to come down and identify the bodies of their children. There would be five coffins ordered, five funerals planned, five fewer kids graduating this year, and it was my fault. I'd been too slow, and now they were dead.

"Jesus, Mary, and Joseph," I whispered.

"It's your kids, isn't it?"

I nodded, but said nothing.

"Do you think it's the same guy?" Detective Richards

asked quietly. "This Jeffrey Bragg fellow?"

Eyes burning and my gut in knots, I stared at the detective. What was I supposed to say? Yes and no? It was him, but not really? Hey, give me a day to remove the Djinn and then you can bring it in for questioning?

There was a reason Presence was still an underground organization. There was a reason we worked quietly and in secret. People just didn't *believe*. They couldn't accept that sometimes things aren't easy to explain. They couldn't accept that sometimes supernatural shit happens and your nice, safe, normal world is tipped upside down and tossed into the cosmic blender.

"Ms. Jewel?"

"Okay, listen," I said. Adrenalin pumped through me once more, sending heat to my skin and sweat along my brow. My body shook with the effort of staying in my seat. "You've got to trust me. This is gonna sound crazy, but Jeffrey didn't do this. Not really. I mean, he may have had a very small part to play in it, but it isn't his fault."

"You're right," Richards said, "it sounds crazy. It also sounds like I should bring this guy in."

He reached for his phone. Before I knew what I was doing, I'd stood and I'd pressed my hand over the top of his, preventing him from lifting the receiver. I gave solid eye contact and I pushed some of my power into that gaze hoping he'd feel it, hoping he'd understand how serious I was.

"Give me some time," I said. "I'll get to the bottom of it. I'll get you an answer."

Detective Richards shook his head. "You know I can't do that."

I sat down and watched his jaw clench beneath tanned, beard-stubbled skin. No, technically he couldn't put his case on hold just because I'd asked him to, but he wanted to. I could see his struggle in his expression, feel it in the air between us, with or without Insight. Maybe I just needed to push a little harder. But what if I pushed too hard? An innocent man's life hung in the balance, dependent on me handling the situation properly. Shit.

"Please," I begged because I didn't know what else to say.

Richards looked down at his desk, averting his eyes from my pleading ones. "If Jeffrey Bragg did this," he said, "he's going to be put up on murder charges. He's going to go to prison and probably be executed."

"Give me a little time," I said. "Just—"

Richards' face went red and he shouted, "Look what he did!" He shoved the pictures across his desk, knocking one into my lap.

I looked down to see Missy Edwards sprawled out in a nondescript field, her chest blown open. I could see the dull white of her spine and the remains of a couple jagged ribs through the hole. Missy's clouded eyes were wide, her mouth opened in a silent scream, terror frozen forever on her precious face. My whole body tensed as my stomach threatened to empty.

Missy's mother was oblivious to everything right now, in her neat little uptown office, asking a client if they'd thought about their future. Missy Edwards didn't have a future. Not anymore.

"Please," I breathed, tears welling up in my eyes. "Jeffrey isn't responsible for this."

I don't know why I felt so strongly about Jeffrey's innocence, but I did. I swallowed and said, "You've got to believe me. You've got to trust me, Richards. Give me the rest of the day. I can get you an answer by this afternoon. I promise."

I looked across the desk, pleading with my eyes.

Detective Richards stared at me, his eyes intense, deep lines creasing the corners and between his brows. Richards wasn't the kind of guy who believed in the supernatural, but he believed in me.

"All right," he said. "You've got until four p.m. to do what you need to do, and then I'm going after this sicko."

"Thank you!" I jumped from the chair and yanked the office door open. "I promise to call you before four, and you won't have to arrest Jeffrey."

ELEVEN

~~

By ten a.m. I was back at my house, on my hands and knees, reaching under my front porch. If I'd been smart, I would have changed into a pair of jeans for this little project instead of wearing a long skirt and sandals. Gravel had worked its way between my toes, dug into my knees and palm, and had left my fingers tingling. But I was determined to get that cat. It was more than just my desire to finally pet the elusive little kitty I'd been feeding for the last few weeks. Now the cat had a bigger purpose.

Nafeeza stood on the far side of my porch, crooning and making kissy sounds to coax the cat out her side. I wasn't into the whole nicey-nicey thing so I kept swiping my hand back and forth under the low porch, cursing under my breath, hoping to hit something furry.

Justice stood above me, hands on his narrow hips, smiling.

"Glad to amuse you, Justice," I said through clenched

teeth. "Want to give us a hand?"

He clapped, slow and dramatic. "Yea!" he said. "Go team!" He grinned from ear to ear.

I kicked my left foot back and collided with his shin.

"Ouch!" he shouted, taking a step back. Then he smiled wide and said, "Sorry."

"No, you're not. Now get down here and help catch this damn cat."

"Think maybe it smells the wolf on you?" he asked.

I pulled my arm out from under the porch and glared up at Justice.

"What?" he said with a shrug.

I glanced over at Nafeeza, who stood with her dainty hands folded in front of her, watching us intently. I looked back to Justice and raised my brows.

"Nafeeza already knows about you," Justice said, as if that made it all right. "She knows all about Presence and most of its members. We need her help. No secrets."

"Whatever," I said. "Just get down here."

I didn't think it was Justice's place to tell people about my Lycanthropy. Maybe I didn't want everyone to know I was a Lycan. Of course, if Nafeeza was around for more than a few days, she'd get to see it first hand. Besides, Justice was probably right, the cat could smell the wolf on me, which would explain why it was now hissing and growling when my hand got too close. Maybe I wouldn't feed it any longer, ungrateful little bastard.

"All right," Justice said. "Move back, Mina. You're just making it mad."

Justice stepped forward when I sat up. He smiled at me, his eyes sparkling gold in the morning sunlight, then the next moment he was gone, and his clothes were in a pile on the ground next to me. All black smoke and damp mist, Justice moved into the small space between the steps. I heard the cat hiss again and felt the cool tingle of Justice's energy. Though I couldn't see what was happening under the porch, I knew Justice was probably touching the cat, calming it as his mist enveloped it. He'd done the same thing to me many times—usually when my Fury had gotten out of control—but I hadn't realized his calming gift worked on animals, too. I guess you really do learn something new every day.

Justice swirled out from under the porch, smokey and soft, the little black cat close behind. I stood. As Justice collected himself on the far side of the porch, Nafeeza watched him closely, her head tipped slightly to the right.

Justice's shapeshifting *was* pretty impressive, and I know that I always liked seeing him do it. But something tugged at my insides as I watched Nafeeza. A little tickle of something not-so-pleasant. Something that made my chest tighten once I realized what it was.

Her eyes trailed down the long wisps of my boyfriend as he pulled the last of his essence from under the porch and drifted around to my side. Nafeeza's lips parted slightly, her eyes now tracking his every move as he curled himself up and up, preparing to shift back to his natural form.

What was she thinking? If I thought I could get away with it, I'd have touched her with my Insight to find out for sure, but I really didn't want to get caught peeking in her head.

No, the naysayer whispered in the back of my brain. *No, you're afraid of what you'll find.*

A moment later Justice was solid in front of me again, a light sweat on his forehead. He wiped it away and smiled as he grabbed his shirt off the ground and covered his groin with it.

Typically, a brief shift wouldn't drain Justice like that. The longest he'd been misty was many months ago while he worked to rescue Timothy and some of my pack mates from a poacher. That long of a shift had almost killed him. But five minutes was nothing to Justice, so why was he sweating?

"What have you been up to this morning to get you so drained?" I asked.

"Oh, nothing," he said, shrugging. "I was showing Nafeeza some of the things I can do. No big deal."

I glanced at Nafeeza in time to see the flicker of a smile dance across her lips then vanish.

Justice didn't seem to notice the look as he put an arm around me and kissed the top of my head, the other hand still clutching the shirt covering his lower half.

The cat weaved in and out between Justice's bare ankles, wrapping its long black tail around his legs, the white tip flicking back and forth.

~~

Jeffrey looked nervous. Not that it was any different than normal, but this time I understood his apprehension. He was sitting in my spare bedroom on a comfy padded chair. But I was sure his ass was the only thing comfortable right now. The ropes on his wrists and ankles had to be tight, and I knew it probably didn't feel good, but we had to be sure he wouldn't wriggle out before we were done.

We'd told him ahead of time what the plan was even though the Djinn was probably listening, too. There was no other way to do it. We didn't want to just surprise Jeffrey. Being ambushed, dragged to my house with a bag over his head, then tied to a chair would have given the poor guy a heart attack. He'd already been through enough.

I hadn't told him anything about the five murdered teens or asked him any questions about it. One problem at a time. The Djinn seemed to be the bigger threat right now. And maybe I just didn't want to believe he had anything to do with it.

"All right, Jeffrey, you ready?" I asked.

Jeffrey nodded, but his eyes were wide and his chin trembled.

The cat swirled around his ankles, a silken shadow. It meowed, rubbing its face against Jeffrey's pants. Jeffrey looked down and gave the kitty a quick, faltering smile, then looked up at me again. The cat purred loudly, then sat at Jeffrey's feet like a tiny, fuzzy sentinel.

Nafeeza was in the corner of the room with a small steel bowl full of sea salt and a second empty steel bowl. She'd brought in a carved wooden box that held some strong-smelling herbs and a couple yellowed scrolls, and Jeffrey's book sat open in front of her.

"Hey, Nafeeza?" I said. "How many times have you done this?"

"Once," she said as she looked up at me and smiled. "Counting now."

Oh goody, a newbie.

She'd seemed confident enough as she set the room up and bound Jeffrey to the chair, and maybe she'd been trained to do this over many years and lots of study. But suddenly I didn't feel very good about the whole situation, and my knotting stomach agreed.

Nafeeza flipped a page in the book and the soft scraping sound reminded me of Oliver's forbidding revelation.

Curiosity got the better of me, once again, and I asked, "What is that anyway?"

"The history of the Djinn, written by the Djinn themselves."

I almost didn't mention it, but my curiosity prodded

me further. "Oliver said it wasn't like other books."

"It is not."

"Then what is it?" I asked, though I was pretty sure I already knew.

Nafeeza looked up at me, her expression relaxed. "It is skin inked with blood in the ancient way."

She was so matter-of-fact about it, flipping through the book like it wasn't disgusting. I shuddered at the thought of touching dried up skin and tried not to imagine where it had come from.

Jeffrey didn't handle it so well. His face went pale when he stuttered out, "S. . . skin and blood?"

Nafeeza nodded again. "Yes, but do not fret. It is not human. Not to worry," Nafeeza looked at Jeffrey. "No person lost a life to make this book."

Maybe not to *make* the book, but I was willing to bet more than a few people had lost their lives *because* of that book. But I didn't say that out loud. Jeffrey was already starting to freak out.

"I am ready," Nafeeza said. She set the book down, then carried the two bowls over to Jeffrey's chair.

Jeffrey tensed and moved away from Nafeeza as far as he could, straining against the ropes. He spit at her, then shouted, "Begone, *si'lat*!"

Nafeeza just smiled pleasantly and patted Jeffrey's head. He yelled something I didn't understand and jerked his head back to avoid her touch.

"Do you speak Farsi, Mina?" Nafeeza said casually as she arranged the bowls and one of the scrolls on the floor at Jeffrey's feet. Just a regular day, nothing odd happening here.

"Um, no," I said.

Jeffrey twisted his hands back and forth, straining to yank his arms free of the ropes. I could see his skin getting red and raw, and worried he was going to really hurt himself. Rope burns are nasty and leave ugly scars. I rubbed my own scarred wrist.

"That is good," Nafeeza said. "Then you will not hear the Djinn's threats."

"Threats? Should I be worried?"

"Perhaps," was all Nafeeza said with a shrug of her narrow shoulders.

She stood in front of Jeffrey for a moment, looking down at him, and I wanted to know what she was thinking. Before I could ask, she placed a hand on each of Jeffrey's shoulders. He jerked back but was unable to get away from her touch. His head turned side to side and he started to speak in that strange language again. Farsi, I assumed. Something told me Jeffrey Bragg didn't know Farsi either.

Nafeeza began to sing. Just a soft humming at first, so soft I couldn't make out the tune between the angry shouts of Jeffrey's Djinn. Slowly, Nafeeza raised her voice and the song seemed to fill the room. Jeffrey had stopped shouting words and now just howled and grunted, his hands and wrists twisting madly in the ropes.

I backed toward the door, my hands pressed against it. Honestly, I didn't want to be *in* the room at all. Nafeeza had insisted I stay so I could help with the ritual. And because I was the only friend Jeffrey had, she said I should be nearby. He needed all the support he could get. Though, I wasn't sure how supportive I could be cowering against the bedroom door.

"Mina, the cat please," Nafeeza said in a sing song voice.

"Right," I said, moving forward.

The kitty had retreated to the farthest corner of the room and was growling, the hair on his back raised. He hissed at me and slashed at my hand. I avoided the razor claws and snatched the cat by the scruff of his neck.

"Sorry, Kitty," I said as I took a handful of his tail and yanked downward. The cat screeched and writhed in my grip but I didn't let go. I looked in my free hand and counted quickly in the dim light. More than enough.

I dropped the cat. It ran under the spare bed and growled louder. With my hand covered in black and white cat hair I walked to where Nafeeza was kneeling in front of Jeffrey. I showed her my hand and she very carefully chose seven hairs, dropped them in the empty bowl, then lit them on fire with a lighter.

She stood with the bowl cupped between her hands, outstretched toward Jeffrey's face. He screamed louder, arched his back, thrashed his head from side to side. Nafeeza gently blew the stinking cat hair smoke toward Jeffrey until there was none left, and then she sang louder.

Jeffrey threw his head back and howled like he'd been struck. My heart thudded in my throat. Jeffrey looked at Nafeeza and began speaking again, spit flying from his mouth. His face went red with anger, the veins in his neck standing out, his eyes glowing a deep red.

I pressed myself against the bedroom door, and I could feel Justice on the other side. It was a small comfort knowing he was there, but he'd been instructed not to come in, no matter what he heard happening on this side. Nafeeza and I were on our own, and I was clueless.

Nafeeza smiled gently as she sang and bent to place the bowl at Jeffrey's feet. She rose slowly, used one dainty foot to slide the bowl away from her, then said, "Djinn," as her face morphed to all seriousness. "Spirit of fire! I command you to leave this host. I banish you from this body, this house, this land!"

Nafeeza's voice was no longer soft and lilting. It had become a thing of substance, power, almost touchable in the little room. Jeffrey shouted something in Farsi, gnashed his teeth, a line of spittle rolling down his chin and dripping into his lap. And then his head flopped forward, his shoulders dropped, and his chin came to rest against his chest.

All movement stopped. All sounds silenced.

Nafeeza stood with her arms wide in front of Jeffrey's motionless form, and I held my breath. The seconds ticked by and I wondered if Jeffrey was dead. How would I explain *that* to Detective Richards?

Just as I took a step forward to check his pulse, Jeffrey's head shot up and he screamed, hands quickly clenching and opening, and his eyes had returned to his normal pale blue-green. He screamed and sucked in a ragged breath then screamed again, and I saw a faint orange light burn around him. It seemed to seep out of his skin, his fingers, his face. Everywhere there was orange light becoming brighter like blowing on a glowing ember. Jeffrey appeared to be on fire, smokeless, heatless fire.

"Mina!" he screamed and his eyes locked on mine. "Mina, help me!"

"Oh, shit," I choked and took a step forward.

Nafeeza's tiny hand shot out and grabbed my wrist. "Do not touch it!"

"But it's Jeffrey! He's hurting! It's going to kill him!"

"No, no. Do not touch it, lest it possess you next!" Nafeeza pushed me toward the door and turned back to Jeffrey and his pleading, hurting eyes.

Nafeeza grabbed the bowl of salt and held it near Jeffrey's face. She tapped the bottom of the bowl hard enough that a small amount of salt flew out as she shouted, "Leave this host!"

The salt sprinkled onto Jeffrey's face. I heard it sizzle as it touched him, and smoke rose in tiny puffs as the salt melted into Jeffrey's skin. He howled and threw his head back, teeth gnashing again, more Farsi curses spewing from his mouth.

I sank to the floor, my back to the door, my hands to my mouth. The room smelled of smoke and burning flesh. The air grew warmer, hot, too hot. The orange flame around Jeffrey turned to a deep, hypnotic blue flicker. It crackled and sizzled, the room becoming a choking chamber of sulfur and burning hair. The cat screeched under the bed, and Nafeeza's song filled the room as she knocked more salt from the bowl onto Jeffrey.

The ropes began to smoke, blacken, and fall away. It happened so fast I barely had a chance to stand and brace myself before Jeffrey jumped from the chair. He grabbed the front of Nafeeza's blue *abaya* in one fist and tossed her to the side as if she weighed nothing. She flew a few feet before she hit the night stand and fell to the floor. Jeffrey took three long steps and was in front of me, leaning into my face, that wicked blue flame flaring up around him.

"I am not through, human!" Jeffrey shouted inches from me. Then he threw his head back and crumpled to the ground.

My back was pressed to the door, my breath coming in ragged bursts, and sweat streamed down my face and between my breasts. Nafeeza was a motionless pile of blue cloth, shimmering black hair, and tiny black shoes. Jeffrey was as still as death.

In the silence that followed, the cat poked his head out from under the bed. When I looked his direction, he gave a short, questioning meow, then bolted toward me and hid behind my legs. I guess faced with the option of an unconscious Djinn or a fully-awake werewolf, the cat thought the werewolf was the safest bet. After what I'd just witnessed, I had to agree.

TWELVE

~~

Nafeeza ended up with a fractured wrist and some bruises, nothing more. Jeffrey wasn't so lucky. He was laid out in my spare room with bad burns on his face and hands, and nasty rope burns on his wrists. He hadn't woken since the ritual, but the little black cat had stayed curled at his feet, offering what comfort he could.

Bernie stood over Jeffrey, writing in his green leather-bound book. I had a journal just like it, as did every Presence member, but I hadn't touched mine in many months.

"Can't you fix him while he sleeps?" I asked.

I'd stayed in the room while Bernie examined Jeffrey. I felt like a fretting mother hen looking over Bernie's shoulder. But I didn't feel right about just abandoning Jeffrey, even if he wasn't conscious and aware of me. It was, after all, kind of my fault he was here in the first place.

"No," Bernie said. "Healing while he's out could do

more harm than good; too much shock to the body within a short period of time." He looked up from his book and glanced at me. "Besides, these burns are unusual. You said your hands and face didn't heal right after a previous run-in with Mr. Bragg, correct?"

I nodded, absently rubbing my arm. "Even after I tried to heal myself, it took a few days for the pain to stop and my color to go back to normal. It was like a really deep sunburn, just minus the skin cancer and peeling skin."

Bernie pushed his thick glasses back up his long nose with one finger. "I'm not sure if I'll be able to heal these injuries any better than you did for yours."

"But healing is your specialty, Doc. I'm an amateur."

Bernie smiled and said, "True. However, the Djinn's power is far different than anything I've experienced before. It's not psychic energy that did this to Mr. Bragg, but something. . . otherworldly. And that isn't what my powers are attuned to. Even *I* have limitations."

"Well, that doesn't sound good," I said with a frown. "Jeffrey's not gifted or anything, is that going to cause a problem, too?"

He looked down at Jeffrey's still form. "No, he'll be fine. Even if I can't heal things up as well as I'd like to, natural healing should take care of the rest."

Before I could pester Bernie any further about Jeffrey, he cleared his throat and settled kind, dark eyes on me.

"I don't mean to intrude on your personal life, Mina," Bernie began, "but it's been a while since you've come to see me."

I gave a weak smile and looked away. "Yeah, I've been hearing a lot of that lately."

"After all you've been through, I think it would be wise to continue your sessions. You've got a lot of pressure on you from work, and a lot of personal grief and anger you haven't addressed."

Heat blazed through my body, lighting my insides on fire. Even my skin felt hot. "Listen, Bernie," I said, surprised I was able to keep my tone friendly with the sudden burst of Fury in my gut. "You helped me adjust to the world outside of the Congregation, and the world outside of the loony bin, and you've even helped me deal with some *normal* people issues. . ." I licked my lips and continued. "And I really appreciate all that. But there comes a time when people have to learn to deal with their own shit, right? I really can't expect you to always fix my life for me."

"Talking to your doctor isn't the same as asking someone to fix things *for you.*" He took a step closer and touched my shoulder. "Talking out your frustrations to a safe person is one of the very best ways to fix *yourself.*"

The heat in my belly subsided. He was right, of course. Bernie Stevens had been there for me for more than a decade. He'd never steered me wrong, and he always tried his best to help me help *myself.* I gave a small laugh. "You're always so damn understanding."

He smiled and shrugged. "It's what I do." Bernie's brows furrowed slightly when he said, "Something is bothering you, and it's starting to affect how you deal with people and situations, even those unrelated."

"Is it that obvious?"

Bernie nodded once. "Some members have come to me, concerned for you."

Scowling, I said, "Was one of them Justice?"

"Yes. But I suspect. . ." Bernie shook his head, sending his glasses sliding back down his reddened nose. "Nevermind what *I* suspect. How about you tell me what *you* think is going on?"

I stared at Bernie for a few breaths, wondering how much I should say. I didn't want to dump all my problems on him, but I also knew he'd always been there for me without a stitch of blame or judgment, and he'd always given me the tools to deal with my issues. So why was I so reluctant to tell Bernie what was on my mind?

I knew the answer, I just didn't want to admit it. But I *did* want this pain to stop. I *did* want to stop feeling so desperate and lost.

"What do I think is going on?" I said to Bernie at last. "I think Justice is. . . messed up."

Bernie nodded, not in agreement, but in acknowledgment of what I'd said. "And you believe that his actions recently are a result of unhealthy thinking?"

"Not just him," I said softly. "I'm repeating the same mistakes over and over."

"What kind of mistakes, Mina?"

"Remember Joseph from a couple years ago? I fell for him, and he turned out to be a selfish ass using me for his own personal gain. Then, I fell for Vincent who turned out to be an *evil* ass, also using me for his own personal gain. Then, I fell for Justice, who turned out to be just as nasty as the other men in my life."

"I see."

"You'd think I'd have seen it coming," I said, fighting an urge to yell. "You'd think I'd have recognized the signs sooner. But I didn't."

"You were raised in an unhealthy environment which resulted in you not understanding what normal, healthy relationships look like. It isn't your fault."

"But I should know better!"

"And you will, Mina. It takes time to undo all the bad in your past."

I chuffed and said, "And it takes even longer when

more bad things keeps piling on top of the old shit."

Bernie paused, then said softly, "Do you think your recent loss is the root of your issues with Justice?"

I rubbed my hands over my face and fought back the sudden tears threatening to spill over. Shaking my head, I ground my teeth together. I didn't want to talk about that. Ignoring it hadn't done me any good so far, but even if I did talk about it, the issue with Justice had nothing to do with losing the baby.

"No," I said in a low, rough voice. "I thought so at first. But the more I look back on things from our past, the more I see that his bullshit has always been there." I shook my head again and looked down at the floor. "I should know better, Bernie. Why didn't I see it? Why didn't I stop it before it got this bad? Is Justice right, and I'm asking for it? Is it really all my fault that he acts so. . . cruel?"

Bernie took my hand and patted the top of it gently. "You know the answer to that, Mina."

"Right," I said. "It's not the victim's fault. But dammit, Bernie, he's really convincing!"

"They always are," he said. "Abusers are very good at twisting the truth just enough to make their side seem plausible. It makes you doubt yourself and what you're seeing, hearing, or feeling."

For a moment I stared into Bernie's dark, kind eyes. Had he just confirmed my suspicions?

"Bernie," I said quietly, "are you saying you believe me? There's something wrong with Justice?"

Bernie pursed his lips for a moment, and I could see him thinking hard about what he was going to say next. Logically, I knew he was in a difficult position. Being the one and only doctor for Presence meant that doctor-patient confidentiality could get a little cloudy when the members mingled intimately like Justice and I had. But my heart did not care about logic. It wanted Bernie to give me an answer.

"I'm saying," Bernie said quietly, "that I believe you're seeing the world as it really is. And I believe that you and Justice both have been dealt more pain and adversity than any one person should ever have to deal with."

"That was very diplomatic," I said, scowling.

"Then let me clarify for you," he said. He pushed his glasses up again. "I believe that you both have some issues to deal with. You have been a victim for so long, you almost seek those situations out now. But you recognize that in yourself and you *are* working hard on changing it."

"And Justice?" I pressed.

Bernie sighed and looked sad. "And I believe Justice has also been a victim. Rather than learning from the evil done to him, he is now continuing the cycle. The victim has become the abuser, and he refuses to see himself as such."

Though Bernie had confirmed what I'd already known, it didn't bring me any joy. Instead, I felt my heart break and my stomach grow tight.

"Can he be fixed?" I said through choked tears.

"Abusers can only be fixed if they *choose* to be. He'll have to admit it to himself first, *truly* admit it, and then he'll have to work hard on changing himself."

"So, there's hope for him?"

Bernie fixed me with an intense look and said, "That's completely up to Justice."

~~

"When will he wake up?" I asked as Bernie came back in the room.

He'd left shortly after our discussion, leaving me to ponder all we'd said. I'd sat on the edge of the bed, watching Jeffrey sleep, letting my brain absorb the revelations of the day. After an hour, Bernie had come back in to check on his patient.

"Soon," Bernie said. "He's no longer deeply under. In fact I think he can hear us if we try to reach him. Talk to him, Mina. Let's see if we can draw him out."

I moved some of Jeffrey's short, sandy hair from his face. His skin was warm and soft. I said, "You in there, Jeffrey?"

His face tightened under my touch, and his closed eyelids fluttered. He turned onto his side and scooted closer to the edge of the bed. Closer to me. Then he was still and quiet for several minutes.

"Jeffrey? Time to wake up."

"No," he mumbled.

I grinned and stood. "Come on, get up, lazy ass. I wanna talk to you."

Jeffrey rolled onto his back, groaned, threw a long hand over his face. "Yeah, I'm up," he said, his voice deep and gravelly. I was surprised to realize I found it kind of cute. "I've got a killer headache," he added. "And my face hurts." He pulled his hand away and cracked his eyelids open.

Jeffrey blinked and held his hands in front of his face. "What the hell happened to my hands?"

"You don't remember what happened?"

He shook his head. Slowly, he sat up, bracing himself against the headboard. "Last thing I remember is Nafeeza coming toward me with those bowls, and then nothing. The Djinn just ripped me out of my body and tossed me aside." He looked up then, eyes wide. All sleep suddenly gone from his voice, he said, "Did it hurt anyone this time?"

I shook my head. "Not really. Nothing permanent at least. Is it gone, Jeffrey? Can you feel it?"

He paused, glanced up at the ceiling, then shook his

head, a smile blossoming. "It's gone. Jesus, Mina, it's actually gone!"

Jeffrey sprang from the bed and grabbed me, gave me a firm hug, then promptly lost his footing and fell onto the bed, dragging me down with him.

Laughing, I peeled his weakened arms off of me and started to stand when Justice came into the room. He looked at me, then Jeffrey, and his face went dark.

"Am I interrupting?" Justice said.

I shook my head. "No, of course not. Jeffrey was just giving me a thank-you hug." I got up and went to Justice. "He says the Djinn is gone. It worked!"

"That's good news, at least."

I frowned at Justice. "Why so glum?"

"Because Nafeeza thinks the Djinn is loose somewhere."

"What the hell are you talking about? I saw the ritual complete and the Djinn leave."

"Actually, according to Nafeeza, what you saw was the *middle* of the ritual. She didn't get a chance to complete it because Jeffrey knocked her out."

"The *Djinn* knocked her out," I said, "not Jeffrey. He was out for the count when that thing took over his body."

"So he says," Justice mumbled as he left the room.

Jeffrey watched the door close, then he turned to me. "What was that supposed to mean?"

"I have no idea. Justice can be moody at times; it'll pass."

But I wasn't so sure it would. I looked at Bernie and all he could do was shrug.

~~

Nafeeza was on my couch talking with Justice when I

came out of the spare bedroom and down the hall. Jeffrey followed close behind checking out the pictures on my walls. He bumped into me when I stopped at the edge of the living room.

"So what's this I hear about the ritual not being complete?" I asked as I crossed the living room and squeezed in between Nafeeza and Justice.

She moved over to the end of the couch and Justice frowned at me.

"When I lost consciousness," Nafeeza said, "the spell was broken. Jeffrey was freed, but not because of my ritual. The Djinn decided to leave, but I do not understand why."

"Maybe Jeffrey wasn't worth the effort," Justice said.

Jeffrey didn't notice the insult. He was standing at the edge of the living room examining a painting of a knight on a black horse and a little red-headed fairy dancing at the horse's feet. I gave Justice a warning glare and he turned away from me.

"Perhaps, or it had a better host in mind." Nafeeza looked at me intently. "How do you feel, Mina?"

"Me?" I laughed. "I haven't been possessed by a Djinn if that's what you're getting at."

"How would you know?"

"Because I've already got more than my fair share of demons, thank you very much."

Nafeeza's dark brows came together and she looked at Justice. "What does she mean by demons?"

"Mina has a lot of inner turmoil," Justice said. "She doesn't mean *real* demons, just her own issues."

I wasn't sure if he was still being snippy or not so I let it pass. It wouldn't do any of us any good if I pointed out Justice's issues anyway.

Jeffrey finally came into the living room and flopped into one of the recliners. "Well, I feel like a million bucks!"

He held up his hands and touched his face and wrists. "That doctor of yours is a miracle worker, plain and simple."

Normally, when working with mundanes, Bernie would use a tube of regular antibiotic cream, and while he rubbed it in he'd pulse some of his healing energy into the person. Most of the time they'd think it was the medicine tingling and not even realize it was supernatural gifts giving it a little kick start. Bernie would always leave a small wound on the mundanes so they wouldn't get freaked out by an instant heal. This time, the light wounds left over weren't a result of Bernie's trickery, but of the Djinn's influence. Jeffrey didn't seem to mind.

"So," Jeffrey said. "What's up?"

"Nafeeza thinks the Djinn picked me for the new host," I replied.

Jeffrey shook his head. "Naw, it's gone. It's not even in this house as far as I can tell."

"How would you know if it's around?"

"It's left me before, just for short little stints. I don't know what it was doing during those times, but I always knew when it was coming back. I could feel it in the room." He shook his head again. "Nope, it's not here. There's something here, but it's not my Djinn."

Something in the room? He must have been feeling either my power or Justice's, but I wasn't about to ask or call attention to it. Jeffrey didn't need to know. Instead I asked, "How long did you have the Djinn? I know you told me you were always unlucky, but for how long?"

Jeffrey rolled his eyes to the ceiling and screwed up his face, scrunching his nose. "I was probably seven or eight. Stuff always happened around me, but *I* didn't really notice things until my cousin came to live with us. Even then I didn't know what was up, *he* was the one to really notice it."

"What do you mean?"

"He'd have these intense nightmares. I'd sit awake at night and watch him sweat and toss and turn. It seemed to happen every night at least once."

"Kids have bad dreams," I said with a shrug. A twinge of memory pulled at my mind, just out of reach.

"Yeah, but these were *really* intense. Thrashing around, screaming, talking, crying. I asked him one morning what he was dreaming about. He always said it was the boogeyman but that he couldn't remember anything else. Well, that night he started having the dreams again. I watched him for a little while, and then decided to wake him up. I went over, shook his shoulders, said his name over and over. Finally, he opened his eyes and looked at me. He smiled, but then his eyes got real big and he screamed. So I turned around real fast and caught just a glimpse of this orange flaming man evaporating into thin air. Just like that, it was gone."

Again, that nagging memory tried to surface. What was it? This was familiar somehow.

"Wow," I said, "so that was the Djinn?"

"Yeah, I'm pretty sure it was. Well, at least now I am. I didn't have any idea what it was until last year, like I said. My cousin was never the same after that. My parents ended up putting my cousin in an institution; haven't seen him since."

And with that last statement, the full memory slammed into me like a big rig truck:

"What's he look like?" I asked.

"Nobody's seen him and lived to say." Marie swung her legs back and forth on the playground bench, one white sock scrunched around her ankle, the other pulled up to her scabbed knee. "But I heard Jeffrey Bragg's cousin saw him once. He's in the looney bin now.

Won't turn off the lights in his room no more."
   "So he's really, really, real?"
   "Of course he's real!" Marie rolled her eyes. "Honestly, Mina Jewel, were you raised under a rock? I never met any kid who didn't know nothing about the boogeyman."

"Jeffrey Bragg!" I shouted and sprang from the couch.

Jeffrey's eyes went wide and his long, thin fingers gripped the arms of my recliner. "What?" he said, looking around the room.

"You used to live around here, didn't you? Went to school in Port Orchard?"

"Yeah, so?"

"My god, I knew you. Well, sort of."

He relaxed a little, sitting back in the chair, but his hands still gripped the armrests. "I didn't know anyone named Mina Jewel." Jeffrey shook his head, then added, "And I think I'd remember *you*."

"What about Marie Oswald? Did you know her? Little blonde girl about five years old?"

"I knew *of* her, didn't know her myself. She'd have been in kindergarten when I went to school here. I was almost nine when we moved away; that was a bit after my cousin went loopy."

"You were a big story back then, Jeffrey. Kids were talking about you all the time. Everyone heard about your cousin. They all thought he'd seen the boogeyman. But that's not what he saw at all!"

"Huh," he said. "I never thought I'd be a celebrity." Jeffrey shook his head. "That Djinn has been tormenting me for as long as I can remember. I'm just glad it's gone."

~~

While Justice took Nafeeza back to Page's Pages, Jeffrey and I took a walk around my property. We spent the time talking about his past with the Djinn and what it was like learning to live with it. I got to know him pretty well during that conversation and started to feel bad for the way I'd treated him at first.

"I need to apologize, Jeffrey," I said.

"What for?"

"For being so mean when we first met."

He shrugged. "I didn't think you were mean."

"Well, I wasn't very nice."

Jeffrey smiled, his eyes sparkling with good humor. "I can't blame you for not trusting me. You thought I murdered some guy, right? You thought you were tracking some creepy psychic butcher or something?"

"Yeah, something like that," I said and tried to hide my grin.

"Wouldn't that just be a hoot?" he asked.

"What?"

"A psychic psychopath. I mean, psychic powers," Jeffrey laughed and looked up at the sky. "Who'd ever believe that, huh?"

"This coming from the guy who was possessed by a Djinn."

"Oh, come on now, you can't tell me you believe in that psychic crap."

"Well, I didn't believe in the Djinn until I met *you*."

Jeffrey stopped walking and turned to me. "Are you saying you believe in psychic abilities?"

I studied his face, trying to read him. All I could tell was that his good cheer was quickly slipping away. He didn't give me the suspicious look, but the subject was definitely making him wary. That wariness made *me* uncomfortable.

We were treading too close to secrets he had no business knowing.

Though we'd recently peeked our heads out a little bit through my private eye gig and Bernie's hospital, Presence as a whole was still very much underground. We were sworn to secrecy and only allowed to talk about the society to gifted people or those who were friendly to our cause. I didn't know Jeffrey all that well. Sure, we'd gotten to know one another and I considered him a friend now, but I didn't know enough about him to consider him a *safe* person. Besides, the whole supernatural thing seemed to bug him, not that I blamed him one bit for that considering his past. Being possessed tends to make you leery of anything out of the norm.

"You *do* believe, don't you?" he said quietly, his face growing dark.

Oops, guess I'd waited too long to answer. Damage control time.

"I wouldn't say I believe so much as that I have an open mind about it, ya know? Maybe there's something more to people than we realize. Maybe there really is other stuff going on that we just don't know about. Hell, you were possessed by a Djinn, why not psychic murderers and all that, too?"

Nice, the naysayer said. *Reveal a truth that could cost the lives of thousands of people and destroy hundreds of years of carefully guarded secrets. Well done.*

My heart thumped too hard and my cheeks grew warm. If he sensed the lie, I was screwed. We were *all* screwed.

Jeffrey looked down at me for a few breaths, then shrugged and started walking again. "Yeah, I guess you're right. The world may never know. Frankly, I don't want to be involved with anything else weird. I'm willing to just forget all about that stupid Djinn and move on with a normal life. . . Like yours. I envy you."

Before I could stop myself, a small laugh sprang from my mouth. Normal? I wasn't even sure what that word meant. Nothing in my life had been normal.

Thankfully, Jeffrey didn't ask what the laugh was about. He just grinned and walked with me back to the house.

We were coming through the front door when my cell phone rang. I snatched it out of my pocket and touched the button to answer the call without checking the caller ID window.

"Mina Jewel," I said.

"It's five to four," Detective Richards said.

My heart skipped a beat. I'd forgotten all about my promise to the detective. "Shit," I said.

"I take it you don't have any good news?"

"Actually, I have some great news for me, not so good for you. And of course, you probably won't believe me anyway."

"Try me."

I swallowed and licked my suddenly dry lips. "Well, Jeffrey Bragg didn't do it, and I know who did."

"And why is this bad news for me?"

Detective Richards sounded suspicious. And rightly so. I was about to tell him he had no suspect he could arrest, nobody to bring before the courts, nobody to strap to the table and give the lethal injection to. Six murders would go unsolved, and it was all my fault.

"Because your suspect is out of town." It was the best I could come up with. It wasn't going to fly, and I knew it, but maybe I'd bought myself a few precious seconds to come up with a better lie.

"And *who* is my suspect?"

Shit. I'd always been a terrible liar.

I closed my eyes so I couldn't see Jeffrey's worried, questioning expression. "You won't believe me if I tell you."

"You don't have much of a choice here. I pulled you into this case to help me. If you hinder the investigation I'm going to have to arrest you for obstruction, and you could be charged with accessory if there's another murder." Detective Richards' tone was low and dark, making his words that much stronger.

"Okay," I said quietly. "It was a Djinn."

Richards said nothing for so long that I thought we'd been disconnected. Before I could ask him if he was there, he sighed. "A genie? You want me to believe all these murders were committed by some kind of demon from the Middle East?"

"Yeah."

The detective sighed into the phone. "I'm picking up Bragg. I know he's at your house. I've got a car on the way now; they should be arriving any minute. Don't try to stop them."

I felt the desperation well up from my belly and burst into my chest. "How can I prove this to you?"

Jeffrey was going to be charged and convicted. An innocent man was going to die because I couldn't spill the whole truth. One man's life for the safety and secrecy of thousands? It didn't seem fair. And why the hell did *I* have to make this choice?

"If it's the truth," Richards said, "then you won't have to prove it to me. It'll come out. But you can't expect me to believe this. Even *you* can't believe this." And then he hung up.

Shaking my head, my throat gone tight with frustration, I turned to Jeffrey. "I'm so sorry."

The police car pulled around the final bend in my driveway just then, and Jeffrey's face fell. The color drained from his cheeks and the light went out of his eyes.

He'd been freed of the Djinn just in time to be taken into custody by the police.

And once again, it was my fault.

THIRTEEN

~~

Jeffrey's cell was tiny. Not that I'd expected the police to put him up in lush accommodations, but the jail cell seemed so. . . enclosed. It was only a holding cell until he could be processed. He'd either be released or moved into a bigger cell, but still, this one seemed so small, and I felt terrible for being responsible for Jeffrey's arrest.

Jeffrey tried to assure me that he didn't blame me one little bit, but it didn't do much to ease my guilt as I watched him shuffle back and forth in front of his dull steel toilet sticking out of the brick wall. He'd made a call to his parents, but they'd refused to help him, yet again. No lawyer was on the way.

"I'm going to get you a lawyer," I said.

He shook his head and turned away from me. "You don't need to do that."

"Yeah, I do. I didn't just bust my ass getting rid of that Djinn to watch you rot in a prison cell because your public defender didn't know his ass from a hole in the ground."

"I can't expect you to pay for my lawyer. You barely know me. Why would you help me?"

I laughed, but it wasn't a happy sound. "Maybe you're one of the first decent people I've met in a long time. Maybe you've had enough crap in you life, and I think you deserve a break. . . Maybe I just like you."

Jeffrey looked at me and smiled. It was a weak, trembling smile, but it was genuine. His pale eyes softened and the tense lines around his mouth relaxed a little.

I don't know what made me do it, but I reached through the bars and put a hand to his cheek. He nuzzled into my palm and closed his eyes.

Detective Richards came around the corner with his tan coat hanging loose in his hand. "Come on, Mina. You have to get out of here."

Slowly, I pulled my hand away from Jeffrey. He opened his eyes and watched me step away from the cell.

"Take my help, Jeffrey," I said. "Trust me." Then I turned and followed the detective out of the room.

In the hall, Detective Richards seemed off. Though he wasn't all droopy and loose and obviously dejected, his head wasn't held as high as usual, and he walked a little slower, his hands deep in his trouser pockets.

"Why are *you* so down?" I asked. "You should be bouncing off the walls that you caught *the bad guy*," I said and made quote marks in the air with my fingers.

"You really think this guy is innocent, don't you?"

"Yeah, I do. I wouldn't be putting my neck out like this if I thought he did it. Have you ever known me to lie? To protect bad guys? Especially *kid* killers?"

He shook his head but didn't look at me.

"Why are you so upset? Seriously, you wanted Jeffrey

behind bars. You wanted this case to be solved. You've got your *attaboy* and your pat on the back and your good press. What's got you all bummed?"

The words may have been concerned but my tone was burning with anger. Detective Richards wasn't a bad guy, but I couldn't help feeling like he'd betrayed me somehow. It wasn't logical, I know, but neither was any of the shit that had happened and it felt as if everything was spiraling out of control.

Detective Richards stopped in front of his office door, his hand resting on the knob. He took a deep breath and looked at me. "I'm unhappy because you're so angry with me, okay?"

I blinked at him, some of my anger cooling and settling in my belly. The big tough detective had his feelings hurt. I gave my head a quick shake to try and straighten out my thoughts, then I followed Richards into his office, closing the door behind me.

"Hey," I said, my tone softened a little. "Why does it matter to you if I'm upset or not?"

Detective Richards fell back into his chair and put his forearms on his thighs, dropping his head low. "You're the reason so many of my cases get solved. You're the reason so many kids come back home in one piece. You're the reason we catch the weirdest bad guys." He shook his head. "Hell, Mina, if it weren't for you, we'd be up to our eyeballs in supernatural crap."

It had been hard for him to admit. He wasn't one to believe in psychic abilities, or so he always told me. He normally just shrugged and pretended none of the weird shit ever happened. But now, he'd just acknowledged that the cases weren't just weird, but actually, truly *supernatural*. I didn't know what to say, so I just looked at him.

"If I follow my gut on this one," he said, "I look like

a freak. I look like I've lost my mind, and I get laughed out of a job. If I follow my head and this guy gets convicted, I'm a hero and my life continues on as it has been. . . but it would be a lie."

He lifted one weary arm and ran his fingers through his mussed, dark hair. There was a little brown stain on his white shirt sleeve—probably coffee—and his slacks were creased funny. This was the first time I'd seen Detective Richards looking less than presentable. It softened me to see him struggling with his conscience. Maybe I could get through to him.

"You could just let Jeffrey go," I offered.

He shook his head. "Can't do that, Mina. I wish I could. All the signs point to this guy. All the signs except what you've told me." He looked up at me and he seemed so tired I just wanted to tuck him into bed and turn off the lights.

"I'm right, Randal," I said quietly. "You've got to believe me."

It was the first time I'd ever used his first name, and I think it caught his attention. He glanced up at me, then down to his lap. "That's just it," he said softly. "I *do* believe you, but how do I prove it to everyone else?"

"You believe in the Djinn?" Maybe it was too much to ask for, but one could always hope.

"I believe *you* believe in the Djinn. I believe you think something or someone else did this and that Jeffrey Bragg is innocent. And when *you* believe something, Mina, it's usually true. At least in one way or another."

I creased my brows. He believed me. . . sort of. That was better than not at all. It's all I could ask for at this point.

"Let Jeffrey go."

"He's got to stay until his lawyer gets here and we can

question him."

"That could be hours."

"Yeah, I know." Detective Richards nodded. "I'll do the questioning myself, and I'll go easy on him because I think you're right. I'll let him go right after I talk to him. But Mina," he locked his eyes on mine and clenched his jaw for a moment. "We don't have much time to prove his innocence. Work your magic. Fast."

FOURTEEN

~~

By six o'clock I had Justice, Timothy, Oliver, Alex, and Beckett waiting quietly in their chairs around the meeting table under Page's Pages. The Ardell twins were on a much needed vacation, and I had no idea where Zia had run off to, but I had good people with me and I was confident we could fix this.

"Here's the deal," I said. "Nafeeza thinks the Djinn is on the loose, maybe looking for a new host, maybe just waiting for our search to slow down before it pops up again. We could wait it out and grab it when it possesses someone else, but that could take months. We don't *have* months."

"Why not?" Alex asked. "Sometimes the best approach is to wait for the perfect moment. Patience, you know?"

"Because Jeffrey is in jail right now being questioned about his involvement in the murders of those kids and

Walter Garrot. Given enough time, the police can find enough evidence to link him to the crimes and get a conviction."

"And," Justice said, "Mina doesn't believe he's guilty."

"Do *you*, Justice?" I asked, my skin vibrating with a sudden surge of anger.

"I don't know enough about the guy to say positively yes or no. . . and neither do *you*."

My hands clenched at my sides, I said, "We're not gonna argue about this right now. Save it for our downtime."

"We don't *get* downtime anymore."

We'd obviously moved onto the less pleasant stage of Justice's cycle. It didn't matter what I did or said, he was going to be angry and he was going to blame it all on me. But I didn't have time to deal with it. And thanks to Bernie, I now knew it wasn't my responsibility anyway. Right now I had to prove Jeffrey's innocence and stop a Djinn from hurting anyone else. Justice would have to find his own path. I wasn't going to let him beat me up any longer. And that realization cooled my anger in one swift wave of logic.

I relaxed my hands and laid them flat on the meeting table. "Help or not," I said calmly, "just don't get in my way."

Maybe I could have been a little gentler. Maybe I could have tried to stem his impending tide of anger and cruel words, but I just stood and watched Justice's face go through subtle changes, subtle emotions that I didn't think anyone else caught.

"I'll help you, Mina," Justice said, dropping his eyes to the table. "I'll always support you."

It was a pretty lie, but it was good enough for now.

~ ~

"Police. . ." Alex said under his breath as he knelt in the flattened grass. He crawled forward a few feet and touched another depression in the plants. "Police. . ." He moved forward again, crab crawled to the left to avoid a damp patch, and touched another flattened area. "Police. . ."

He'd been at it for an hour, slowly making his way from the center of the field, working in a circle outward. When he'd first started, he'd touched the ground where one of the bodies had been found. He'd jerked his hand back with a whimper, closed his eyes, and wiped his hands on his jacket. He'd shaken his head and choked out, "Body," before tentatively touching the ground again.

I stood in the warm evening breeze watching my friend crawl on hands and knees through what must have been a nightmare of images. Alex had explained to me that as a touch psychic everything came to him as bursts of pictures, like images in a flash of lightning. He had to piece them all together before he could get any answers. Sometimes it took longer than others. Like today.

"Is there anything I can do to help?" I asked.

"You want me to hurry up?" His eyes were closed and he was crawling forward again, fingers caressing the grass in front of him, feeling his way like a blind man lost in a new place.

"I didn't say that. I just feel useless right now. Is there anything I can do to help?"

"You can shut up."

Normally I'd have ripped him a new asshole for talking to me like that, after all I was his boss at work and his superior in Presence, but today he got a free pass. I didn't really want to be crawling around on a murder scene, and I was pretty sure he didn't want to either. It must be like watching your own personal horror movie play out in your head.

Now, I'm no prude. I like horror movies. I can always turn my head or close my eyes if I'm scared. And it's easy to remind myself that it's all make-believe. Alex didn't get that luxury when he worked a case with me.

"Police. . ." he said quietly again.

He was moving a little faster now, hands flying over the ground, touching each blade of grass, each crushed flower. It was almost hypnotic to stand and listen to his whispered chant over and over, the rustle of his movement in the grass.

I'm not sure how much longer I'd stood there listening when Alex gasped and jumped up. He staggered back a few steps.

The hairs on the back of my neck jumped up. "What's wrong?" I said.

"He was there," Alex said. "Right there." He pointed to the place he'd just been kneeling on.

It looked like all the other flattened grass to me, but the way Alex stared at it, eyes wide, lips trembling, made me think twice about getting any closer.

"You said *he*, not *it*."

Alex shook his head and closed his eyes. He rubbed his upper arms like he was cold. "It wasn't the Djinn," he said and opened his eyes to look at me. "It was Jeffrey."

~~

"You fucking liar!" I screamed. My fist was getting sore from pounding so hard, but I didn't care. I was pissed. Better to pound Jeffrey's door than his face. "Open the God damned door, Jeffrey!"

I heard the bolt slide out, a fumbling at the doorknob, then the door cracked open.

"Mina? What's wrong?" Jeffrey said.

He opened the door wider and I pushed my way past him. His apartment was sparsely furnished with a fading rocking chair, brown card table and two folding chairs, and a gray milk crate to hold his small television.

I turned to Jeffrey and glared at him. "Alex said you were there the night those five kids were murdered."

Jeffrey's face went pale and he shook his head quickly. "No way, Mina." He closed his door and took a step toward me. "I didn't do it."

"Alex saw you there, he touched the very spot where you stood and killed those kids!" I could feel the heat rising to my cheeks, bubbling in my belly like lava. "Why did you do it? What could you possibly gain from killing a bunch of kids?"

Jeffrey's brows creased. "What do I have to say or do to convince you I didn't do this?"

He took a step toward me and I backed against the wall. "Don't get any closer, Jeffrey."

"Or what?"

I chewed the inside of my cheek and stared at Jeffrey's sad face. He wasn't moving anymore, just standing there looking at me, waiting for me to speak. I licked my lips. Even after hearing the gruesome details from Alex, I just didn't get the evil vibes from Jeffrey. He was harmless. Normal.

Jeffrey gave a delicate, hopeful smile. "You don't think I did it."

I shook my head and relaxed my shoulders. Jeffrey relaxed his too and let out a long sigh.

"You packing a weapon or something?" he asked after a moment.

"No," I said. "Why do you ask?"

Jeffrey hadn't killed those kids, but I was still

suspicious. Hell, I was suspicious of everyone, even other Presence members sometimes. My troubled past and all that.

Jeffrey gave a short laugh and moved toward one of the brown folding chairs. He sat and looked at me. "You had this serious look on your face like you were gonna draw some big gun from under your arm and blow me away."

"I don't do guns," I said.

What I didn't say was that I didn't *need* guns. I'd killed with just a thought. Less than a thought on one occasion. But I couldn't say that out loud. Jeffrey still thought I was normal. He thought I was just a simple private investigator who went home at the end of each day and ate dinner and watched a little television and crawled into my bed to dream normal people dreams. He didn't need to know the reality of my life.

And honestly, it was nice to be thought of as normal for a change. I had no intention of shattering that illusion.

"Well," Jeffrey said. "I do guns."

I followed the line of his gaze to the television. I hadn't noticed it at first, but now that I was calm I saw the small black pistol sitting next to the television.

"Why do you have a gun?" I asked. It didn't seem right that gentle Jeffrey would have something like that in his house. It made me uneasy knowing the weapon was in the apartment.

"With all the bad things the Djinn has done," he said, "I guess I just needed to know I always had a way out."

Frowning, I asked, "A way out of what? Out of trouble?"

Jeffrey didn't answer, he only stared at the gun.

FIFTEEN

~~

Nafeeza cradled her broken wrist next to her body. Though Bernie had given her a sling to use, she chose to make one out of a brightly colored silk scarf that matched her outfit. It did a crappy job supporting the wrist but it sure looked pretty. I rolled my eyes when I saw her wince.

"You know," I said, "Bernie can fix that in less than a minute."

Nafeeza gave a dainty smile and a tiny nod of her head. "I prefer to let my body heal naturally. I am not used to your magic to mend bones and flesh."

Should I point out the hypocrisy of refusing to use "magic" to heal an injury after what she'd just done to banish a Djinn? Nah. I wasn't *that* big of a bitch.

After Justice finished fussing over Nafeeza and took his seat, Oliver passed out small cups of something steamy and warm. I looked in the cup hoping for coffee. It was tea. My nose wrinkled at the sweet and spicy aroma. I set my cup on the table without taking a drink.

Nafeeza picked up her cup, took a sip, then looked around at all of us waiting. "I believe the Djinn is actively searching for a new host. It is not waiting like I thought it would. I think maybe it is growing weak and needs to find a new host before it fades."

"Hey," Timothy said, "what if we stop it from getting into a new host? Won't it just go *poof*?" He wiggled his fingers in front of him for effect.

Nafeeza shook her head, her silky hair shimmering with the movement. "We cannot stop it from possessing another. Not for as long as it would take for its essence to go. . . *poof*, as you say."

Timothy shrugged. "So, how do we kill it?"

"There is little said about killing the Djinn."

"Why not?" I asked. "It's a demon from your homeland, and you obviously know it exists, so why not research it?"

"It is not something widely spoken of in my land. The Djinn are still considered supernatural. There has been no research done to find the truth in the legends, and so no true research on killing the Djinn."

Presence did their damnedest to catalog and research all myths and legends, no matter how far-fetched, so we would be prepared if they turned out to be true. Nafeeza ignoring the Djinn seemed like a really stupid idea. It was akin to a child putting their fingers in their ears and closing their eyes, pretending the neighbor kid didn't exist because they'd gotten in an argument about whose turn it was on the swing.

But I didn't ride Nafeeza's ass about it. We only had one Djinn to deal with, and once it was gone, Nafeeza would be, too. As much as I was starting to dislike Nafeeza, as soon as the Djinn was dead Nafeeza could go back home and put her fingers right back in her ears. But for now, we needed her help, and any info she could provide would be useful.

"So what do the legends say?" I asked.

"It is said that the Djinn can only be killed while it is bound to an object. When it is bound you must kill it with the stone of a fruit."

"What does that mean?" Timothy said.

"The. . . seed?" Nafeeza turned to Justice, the question in her eyes.

Justice nodded and gave a small grin. He thought it was cute. He used to smile at me like that.

I frowned. I didn't buy the game of her not knowing English words. She'd been speaking just fine until now.

Timothy laughed. "So all we gotta do is throw fruit at it?" He laughed again and shook his head.

Nafeeza smiled. "It is not as simple as that, Timothy." She said his name in three separate syllables: Tim-oh-thee.

I rolled my eyes. Oh, gag me.

"The pit must be thrown hard enough to kill," she added.

"Not a problem," Timothy said with a wide grin as he clenched a meaty fist.

"I do not think even a Lycan can throw the pit hard enough to kill the Djinn."

"What do we do then?" I said. "Peach pit guns? Avocado cannons?"

Nafeeza looked at me, blinked twice, then looked back to Justice. "I am. . . unsure."

"All right," I said, "one problem at a time then. You said we have to bind it to an object. Like the magic lamp in the story?"

"It does not have to be a lamp. Any object will do. One from its homeland would be best, I think."

"How are we going to get something from Saudi Arabia as quickly as we need it?" Justice asked.

Good question. The only person I knew who could help us, was someone I'd rather not ever see again.

As if he knew what I was thinking, Justice looked at me and gave a single, decisive nod.

Crap.

~~

The next morning Mr. Boad was waiting for me at the pier just like I'd asked him to. He didn't seem very happy about seeing me. At least we agreed on something. He wore a dark suit and his blue fedora, as always. Did he wear the hat to bed? In the shower? Did he have an entire closet full of blue fedoras or just this favorite one?

"Ms. Jewel," he said with a nod.

"No small talk, no nicey-nicey," I said. "I need an object from Saudi Arabia."

Boad raised his eyebrow. "Oh? The mighty Mina Jewel needs a favor now?"

"Listen asshat," I said through clenched teeth, "this isn't about you or me or even Presence. This is about stopping a nasty little demon that *you* probably helped bring here. Now, you're going to get me a suitable object and you're going to do it soon, or the next death is on *your* hands."

Boad didn't flinch. I narrowed my eyes at him and stepped close enough kiss him.

"Zia is just a phone call away," I whispered.

His jaw tensed and his face went a shade paler, but otherwise his expression didn't change. Even without obvious signs of distress, this close to the full moon, my wolf could smell the fear on him. I wouldn't eat him, but maybe I'd tell Zia about his return anyway, just to see him squirm.

Vindictive? Me? Nah.

~ ~

An hour later I held a small clay pot. It was plain, brown, chipped, and ugly, but Boad promised it was authentic and expensive. Nafeeza took it gingerly from my hands, holding it as if it were the holy grail itself. Her eyes were wide with wonder as she gazed upon the pot, her fingers moving gently over the rough surface.

There's no accounting for taste, I guess.

"This is just what we needed," she said quietly.

"All right, now all we need is the Djinn." I turned to Timothy. "Any word from Latrator?"

Timothy nodded. "Yeah, he says he tracked it to a shopping center in town. A two story building in the business section between the Mile Hill roundabout and KFC."

"Thanks," I said.

"Oh, and Mina," Timothy's expression went serious. "Latrator said he'd like you to make an appearance one of these days."

"You always seem to have a message for me from someone who's pissed," I said. "Why is that?"

Timothy grinned and said, "Better to ask why you always piss people off."

I smirked. "You sound like Latrator."

~ ~

It only took ten minutes to get to the shop Timothy

had indicated. It was nestled on the top floor of a two-story yellow building off the main road. Timothy, Justice, Nafeeza, and I went around the back of the shop and explored the jumble of cardboard boxes, old newspapers, garbage cans, and recycling bins. There weren't any signs of life at all. It looked like people just tossed their junk out the back window and let it rot there.

We'd given the area a good once over and were heading back to the front of the building when Nafeeza dropped to her knees on the concrete. She gave a small whimper and covered her mouth with one hand. Justice moved forward to help Nafeeza up.

"It is here," she whispered.

At that moment I felt a blow to the middle of my back. I lurched forward. I'd have fallen on my face if it weren't for Timothy's iron grip on my hand. He yanked me to standing and whipped around, a low, animal growl rumbling in his throat.

After steadying myself I went into a defensive stance with my knees and arms slightly bent, elbows out, and fingers clawed. I narrowed my eyes, my back against Timothy's, waiting for the next strike while Justice held Nafeeza protectively against his body.

Several tense moments passed with nothing but the sound of an occasional passing car. I was relaxing my stance when I heard a rustle to the left. Timothy and I both sprang toward the sound, ripping boxes and garbage out of our path. I heaved a heavy box to my right just in time to see the end of a thick, silver and gold-speckled tail slither into a hole in the foundation of the building.

"That was it!" Nafeeza said. She pointed at the hole, her eyes wide.

"You didn't tell me it could shapeshift," I said, and it sounded as accusing as I'd meant it.

"I did not think it was important."

"Well, you were wrong. . . Again."

"It should not be able to do that." Nafeeza shook her head and looked up at Justice. "Separated from its host, it should not have enough power to change form."

"Okay," I said, "the thing knows we're here. It's not going to come out any time soon. What do we do? We can't just sit here all night. Eventually the store owner is gonna come out here and chase us off."

"The store has to close eventually," Timothy said.

"True. But then what?"

Timothy shrugged. "I'm not the thinker here."

"Timothy," Justice said, "I want you to shift to wolf and sit out here until the businesses close. We'll be back after closing time and we'll fish that Djinn out."

Timothy grinned and nodded. He loved being a wolf. He jumped at the chance to run around with fur and fangs. Sometimes I wished I was that enthusiastic about it myself.

SIXTEEN

~~

As promised, Nafeeza, Justice, and I were back just after the last business closed and the building went dark. We found Timothy waiting where we'd left him, his gaze locked on the hole the Djinn-snake had slithered into. Timothy's bushy gray and auburn tail swept back and forth across the concrete when we came around the corner, but he never took his powder blue eyes off the hole. I resisted the urge to rub his belly and say, "Good boy!"

Nafeeza held the ugly clay pot under her left arm and clutched a yellowed scroll in her right hand. Justice walked between us, head swiveling side to side, watching for interruptions. Nafeeza went about her work, quickly setting up the pot and her scroll in preparation of the binding ritual.

"What if it's gone inside the building?" I asked.

She didn't look up as she said, "As long as the Djinn is within my range it will be bound."

"And your range can go through solid concrete walls?" I doubted it, and my tone said as much.

Nafeeza looked up and smiled at me like I was an amusing little child. I was *really* starting to dislike her. Justice looked from Nafeeza to me and shook his head.

"I am ready," Nafeeza said. She stood and looked around. "Everyone please stay back so you are not pulled into the ritual on accident."

We'd barely moved away when words began spilling out of her mouth. I didn't understand a single one but it sounded like the same language Jeffrey's Djinn had been spewing during the ritual at my house. She spoke that strange language, scooping the air toward her with her good hand cupped as if she were pulling water around her. After a moment I felt the air grow thick and I could feel the current of energy Nafeeza had created.

She'd been claiming all along that she possessed no special powers, but I could feel the tug of that energy drawing me closer to her. Rituals held power, but it was rare to find one this strong.

I took Justice's hand and Timothy wrapped his tail around my left ankle. Nafeeza continued to pull the air toward her, making it circle around her, the words lost in the strong torrent of energy and wind. My hair whipped around my face, tangling with Justice's, but Nafeeza's was still and smooth down her back like a cape, not a hair disturbed by the tempest.

The air grew warm, thickening more, and it became harder to breathe. Justice looked calm and relaxed. I looked down and saw Timothy panting, but not like he was struggling for air. Squeezing Justice's hand, I tried to slow my breathing, relax my tightening throat. Maybe it was my nerves. Or maybe Nafeeza was trying to be sneaky and hurt me. Or maybe I was just paranoid.

All at once the wind stopped and the air thinned again. Nafeeza stopped chanting, the swirling cardboard scraps settled to the ground, and the grass stopped swaying. Nafeeza turned to us, her mouth open and trembling. She shook her head and dropped the pot. I watched it shatter, the pieces flying in all directions.

"What's wrong?" Justice said as he let go of my hand and moved toward Nafeeza.

"It did not work," she said quietly. "And it will never work."

"Why not?" I asked. "You said we could bind it and kill it. Why didn't it work?"

"We should have been able to bind it. We should have been able to trap the demon in the pot for all eternity."

"For all eternity?" I asked, my anger flaring to life.

I took a step toward Nafeeza. I was getting tired of this bull. I was tired of the games. I didn't trust Nafeeza. She'd been wrong too many times, and each time something bad had happened because of it. We didn't have time for more wrong; Jeffrey's life was on the line. My energy crackled along my skin, and I felt the burn in my belly that had nothing to do with the Djinn.

"What about killing it?" I said in a voice gone low and dangerous. "You said we were going to kill it. What's changed?"

Nafeeza backed away from me, shaking her head.

"It's time to tell the truth, Nafeeza."

She looked from me to Justice, then said, "I was sent to bring the Djinn back home."

"So you lied to us," I said. A flash of anger fed my Fury, and my skin itched with the need to let it go.

I blew a breath out slowly and willed the Fury to settle. Nafeeza's betrayal wasn't worth my losing more control. I wasn't going to waste my energy on her.

Timothy growled and took a step toward Nafeeza, staying against my leg like a protective pet. It was nice to know someone finally agreed with me.

"You must understand." Her voice was breathy, light. She sounded scared. "I was only doing what I was told to do. I had no choice. I had to come and take the Djinn back!"

"There's always a choice," Justice said.

"Why not do what you said and just destroy it?" I asked. "Why does it have to go back with you? It's evil. It's killing people for no reason!"

Nafeeza gave a small, humorless laugh. "It has a reason."

I stopped moving. Something inside of me screamed that I should plug my ears. Something told me I wasn't going to like what I heard next.

I've never been good at listening to that part of myself.

"It is clear," Nafeeza said as she straightened her sleeve. She bent and casually picked up her scroll from the ground, then looked me square in the eye. "The Djinn is taking revenge."

"What? Revenge for what? It's been here killing people. People who didn't do anything to deserve it!"

"It is taking revenge for its imprisonment."

Shaking my head I said, "I don't understand."

"Did you really think the Djinn was killing randomly? Did you really think a being of such power and ability would simply go about killing just anyone?" Nafeeza laughed. "This Djinn has eluded us for decades. It was not until Oliver called me that we even realized the demon had come to America at all!"

"Okay." I shook my head harder, my hand over my forehead. "Just stop a second and let me catch up."

I counted in my head, trying once again to calm the Fury that now bubbled in my belly. Justice put a hand on my shoulder and I felt some of that anger, that feeling of betrayal melt away. I hated him for controlling the part of me that *I* struggled to control, but I was also thankful he was there to stop me from tearing Nafeeza's lying lips from her pretty little face.

"So why couldn't you bind the Djinn?" I asked. "Or is that a lie, too?"

"The Djinn cannot be bound to two objects at once."

"But it's not bound to anything now," Justice said.

"Oh, but it is," Nefeeza replied. "The Djinn is still bound to Jeffrey."

SEVENTEEN

~~

"But, it isn't," Jeffrey said, shaking his head. "It's not here. I can't feel it at all, I swear!"

At least he'd stopped pacing. Seeing him wander back and forth in his living room had been driving me up the wall. I sat in one of his folding chairs, he sat in the other. I had his softly shaking hand between mine. It was the only thing I could think to do, and it felt lame and inadequate under the circumstances. But the moment I'd taken his hand and looked him in the eye, Jeffrey had settled into the chair and started speaking slower.

"I don't understand how this happened, Mina."

"I don't get it either," I said.

"What did Nafeeza say?"

I bit my tongue. I could have said all kinds of nasty things about Nafeeza, but none of them would help Jeffrey right now. He looked at me, lost, frightened. He needed me to help him. He needed me to be strong, not petty or angry or vindictive. I *would* be strong for Jeffrey. He deserved better than what life had handed him.

"She said the Djinn's possession was secondary. That it had been bound to you when you were very young. She said that after a while the Djinn was tired of being a prisoner, and it possessed you, eventually learning to take complete control."

My heart ached for Jeffrey. Not just because his situation sucked, but because I understood it all too well. My Fury, his Djinn, the same result if either one of us lost control. I knew his pain and I understood it, but Jeffrey didn't know about mine. He didn't know, and I prayed he never would.

Jeffrey nodded once. "So it was doubly bound to me."

He'd caught on quick. Small blessings that I didn't have to try and explain it in great detail. I wasn't sure I could explain it any better, not without telling him about my own demons.

He squeezed my hand and took a breath. "So what do we do now? I want it gone."

"We've got to kill it."

Jeffrey nodded, his eyes going wide. "You'll help me, right?"

"Of course. What kind of friend would I be if I didn't plan on helping you?"

"Then what does Nafeeza say we need to do next?"

I paused and studied his face. He was so scared I could taste it, but he was being brave and trudging forward straight into the unknown. He'd looked to me for guidance, and in turn I'd looked to Nafeeza. But now Nafeeza's true intentions were known and I was left clueless. But did Jeffrey need to know that? Would his trust and willingness disappear knowing that Nafeeza wasn't going to help? How much should I tell him? How much did he really need to know?

The whole truth. He deserved nothing less. It was *his* life, after all.

"Nafeeza doesn't want to kill it," I said flatly.

"What?" He let go of my hand and stood up. "Why not?"

"She wants to take it back home."

"That's insane!"

"I agree. And thankfully, so does Justice. We aren't going to let her take the Djinn back. We're going to kill it, with or without Nafeeza's help."

~~

"You do not understand what you are doing!" Nafeeza yelled between the bars.

My back rested against the cool brick wall just outside the cell, my arms crossed over my stomach. I couldn't stop the smug grin, and frankly, didn't want to.

Three years ago this very cell had been home to a nightmare. After getting rid of the zombie—a long story— we'd cleaned out the cell, cemented over the dirt floor, removed the chains, and replaced the stained bricks. But the smell was still there. Damp old rot. It had been my idea to stick Nafeeza here, and though Justice and Oliver protested, I'd won. I'd reasoned that there weren't any other cells at Presence headquarters, and we couldn't let Nafeeza get away. Of course, what I didn't say was that I liked the idea of Nafeeza suffering down in the cold, smelly cell.

"I understand that I've got a traitor behind bars. That's all I need to know," I said. "You're lucky I didn't treat you the way I've treated other traitors."

Nafeeza laughed, cold and angry. "You threaten me?

After I have helped you, you make threats?"

I pushed away from the wall and took two steps toward the cell, my anger a hot aura around me. "Helped? You think you helped us by tricking us into letting you release that thing? Jeffrey has *no* control over it now. It's feeding off of him and yet it's free to go around doing whatever it wants to! That's helping?"

"It is only seeking revenge. And rightly so!"

"Bullshit!" I grabbed the bars and put my face as close as I could so Nafeeza could feel the heat of my anger. I hoped it singed her dainty eyebrows.

"You think killing five kids is okay?" I said. "You think murdering Walter Garrot is justified? If you truly believe that, Nafeeza, then you belong in a real cell. I should tell Detective Richards what you've done."

The piercing ring of my cell phone made me jump. I snatched it from my pocket.

"I'm a little busy!" I shouted into the phone.

"Mina," Alex said. "I think you better get down here."

~ ~

Evan Johansson was tall for sixteen, close to six two even if he hadn't been wearing thick black combat boots. His mop of dark curls fell over his piercing blue eyes. When I came into the office, Evan watched me closely as I sat behind my desk. A slight blush tiptoed over his cheeks when he realized I knew he was looking. Like most boys his age, he was trying to grow a mustache. He ended up with that super soft, baby-fine fuzz on his upper lip and even a small patch on the end of his long chin.

Mrs. Johansson's eyes were red-rimmed and bloodshot behind tasteful, light glasses. The skin around her eyes had become puffy and raw. She held her little black purse in both hands, perched on her lap like a shiny, patent leather lifeline anchoring her to the chair.

"Tell me," I said. There was no point in detailed questions; we all knew why we were here.

"Evan came home late last night," Mrs. Johansson said. Her voice was rough, probably from all the crying. "But he won't even talk to me now. Won't say a word!" She covered her mouth with one thin hand and sobbed.

I turned to Evan. His cheeks burned deep red and he turned away from his mother, his expression one of forced blankness.

"What's up, Evan?" I asked.

He shrugged thin wide shoulders and shook his head, shining ringlets bouncing with the movement. One boot-clad foot shuffled back and forth under the chair. Teen angst at its finest.

"Mrs. Johansson, would you leave us alone for a few minutes?"

She stopped crying and blinked at me. She shook her head and reached for her son's hand. He snatched it away and folded his arms tight across his chest. With a wounded look, she whimpered and stood. She went behind the chair, reached for the shorter curls on the back of Evan's head, and stopped before she touched them. Pulling her hand back and clutching her purse, she left my office without another word.

"Will you talk to me now?" I asked quietly.

Evan gave no indication that he'd heard me speaking. He didn't even flinch, but I wasn't going to give up.

"What were you guys doing out there? Coloring books and building blocks?"

He scowled. "It was a party." The voice was almost done, almost mature. A few more months and he'd be a deep, rich bass. Right now it cracked and strangled out with the effort to keep his emotions under control. "Just a party like all the others." Evan rubbed his eyes like a sleepy little boy. "We'd have parties like, every month or something. Sometimes more. All get together and drink and smoke." He looked up at me through all those curls, eyes distant and knowing. No more little boy. "We'd do drugs sometimes, too. And then we'd. . ."

A few silent moments passed. I could hear the clock ticking away on my wall. Whatever it was, he didn't want to say it, but I was pretty sure it was important.

"What?" I prompted.

"We'd all have. . . sex." Evan shrugged. He tried to be casual about it, like it was no big deal, but his face went bright red again and he wouldn't meet my eyes.

My own face grew hot. I didn't want to know how bad the teen sex issue had gotten. That wasn't my problem, not until I had kids of my own—*if* I ever had kids of my own. Besides, with all my issues, I was the last person to talk to about sex.

"I don't need to hear any of that," I said.

He swallowed hard and his eyes flicked to the door. His mother was speaking to Angie out in the lobby. Her voice trailed in through the door, high and scratchy, obviously unhappy about being asked to leave my office. Poor Angie.

"I won't tell your mom," I said.

His face relaxed a little, but he stayed quiet.

"So what made this party different, Evan?"

"There were only a few of us that night. Usually had like twenty or so. But that night there was only the six of us. We were all getting ready to, ya know. . . and then everybody just stopped moving and talking. I thought I was having a bad trip or something."

"Then what?"

He paused. I think he even held his breath. Then suddenly he was on his knees on the floor, his face buried in his hands, sobbing.

I got out of my chair and came around the desk. For a moment I just stood over him, looking down at his shuddering form. I'd never been good with teens. Did he need comfort? Space? Valium?

I was fresh out of Valium and I wasn't about to leave him alone. That left comfort. Crap.

I knelt beside him and rubbed his back like I'd done for Jeffrey. Evan trembled under my touch and scooted closer to me. The next moment his arms were around me, his face buried against my neck, crying into my hair. He sniffled a few times, lifted a hand to scrub at his face, then went back to sobbing against my neck. Minutes passed and his sobs eased, his breathing slowed. When he finally stopped shaking, he pulled himself away from me and wiped his face on his long sleeve.

At that point I'd expected him to act all macho, to pretend he hadn't just been bawling like a baby in front of a stranger. But he leveled his gaze on me, as if daring me to look away or laugh or mock him.

When he saw I was keeping eye contact he whispered, "He made me watch."

"Who made you watch?"

"That skinny guy with the dead eyes." Evan sniffed and wiped his nose on his sleeve. "He made us all watch."

"Made you watch *what*?"

Evan dropped his gaze to his lap and fumbled with the edges of his sleeves. I heard him swallow hard. All I could see was the shiny, hanging curls covering his face.

"He made us stand there and watch him kill Missy. He. . . he never touched her, but I know he did it. I *know* he killed her."

"How? If he didn't touch her, how did he kill her?"

It's not that I wanted this boy to relive every painful memory, I just needed to know how it was done. I needed to hear how the Djinn had used Jeffrey to do those awful things, because Jeffrey didn't deserve to die for something he didn't do. If Evan's story could shed some light on the *how*, I had a better chance of figuring out the *why*, and a better chance of keeping an innocent man alive.

"He just stood there and pointed," Evan said. "And when Missy started to scream, he laughed. She fell backwards and went all stiff and then she grabbed at her chest and I saw—" Evan's words were cut short by his sudden sobs. He lifted his hands to his face and wept into them.

I leaned forward to try and see his face. I moved his hair and lifted his chin. Evan looked up at me then, the tears still wet on his cheeks. His eyes were haunted, filled with such horror my heart ached for him. I'd had those eyes for a long, long time and I knew how he felt now. He was weak and powerless. It was all his fault.

"It's not your fault, Evan," I whispered into his ear as I hugged him to me. "It's not your fault. You couldn't have stopped it even if you'd tried."

"I *should* have tried!" Evan wailed against my neck.

"It would have been you next if you'd have tried. But, Evan," I pulled away from him and lifted his face to mine once more. "I promise you, *I* can stop it."

Evan stopped sobbing and stared into my eyes. He looked deep, probing, as if he had some inner gauge of who I was way down inside. I was uncomfortable with the closeness, the intimate gaze, but I kept eye contact. Finally, he wiped away the last of the tears and nodded once, as if to say I'd passed his test.

EIGHTEEN

~~

The connection between Walter Garrot, the dead teens, and Jeffrey had me stumped. Jeffrey and I sat at the Bremerton branch of the Kitsap Regional Library searching through public records and news stories for anything that might hold a clue. Thankfully, everything had been transferred to computer, so at least the research was easier than rummaging through old files and boxes of crumpled papers. That always made my allergies act up, and I was pretty sure my swollen eyes and red, runny nose wouldn't put fear into the heart of the Djinn if we ended up going toe-to-toe with it.

After an hour of fruitless searching I'd sent Oliver and Angie back to Page's Pages to see if one of the thousands of Presence journals stored there might have some kind of clue. I didn't think there would be one, but it never hurts to look. How embarrassing would that be if our answer had been right there in one of the journals all along and we'd ignored it? Better to cover all our bases than end up looking like fools.

Hours of further research netted me absolutely zip, and Jeffrey had the same results. None of the teens were related. Their families didn't know one another, didn't work together, didn't go to the same churches or bars or social clubs. They didn't even live in the same neighborhoods.

We'd thought we may have caught a break when Beckett found one news article that seemed promising. Ten years prior, the deli had its grand re-opening. There was a picture on the front page of the newspaper showing the first patrons enjoying their sandwiches. Missy Edwards and Evan Johansson were both there with their families, but sitting on opposite ends of the restaurant, oblivious to each other. More digging and we realized there was no other connection between the two. Missy and Evan wouldn't officially meet until years later at some crazy teen sex party.

After that lead had flopped, Beckett excused himself and went to help Oliver at the book shop. That left Jeffrey and I alone in the library combing through the most obscure and least-likely sources, hunting for that one elusive clue that would crack this mystery wide open.

What was I missing? Where was the link? I hadn't even seen anything in the archives about known Congregation members. Not that the news people would know about the cult, or Jeffrey for that matter, but I knew their names and all about them. I'd search for their names, their relatives, and their known affiliations, but not a single one had been mentioned anywhere in connection with any of the victims' families.

"You sure you don't recall the name Walter Garrot?" I said over the top of my computer monitor.

"Nope." Jeffrey shook his head without looking up from his screen. "Doesn't ring a bell."

I sighed, tapping my fingers on the desk. Walter had not been a Port Orchard native and didn't have any ties to Washington. Or at least any that I could see right off the bat. He'd moved to the area well after Jeffrey's family had moved to California. That was a couple years after the night Jeffrey's cousin saw the Djinn.

My head snapped up. Holy crap.

"Your cousin!" I jumped from my chair and leaned over the monitor to get Jeffrey's attention.

Jeffrey looked up at me. His eyes were watery and dark circles had started to appear below them. "What about him?" he asked.

"Is he still up at Gentle Arms Institution?"

"Yeah, but what does that have to do with anything?"

"We've got to go see him."

"He hasn't spoken to anyone in more than twenty years, Mina. What makes you think he'll talk now?"

My smile widened. "Because I know someone who can stop his nightmares."

~~

I knew the way to Gentle Arms Institution by heart. My mother lived there, and I was there once a week for her therapy sessions and a nice visit. There wasn't a whole lot of Mama left, but I think she appreciated that I was there for her, even if she was just a shadow of the woman I remembered trying to shield me from my stepfather's wrath.

Nurse Bridge was never happy to see me, so the scowl she shot me as I came through the door was no big surprise. She was maybe in her late fifties, thin, pale. She had to look up to meet my eyes, so she couldn't have been much over four nine with her stiff, white shoes on. Her features were sharp enough to cut if you got too close, all angles and points and severe lines. Her cheeks were slightly sunken and her eyes seemed too round to fit in her tight-skinned face, yet they managed to look small and squinty at the same time.

"You're mother is sleeping, Ms. Jewel," Nurse Bridge said with her usual caustic tone. "You are three days early for your scheduled visit. You can't disturb her rest."

"I know," I said. Then I smiled sweetly. "I'm here to see someone else."

She narrowed her eyes. "You've come to make more trouble for my patients?"

I grinned wider. "Would I do that?"

"Who did you want to see?"

"Gabe Hamm. He's in room four-twenty." I gave my most helpful, friendly smile. It might have worked if Nurse Bridge didn't know me so well and hate me already.

"Mr. Hamm has a no contact clause in his agreement." The nurse grinned with a triumphant, vicious turn of the lips. "Only *family* may visit."

"Well, I'm in luck then," I said. "I've got his cousin right here."

I pulled Jeffrey forward, and he gave a nervous smile and a clumsy, flopping wave of one big hand.

"Jeffrey Bragg," I said as I elbowed him in the ribs.

He placed his ID on the desk. Nurse Bridge frowned. She looked Jeffrey over and then looked in her big book of names. She scanned the page, running her sharp fingernail down the list. She gave a grunt and slammed the book shut.

It took all I had not to beam and throw the one-finger salute to the wretched hag. See? I can be mature.

"Mr. Bragg, sign here and follow me." She pushed a guest book toward him and then stalked away down the hall toward the elevator without giving him a chance to comply.

Jeffrey grabbed the pen and scribbled his signature, then ran after the little nurse with Justice and I close behind. I tried to stifle my laughter while Justice shook his head.

~~

Gabe Hamm sat quietly in the middle of his bed with the sheet pulled up around his chin. Everything was white from the walls to the sparse furniture to the clothes on Gabe's body. It sort of bleached the happiness right out of you just walking into the room. I glanced around as Justice closed the door behind us, and I noticed Gabe's small closet door was secured with six different deadbolts and one chain. Nightlights burned in every outlet even though it was still daytime, and when Gabe moved in his bed, the blankets shifted enough to show that the bed frame was one solid piece.

I got it. No space beneath the bed meant no boogeyman yanking your ankles and pulling you into his underworld nightmare. Nightlights on, even in the daylight, meant there was no chance at all for the master of darkness to materialize. And the tricky fiend certainly couldn't undo all those locks from *inside* the closet.

Holy hell, Gabe was a piece of work. But what did that say about me that I understood his madness? Self-analyzing aside, seeing all that, I started to worry my plan wouldn't work.

Gabe's eyes were large and round, his face gaunt with years of sleepless nights. He blinked at us but gave no indication he actually *saw* us. Jeffrey stepped forward and extended a hand. Gabe just stared at it.

"Gabe, do you recognize me?" Jeffrey asked. His voice seemed small, lost in the blinding white hole of the room.

The situation reminded me of the first time I'd come to see my mother here after nearly a decade apart. It had crushed me to see her broken, frightened, lost. My heart ached for Jeffrey knowing he was probably feeling the same way.

Gabe blinked once but said nothing.

"It's me. Jeffrey. Do you remember?"

Gabe's face went rigid at Jeffrey's name, and his wide eyes darted from Jeffrey to the door and back again. He shook his head and said, "No, no, no!"

Jeffrey stopped moving forward and dropped his hand to his side.

"Is it with you? Did you bring it with you, Jeffie?" Gabe stood in a swift motion, throwing the sheet to the floor. His hands clenched defensively into tight, pale fists in front of his chest.

"No," Jeffrey said. "No, it's gone. I came to tell you it's gone."

"Really, truly gone, Jeffie?"

"Yeah, it's gone. It's okay," Jeffrey said quietly, but his face betrayed his true feelings. Jeffrey was spooked.

"I can sleep now? It won't come to me anymore?"

Jeffrey nodded but didn't move any closer to his cousin. "You can sleep now. I've brought someone who can help you sleep."

Gabe's shoulders relaxed and his hands uncurled, but he kept them protectively in front of his chest, the knuckles of his right hand *tap-tapping* gently against the knuckles of his left.

"I've been awake for so long," Gabe mumbled, his eyes darting around the room.

"I can help you sleep," Justice said. He took a step closer to Gabe. "Will you let me help you?"

Gabe looked up at Justice, maybe seeing him for the first time since we'd come in the room. He tipped his head to the side and studied Justice's face. "You're different," he said.

Justice nodded. "Yes, I'm different." He moved a hand slowly to his face and removed his dark sunglasses, leaving his golden serpent eyes exposed. "I can help you. Will you let me help you?"

I'd expected Gabe to freak out. I'd expected a panicked scream, hands lashing out to ward off the strange, serpent-eyed man standing in his room. I'd expected a frightened wail as Gabe fled to the far corner. Justice's appearance shocked most people: The yellow eyes, the pale, almost blue skin, and even his shining black hair brushing his waist. Justice screamed *otherworldly*, but Gabe was unfazed.

Gabe sat on the end of his bed and folded his hands in his lap. "You'll help me sleep? You'll keep the boogeyman away?"

"Oh, yes," Justice said quietly, calmly, as if speaking to a wild animal. "I'll keep him away for good."

Justice sat next to Gabe and lifted his left hand to Gabe's temple. A tingle of calming energy built in the room as Justice released his gift. Gabe's eyes fluttered and then closed. A moment later his tense lips relaxed, then spread into a content but weary smile, and slowly he laid himself down on the bed, Justice's hand still to his temple. Moments later the muscles in Gabe's jaw relaxed as he sank peacefully into calm sleep for the first time in twenty years.

Jeffrey watched all of this with a look of shock and a thread of fear. He took a step back and shook his head. He may have suspected something was wrong with Justice before, but now there would be no doubt in Jeffrey's mind. But I couldn't explain it to him. Not because of the secret of Presence and the oath I'd taken, but because explaining Justice's powers meant explaining my own, and I didn't want Jeffrey to know the truth about me.

Selfish? Yes, but dammit, he thought I was normal, and when I was with Jeffrey I *felt* normal. I'd never felt normal before. I wasn't going to just throw that away, even if it might help calm Jeffrey's nerves.

~~

"I've never seen anyone so scared in my life," Justice said as we drove back to Port Orchard. "Not even when I first met you, Mina. You were messed up, but Gabe is something else."

"That bad?" I asked.

"I couldn't find many happy memories buried in there. It was tough to build him any good dreams."

"But you did it, right?"

Justice nodded. "I gave him enough happy memories to cover up the trauma of his past."

Jeffrey leaned forward from the back seat. Though he was between the seats, he leaned closer to me than to Justice. I watched him in the rearview mirror as he looked at the side of Justice's face. He definitely didn't trust Justice, and he made no efforts to hide his dislike.

"So," Jeffrey said quietly, "did. . . did you fix him?"

Justice didn't turn to look at Jeffrey, but I knew he could sense the other man's unease. A lifetime of being judged and treated unfairly had honed his senses to pick up that kind of discomfort. That sense of others' reactions to him had helped Justice survive for so many long years, but it had also made Justice's life very lonely.

If Jeffrey's sudden distrust bothered Justice, he didn't let it show when he said, "I don't think Gabe will ever get out of the institution. His problems go deeper than just his scare when you were kids, but at least he can sleep now."

"What. . . what did you do?" Jeffrey asked.

Justice frowned a moment, then said, "He won't remember a thing about our visit or about the Djinn. There's no boogeyman in Gabe's world anymore."

That made me chuckle. I'd once thought of Justice as the boogeyman. That was back when I'd seen him for the very first time more than ten years ago, floating through my house, ripping my abusive stepfather to shreds without ever touching him. I knew better now, but not long ago I'd thought he was one of the bad guys. A bad guy who saved me from my stepfather, but a bad guy nonetheless.

Even with all the troubles we'd been having in our personal life, I knew Justice wasn't really a *bad* guy in the same way that my stepfather had been bad, or the same way that Vincent had been bad. Justice had issues, but so did *I*. Maybe we weren't right for one another, and maybe we shouldn't be together, but I still loved him and I didn't think that would ever change.

I glanced at Justice in the passenger's seat. It was a cool, overcast evening, and I had the car windows open. Why was he sweating? Did he overexert himself helping Gabe? That should have been nothing to him, an easy fix. He did it almost every night, going to the houses of Congregation survivors and slowly eliminating their bad memories while they slept. Then again, how would I really know? I didn't have the same gifts as Justice, and I knew very little about them, to tell the truth. Maybe he just made them *look* easy.

I knew the basics of Justice's gift. He'd gone into Gabe's head and gently pulled the bad memories from his mind, replacing them with good, clean, soft things. The "Reverse Boogeyman" I often called him. He'd done it a million times before with other people who needed his help, but this time, with that extraction of the bad memories, Justice had dug deep and borrowed knowledge. Maybe that small change in protocol was enough to drain Justice so badly. Maybe digging for information like that was more draining than simply wiping out bad dreams.

Justice would never complain though. No matter how exhausted he got, no matter how spent he felt after doing his job, he'd never complain. Justice was one of the few people I knew who'd put his own health and safety on the line to help others. Of course, in light of recent discoveries, Justice would only put his life on the line if a *gifted* person was in danger. Gabe wasn't gifted, but he'd been damaged by something supernatural. I guess that earned him some compassion from Justice. Or maybe the attention he'd given Gabe was all about Justice trying to cover the fact he was a bigot.

I could sit here and ask myself questions about Justice all day, and I'd never come up with any answers, so I decided to focus on the things I *could* figure out instead. Things that would do more than just satisfy my own curiosity or make my own life easier to deal with.

"Did you get anything useful from Gabe?" I asked.

"Yes." Justice nodded and closed his eyes, tipping his head back to rest against the car seat. "He had a lot of information just out of reach, but I got as much as I could without completely wiping his mind clean. You're going love this one, Mina." Justice opened his eyes and smiled triumphantly. "Walter Garrot was Gabe's father."

"That means Walter was my uncle," Jeffrey said. He grabbed the front seats and pulled himself closer to the front. "He was my uncle and I never knew?"

"You said Gabe's parents sent him to live with your family when he was, what? Seven?" I asked, watching Jeffrey in the rearview mirror.

"Yeah, something like that."

"And you don't recall Walter Garrot?"

Jeffrey shook his head. "No. Greg must have been his stepdad then. Nobody ever said anything about it."

"Interesting." I rolled my bottom lip into my mouth and chewed on it for a moment. "I wonder. . ."

"Yeah?" Jeffrey leaned closer, his excitement like an electrical charge against my cheek.

"You said your family had a lot of old stuff in your house when you were little, right? That was the reason you were interested in antiques in the first place?"

"Yeah? So?"

"I've got a call to make as soon as we get back home."

~~

"Walter Garrot was a fine man," Boad said. He'd lost some of that pompous air he usually had, but he still carried himself with an over-abundance of pride.

"Sounds like you knew him pretty well," I said as I tapped my pen on my desk.

"That I did, Ms. Jewel." He folded his hands in his lap and watched me.

"Are you gonna make me ask the questions, or will you just spill the info so I can finish cleaning up your mess?"

Boad cleared his throat. "I would like assurance that you will not be going to the police with any of the information I share with you this evening."

"If you've done something illegal, I'm going to tell the police." I gave an unpleasant smile. "You've got no leverage, Boad, so quit stalling."

He leaned forward and steepled his hands on the desk between us. Shiny, neatly trimmed nails and callous-free skin that smelled like expensive cologne made me doubt Mr. Boad had done an honest day's work his whole life.

"You're correct," he said. "I have no leverage in this situation, or with you in general. I'm surprised to find myself at such a. . . disadvantage."

"Get used to it. Now, tell me what you know about Garrot so you can get out of my sight."

"Walter Garrot was a collector of some standing within our circle. He was able to find some of the most rare and sought after items I've ever laid eyes on. I often envied his luck, but. . ."

"But what?"

Boad went stiff in the chair, cleared his throat, and straightened his tie. "I suppose now that Garrot is gone I can be frank."

"As if you had a choice."

"Garrot's methods weren't always approved of."

"Much like your methods of dealing with me three years ago?" I let the anger seep into my words, and the Fury ignited in my belly.

Boad shifted in his seat, his eyes darting toward the door. He'd seen the aftermath of my anger, but this was the closest he'd come to seeing my Fury in person. He had lost his best guard the day he'd ordered the man to rape me. I'd left that man in a sticky, oozing pile on the floor at my feet.

Boad was a smart man, so I was sure he knew the danger he was in. Angie had gone home hours ago and Alex was on assignment. It was just he and I in my office late on a weekday, and I held grudges.

"Yes, well, all that aside, Ms. Jewel—"

"For now at least," I said through gritted teeth. The

Fury bubbled and moved, slithering inside my belly. I added, "But you better talk fast."

"As I was saying," Boad quickly said, "his methods weren't always within the law. I know for a fact he ordered the detainment of a young Saudie girl some years ago."

"And of course by *detainment* you mean he kidnapped her." The muscles in my jaw clenched. "Did he torture her, too? Maybe threaten to rape her? I'm willing to bet *she* didn't have any special gifts to get her out of that situation. Am I right, Mr. Boad?"

Again my anger seethed at the memories. My Fury bubbled higher, burning its way out. Logically, I knew that if I didn't calm myself I was going to end up killing Boad.

Who cares? The naysayer hissed the question into my brain. *He's a blight. Him and all his friends. They all knew about the poor girl. They all knew about **you**, but they'll never be punished and they'll keep on doing whatever they want to whoever they want. . . unless you stop them.*

I pressed my hands to my ears, still gripping my pen in my right hand, and I squeezed my eyes shut. Maybe I should have called Justice at that point, but I didn't. I was tired of Justice flying in to save the day every time I got a little pissy.

Boad must have sensed my control slipping because he sat perfectly still, holding his breath. Thanks to those wonderfully sharp Lycan senses I could hear his heart thumping madly even this far away. I could smell his fear, too. That delicious, thick, sweet smell of fear. It made my skin tingle and my heart race, my body priming for the hunt. I shook my head and dropped my hands to my lap. I had to calm down or I was going to go fuzzy and eat Mr. Boad.

If it wasn't one problem it was another. My grip tightened on my pen and I heard it snap, the cool ink splashing my fingers, spilling onto my lap, and soaking into my jeans.

"Ms. Jewel?" Boad's voice was a squeak. An animal ready to run from the predator.

"Don't talk, Boad," I said through clenched teeth. Talking would only make it worse.

I heard him swallow and then hold his breath again.

I'm not sure how long I sat there concentrating on calm, but Boad didn't move a muscle. I finally opened my eyes. His face was white, eyes too big, the sheen of a fresh sweat covered his face.

"Now," I said quietly, "about that girl?"

Concentrate on the case and the Fury will sleep again. Concentrate on the issue at hand and I can keep my wolf from coming out. Concentrate, and I can go on pretending to have control.

Keep telling yourself that, the naysayer whispered in my brain. *I'll be here when you finally accept reality.*

Boad swallowed loud again. "Yes, well, the girl was detained and released, but only after Garrot acquired a book from her parents. That book—" Boad flashed an uncomfortable smile. "—was the very same that I sold to Jeffrey Bragg."

"That's the link," I said more to myself than to Boad.

Boad nodded. "Yes, I'm afraid I didn't realize until it was too late and Walter Garrot was dead. You must believe me, I had no idea who Jeffrey Bragg was or that he would come all this way to kill Garrot!"

"I don't give a shit what you thought. No wonder you were worried the police would pin this on you. It's *your* fault!"

"Well, I suppose that depends on how you look at it, Ms. Jewel." Boad's upper lip twitched. "I think it would be rather difficult to prove to a jury that my selling a book to

Mr. Bragg caused the death of Walter Garrot."

"And five teens," I snapped. "Don't forget the kids, Boad."

Boad gave a shrug. "There will always be more children."

I stood so fast my chair shot out behind me and slammed into the wall. I was on my knees on my desk, my ink-stained right hand twisted into Boad's starched white shirt before he could blink an eye. Yanking him from his chair I let loose a low, menacing growl and watched his hat tumble to the floor.

Justice threw my office door open just then. "Let him go, Mina."

"Fuck," I whispered as my teeth began to ache and the heat of the shift burned through my body.

NINETEEN

~~

"I don't want you to meet with Boad alone ever again."

Justice wasn't angry. I would have been. I would have been pissed enough to yell and scream and slam doors. I'd have raged all around the room until the anger was gone and I could think straight again. But not Justice. He wasn't angry, but he *was* demanding.

He handed me a cup of fresh coffee from the pot in my waiting room, then sat on the desk, his knees around me while I shivered in my chair, trying to contain myself.

It wasn't just the quickly subsiding adrenalin that had me shaking so bad, or the fact Justice had knocked me out with a temporary psychic lobotomy so Boad could escape. Even after waking from Justice's grip, my wolf still rolled around under my skin, begging me to let it out, to hunt that meal that had gotten away from us. The Fury had settled to a low boil, but it was still hot in my belly, asking for release to exact our revenge. If both my wolf and my Fury were still battling it out inside of me, even after my Justice-induced coma, I'd been very close to the point of no return.

I took a sip of the coffee, set the cup on the edge of the desk, then leaned into Justice, resting my cheek against his chest. His heart thumped slowly, calmly, the blood pumping in a hypnotic *whoosh-whoosh* rhythm that my heart wanted to mimic. His sweet-smelling hair fell over my face and around my shoulders, and I breathed deeply. If we could stay like this I could get a grip. Maybe I could even pretend I hadn't almost gone on a killing spree.

"The full moon is tomorrow," Justice said. "Having an emotional meeting like that was not a good idea." He rubbed my back.

"I know," I whispered against his chest, hoping he wouldn't ruin the comfort with more scolding words and guilt. Hoping he'd understand that I needed love and support right now, not admonishment and reprimand.

Angry with each other or not, a sign of weakness or not, I *needed* to be comforted. I was willing to overlook all of Justice's stupid jabs and childish behavior and need to control my every move if I could just feel some of that soft, sweet comfort he'd won my heart with so long ago.

I opened my mind to him and tried to show him what I needed right now, but he'd walled himself off months ago. Telepathically, I'd heard almost nothing from him since the day our baby's life ended. Shunned, banned from his mind, I was lost and alone in my own head. That was his way of punishing me for letting the baby die. That alone screamed to me that it was all *my* fault. If I had just listened to him and done what he'd said, our baby would be in our arms right now.

"Then you also know you could have killed him tonight."

I nodded and closed my eyes, his offered comfort slowly slipping away, replaced by shame. A heavy sigh built up in my lungs and I released it, preparing myself for what I knew was coming next.

"And would that have solved anything? Would it have taken back what Boad did to you?"

"No."

I fought back the tears. Tears because he was right, but also because he was hurting me. He'd offered me comfort, knowing I needed it, but then ripped it away so he could scold me like a naughty child. He'd been inside my head long enough to know that what he was doing right now *wasn't* helping me. He'd been inside my head deep enough to know that his words were cutting me to the core, and his little games were tearing me apart from the inside out.

But yet he continued, that soft, soothing voice throwing the shaming words right in my face even as his gentle hands offered me comfort.

"You have to be smarter about things, Mina."

He stroked my hair, trying to soften his words. But the softness was a lie, and I knew it. The comfort was for show. It was there to trick me into believing his words.

But it worked, as he knew it would.

I shook my head, but I couldn't pull away from Justice. Lies or not, I needed something soft and kind right now, and he was offering it. With a side of guilt.

He stroked my hair again and I shuddered. The lies always worked because I craved acceptance, love, and comfort. The things that had been missing from my childhood.

"You can't put yourself into these situations," he said. "If you lose control of either the Fury or your wolf, people *will* die."

Justice put his hands around my upper arms and pushed me gently away from his body. He waited until I met his eyes before he spoke again. "And you can't control if it's the bad guys or the good guys who end up dead."

I swallowed past the lump in my throat and stared into his intense yellow eyes. He was right. I'd done something very stupid. In my hurry to save Jeffrey and stop the Djinn, I'd endangered everyone else. The full moon ruled me, and I had only a shaky hold on the Fury always slithering inside of me. I was a danger to everyone and everything. No matter how hard I tried, people would get hurt and it would be my fault.

I didn't deserve comfort. I didn't deserve softness. "I should be locked up somewhere," I croaked as tears poured from my eyes.

Justice gave a sad, soft smile. He wrapped me in his arms and kissed the top of my head. Comfort. Real comfort, but now I didn't want it. I didn't *deserve* it. Offering comfort now was almost mocking.

"You do so much good for everyone," he said. "What would we do without you? What would all those kids have done without you? They're all home with their families now because of *you*."

"I'm a danger to everyone." Another hot tear rolled down my cheek and I swatted it away.

"You're only dangerous if you let your emotions get away from you. People have lived with the Fury before. They've led. . . happy lives."

I chuffed and pushed away from Justice. "I notice you didn't use the word *normal*. Why is that, Justice? Is it because people with the Fury can't *be* normal? What happens when you add in Lycanthropy? Am I a double danger now? Am I uncontrollable?"

"Calm down, Mina."

"Or what? You think I'll release the Fury on you? Think I'll go fuzzy and chew your arm off?"

Justice smiled. I knew his smile was supposed to come across as compassionate, but I'd seen too deeply into Justice's heart. I had seen the hidden darker side, and no matter how hard I wanted to believe the lies, no matter how soft and comforting he'd just been, I knew that Justice was sick inside and full of hate. I knew that for some reason he got off on making me hate myself and depend on *him* for approval. Drag me down, then build me up, only to drag me down again. Over and over. The same shit.

He gave me comfort, let me sink into it, only to snatch it away as he pummeled me with words telling me how stupid I'd been. It was my fault, and he was only here to help and guide. And look who came to the rescue again before naughty little Mina ate the bad guy.

It had been like this from the start, and I hadn't seen it until recently.

You didn't **want** *to see it*, the naysayer said.

That was true. I didn't want to believe that Justice could be so controlling and cold. Compared to his brother, Justice was a saint. But with Vincent dead and me having learned to judge others by their own merits, I realized Justice wasn't as great as I'd first thought. He was no better than my stepfather beating me, then the next day giving me presents and candy and false love, only to repeat the cycle again.

No more.

Shaking my head, I moved away from Justice. There was too much animosity between us. Too much distrust. And Justice wasn't willing to see his part in it.

"We're done, Justice," I said.

Justice laughed and the sound moved through the room like a gentle, cool wave lapping at me.

"Stop it!" I said. "Just stop. We're done."

His smile dropped away. "Done with the conversation?"

Averting my eyes, I shook my head.

"No." Justice stood and took a step toward me. "No, Mina. We're *not* done."

At his words the anger flooded back into me. I stood and walked to my office door. "Just because *you* aren't done with me, Justice, doesn't mean I'm not done with you."

He shook his head and set his jaw in a stubborn line, crossing his arms over his chest. "No. We're *not* done, Mina. It won't end like this. I won't let it."

"You're not in control of me anymore," I said, squaring my shoulders. "I won't let you abuse me any further. Get out."

"Abuse?" Justice looked sickened for a split second, then pursed his lips and I saw his jaw tighten under his skin. "I'm no abuser, Mina. I've never laid a hand on you!"

"There are many kinds of abuse, Justice." I shook my head. No amount of arguing would make him see the truth. I was done trying. "Just get out," I said.

He came toward me, and before he stepped through the door, he turned to me and said, "You'll want me back. Six months, and you'll want me back."

~ ~

"Calm down, Mina," Bernie said over the phone. "Take a breath and tell me what happened."

I clutched the phone in my right hand, pressing it hard against my ear. "I dumped him."

"You broke up with Justice?"

I nodded, realized he couldn't see me, then croaked out, "Yes."

"Ah," he said softly. "And you're uncertain that this was the right choice."

"Yeah. Did I fuck up, Bernie?"

"That's a question that only *you* can answer."

"I feel like my heart's been torn out of my chest."

"Anything else?"

It was an odd question. I'd expected comforting words, maybe some scientific explanations of why I felt so awful, but not that question. I frowned and asked, "What do you mean?"

Bernie paused, then said, "Look past the immediate pain, and tell me if you feel anything else."

For a moment I closed my eyes and focused on the pain. It was a deep black sludge encompassing all of me, crushing my inner self in a fist of despair. But I knew that couldn't be all there was to it. There had to be more. Concentrating, I pushed the pain aside and looked deeper into myself. Down at the very bottom of my soul I felt a spark. Putting my full attention on that tiny spark seemed to give it fuel, and it grew a little brighter, shedding light in the dark space inside me.

"Hope," I said into the phone. "I feel a sense of hope, that I'm not going to die without him."

"Is that all?" Bernie coaxed.

"And strength. I feel stronger. I feel like I. . . won."

"Because you did, Mina," Bernie said. "You stood up for yourself. You saw what he was doing, and instead of falling into the old pattern, you stood up for yourself and you stopped him."

I gave a small, soft laugh. "I did, didn't I?" Tears welled up in my eyes then and I let them spill over onto my desk. "But if I won, why do I feel like I've lost everything?"

"Growing stronger doesn't come without difficult choices. Nobody said it was going to be easy to rebuild yourself and find your inner strength. But you're doing it, and you're surviving. You *are* stronger than you think. And the next time you're in a rough relationship, you'll see it for what it is and you'll know sooner what you need to do."

I chuffed into the phone and shook my head. "There isn't going to be another relationship, Bernie. I'm done with men."

Bernie chuckled then said, "You say that now, Mina, but you're going to meet someone someday that proves you wrong. There *are* good men out there, you just have to open your eyes to see them. And before you argue, you *do* deserve to have one of those good men in your life."

~ ~

"We're going to play a game, Mina," Cadric said.

He had a handful of my hair, close to the scalp, and he was pulling me behind him. He yanked hard, and I felt some strands of hair come loose, but I didn't cry out. Crying was a sin. Father always said to take your punishment in silence and be glad that someone cares enough to do it. But what had I done to be punished? What had I *ever* done to be punished? Stupid question. My stepfather never needed a reason.

Cadric threw me forward on the cold, packed snow of our front yard. I fell and the air *whooshed* out of my lungs. I coughed and covered my mouth trying to muffle the sound.

Never make a sound. Never show weakness.

Cadric's boot connected with my belly and I sputtered for breath.

"We're going to play a game. You better laugh because I've gone through a lot of trouble to set it up."

Cadric had never wanted me to laugh before.

Laughing was a sin. My head swam. Just minutes before, he'd dragged me from my warm bed and pulled me out here in the dead of night. I was shivering in my thin, teddy bear nightgown.

"Look what I've brought for you, Mina," Cadric said.

My eyes followed the line of his arm as he pointed just a few feet away. A fluffy brown puppy shivered in the snow, tied to Cadric's van. When I looked in its soulful eyes, it thumped a bushy tail on the ground.

Cadric brought me a puppy? My seven-year old mind couldn't comprehend why Cadric would do something to make me happy.

Does it matter? The voice in my head whispered. *He's done it and you're here looking at it. It's real.*

I let myself feel a twinge of happiness, a twinge of rare childhood joy, and I smiled even as I gasped for breath and my gut cramped.

"You want to pet your new puppy, Mina?"

"Yes, Father. May I, Father?"

My thin hands shook from the cold and my excitement. A real live puppy all for me. A real pet for me to love and cuddle.

"Yes, you may pet his head one time."

Tentatively, I reached out and touched the puppy's warm, soft fur. It was damp from the falling snow, but still warm. I'd never felt anything so wonderful in my life. The little dog wagged its tail faster and lifted its head to sniff my hand.

As I smiled, Cadric laughed. Without warning, he drew his leg back and kicked the puppy. I cried out and reached for the whimpering dog. Cadric grabbed a handful of my hair and yanked me to my feet.

"You want to pet your puppy, Mina?"

Hot tears rolled down my freezing cheeks and I

nodded. "Yes, Father. May I, Father?"

The puppy lay curled on its side, tail tucked between its legs and held tight against its belly. Whimpering into the snow, it looked at me with those wide, brown eyes. *Help,* they seemed to say, *help me.* I was sobbing, my hands in front of my mouth trying to hold the sinful sound in.

"You may pet him one time," Cadric said.

He let go of my hair and I went immediately to my knees and pet the puppy long and slow. "Its okay, Puppy," I said as quietly as I could. "Don't cry. Never cry."

It looked up at me and whined.

Before I'd pulled my hand away from the dog, Cadric kicked it again. The puppy screamed and I scooted away from it, fresh tears streaming down my cheeks. I shook my head and cried out. "Please, Father, stop!"

He grabbed my hair again and yanked me to standing once more. Cadric leaned low so his fat face was right next to me. The stench of old alcohol and stale cigarettes came with each of his breaths. I looked away because I was never allowed to look at his face.

"You want to pet your puppy, Mina?" he said slowly, venom drenching each word.

I didn't move. I didn't answer. Was it a trick? If I pet the puppy would Cadric kick him again? It was suffering because of me. Every time I touched it, Cadric would hurt it again. It was my fault the little dog was hurting.

Yes! The voice in my head cried, *Yes, it's your fault! You hurt the puppy because you're naughty!*

With a sinking, desperate feeling in my belly, I shook my head. "No, Father," I sobbed. "I don't want to pet the puppy."

"Oh," Cadric said with mock surprise. "In that case."

And before I could cry out, before I could throw myself in front of the tiny, whimpering dog, Cadric pulled a black handgun from inside his jacket, pointed it at the dog, and pulled the trigger.

Blood spattered my nightgown, gushed red and thick from the dog's ruined head, poured out around it, staining the snow. Something warm and wet slid down my cheek.

"Useless," Cadric said. I barely heard him over my screams. "Useless, just like you."

Then the gun was against my head, pressed into my temple. Cadric forced me to my knees and laughed.

"Why aren't you smiling? Why aren't you laughing? Show me you appreciate what I've done for you!" He pushed the gun hard against my head and I cried.

"Thank me," he growled.

"Thank. . . you. . . Father," I sobbed.

"Not good enough." Cadric pushed me onto my back and stood over me, straddling my body. He looked like a giant glaring down at me, looking over that huge, round belly. He bent at the waist and pressed the gun to my forehead.

"Useless," he said, and he pulled the trigger.

~~

I sat up, clutching the covers, tears wet on my face as the last of my scream faded from my lips. Seconds later Jeffrey stumbled through the door. Dim moonlight spilled into the bedroom from the living room window. Jeffrey's hair was mussed from sleep and his eyes were half closed, but his voice was wide awake, concern accenting each syllable.

"What's wrong, Mina?"

I touched my forehead with one hand, wiped the tears from my cheeks with the other, then covered my mouth with trembling fingers.

"One bullet. . ." I whispered, then gasped. "Only one bullet."

"Did you have a nightmare?"

"No." I shook my head and pulled the blanket closer, tucking it under my chin. "A memory."

"Memory?" Jeffrey came closer and sat on his bed next to me. "Has your life been so bad?"

"My life was. . . bad," I said. "You could say that."

I would have preferred to wake up in my own bed cuddled against Justice and Timothy like I did every other night, but I'd banished Justice from my bed. And it was my shift at Jeffrey's house anyway. We were taking turns keeping an eye on him in case the Djinn came back. Justice had left only two hours before with a promise to return at six a.m. He hadn't even looked me in the eye when he'd left, and my soul ached for the pain I'd caused him. And the pain I'd caused myself.

Jeffrey had witnessed the uncomfortable exchange, but hadn't said a word. He'd offered me his bed and had been sleeping on the floor in his living room since he didn't have a couch.

"What happened?" he asked softly.

My body shook hard enough that my teeth chattered. To my core, I was cold, as if I'd really been laying in the bloody snow again. As if I'd really had the blood cooling in tiny drops on my skin. As if I'd really thought I was about to die just before the gun clicked empty and Cadric dragged me by my hair back into the house for more *fun*.

A violent shudder shook me, and my stomach lurched, turning in on itself. I tried to block the memory of what had happened next that night, but it was too fresh in my mind. Another tear dropped from my eye and landed on the blanket in my lap.

Jeffrey put his arm around me and it was then I

realized he was shaking, too.

"Jeffrey?"

"Yeah?"

I turned in the near-dark and looked at the side of his face. "Did you have a nightmare?"

He paused, his body tensing beside me. Then he nodded. "Yeah. I woke up right before you screamed."

"Was it the Djinn?"

"Hey," he said, squeezing me gently, "this isn't about me. For once, lets worry about you. What was so bad?"

Quickly, I shook my head and set my shoulders. "You don't want to know about me. Trust me, if you're having nightmares already, my stories aren't gonna help you any."

Jeffrey shrugged. "All right, I won't push it. But I have to know. . . Are you going to be okay?"

I nodded even though I knew I wasn't okay. I would never be okay. Peace, solace, happiness. These were things I was never destined to have. I could spend the rest of my life pretending I was happy or I had peace, but deep down I knew it was all a lie. All I would ever have were the terrifying memories that haunted my dreams and the knowledge that I wasn't worthy of anything more.

"You sure?" Jeffrey asked.

"Yeah, I'm just gonna go back to sleep now. Sorry for scaring you."

"Not a problem." Jeffrey stood. "If you need anything at all, I'm just out here. I don't mind being woken up."

"I'm fine, really. Goodnight."

He stepped away from the bed, and I felt something jerk in my gut—a sudden ache, but of what I wasn't sure. His next step put him in the doorway of the bedroom, and the ache grew and my throat went tight. Moonlight tumbled into the room, turning Jeffrey into a moving silhouette. In that soft blue light, suddenly I didn't see Jeffrey the awkward guy who had a pesky Djinn threatening his life. I saw Jeffrey the man with thoughts and feelings and worries and dreams. I saw Jeffrey the man who'd extended the hand of friendship to me even after a lifetime of having his hand slapped away by so many others.

He paused at the door, one hand on the doorjamb, and I knew then what the ache in my body was. My subconscious told me that I didn't really want Jeffrey to go, and that I needed something that only he could give me right now.

I'd had a rough night. I couldn't get comfort from the man I'd loved, and I couldn't leave my post at Jeffrey's to go find Timothy or my Lycan pack. I'd lay here all night reliving the memory if I didn't calm down, and I knew I couldn't calm down here in the dark all alone. There was only one option.

"Jeffrey?" I whispered.

He turned in the doorway. "Yeah?"

"Would you come lay down with me?"

My cheeks went hot the moment the words left my mouth. It was definitely *not* what I'd intended to say, but my subconscious had hijacked my mouth at the last second. Mortified as I was with what I'd asked of Jeffrey, part of me was relieved. Part of me knew it's what I really needed. Human contact. I could have asked him to just sit with me and talk, but that would only go so far in giving me the true comfort I needed right now.

Jeffrey didn't answer right away, and I felt like an idiot. I'd made him uncomfortable. I'd put him on the spot for my own selfish needs.

"You can say, no," I said.

"No," he snapped. "I mean, yes. Yeah, I'll come lay down with you."

He closed the bedroom door, shutting out the moonlight from the living room. I heard his feet shuffling along the floor and his breathing quicken as he drew nearer. The mattress sank as he slowly, carefully climbed on and settled down next to me.

I laid down, rolled onto my side, and scooted my back against his body. He was warm and alive and real. I needed that contact. Even if it wasn't Timothy or Justice or even Latrator and my werewolf pack, I needed the contact. The touch of another living creature could chase away the bad things, chase away the memories.

A moment passed and Jeffrey turned onto his side, scooted close against my back, and slowly put his hand on my waist. With his touch my anxiety eased and my mind quieted. I smiled and closed my eyes, ready to sleep.

Jeffrey's heart hammered against my back, and his hand moved down to my hip. After a few minutes it became apparent that *he* wasn't thinking of sleep. My eyes shot open when I realized my mistake.

I'd been sleeping with Justice and Timothy for so long I'd forgotten that our arrangement wasn't normal. Even after Justice and I started all these damn fights we still slept together nearly every night. And before I'd stopped going to see my fellow Lycans, I'd slept in the big puppy pile which had lots of males in it. Erections were just a natural part of living with men, and for the men in *my* life it wasn't usually a sexual thing. I knew it was out of their control, and I knew it would go away if I ignored it. I'd become accustomed to just pretending it wasn't there, and all the men in my life had grown accustomed to the fact I didn't have sex with *anyone*.

Inviting Jeffrey to sleep in the bed with me wasn't an invitation for sex, but *he* didn't know that. I guess I'd forgotten that most women didn't invite men to sleep with them unless they wanted a little more.

Crap.

"Jeffrey?"

"Yeah?"

I cleared my throat. "Hey, we're not going to—"

"I know," he interrupted.

It felt like I should say something to help diffuse the awkwardness, but what? No matter how I looked at it the whole thing was uncomfortable for both of us. Jeffrey stayed next to me, his hand resting lightly on my hip, his body vibrating with nervous energy, and his excitement poking my back side. Even if I hadn't been a Lycan I could have heard his heart thundering away and his breath coming and going in soft little spurts. I had to say *something*.

"How long has it been?" I finally asked.

Probably not the best thing to say, but at least I was talking. It could still be a casual conversation, even if the subject *was* sex. I just needed to handle it carefully. Taking the focus off the immediate situation and looking at the big picture meant we could slowly ease ourselves out of the uncomfortable spot. Or so I hoped. A lot of it depended on how Jeffrey reacted, and if I could keep my cool.

"Oh. . . uh. . . a long time," he said. "Listen, if this is making you uncomfortable, I can go back to the living room floor."

He said the words but I knew he didn't mean them. He held his breath and stayed perfectly still. His hand still rested on my hip as if he feared any movement would scare me away or make me angry.

"I'm not uncomfortable," I fibbed.

True, I wasn't as uneasy as I had been moments before, but I certainly wasn't relaxed. Even so, I suspected Jeffrey was more embarrassed than I was. Since it was my fault we were here in the first place I thought I should try to ease his mind a bit. I patted his hand and tried not to sound freaked out when I asked, "So, how long is a long time?"

Jeffrey groaned. "You're going to make me answer that, aren't you?"

"Yup."

Jeffrey sighed. "All right, it's been thirty-seven years."

The laugh popped out before I could stop myself, and I felt Jeffrey's whole body go rigid behind me.

"Are you laughing at me?" he asked.

Yes.

"No," I said, "it's just—"

"That I'm a virgin and you think it's pathetic."

In one swift motion, Jeffrey took his hand off my hip and rolled onto his back as far away from me as the small bed would allow.

Well, that didn't go as well as I'd hoped. Laughing at a man's lack of sexual exploits was a definite mood-killer. Sure, we were out of the danger zone now, but I'd hurt his feelings in the process. That was pretty much the exact opposite of what I'd been trying to do.

I turned onto my right side. All I could see was a faint outline of Jeffrey's profile, but I sensed his tension and his hurt.

"Hey," I said, lifting myself on my elbow. "I wasn't laughing *at* you."

"Sounded like it to me."

"It's not like that. I laughed because I've found another virgin."

"What's that supposed to mean?"

He sounded defensive, and I couldn't blame him. This whole night was falling apart, and every time I opened my mouth I made it worse. But I couldn't just leave it. He'd misunderstood me and he was hurt. I had to try and fix it.

"Justice was a virgin when I first met him," I said.

"And he's *much* older than you." By about a hundred and fifty years, but I didn't say that part out loud. Secrets, you know. "And I'm pretty sure Timothy is a virgin." Only because he'd spent twenty years alone in the woods with no contact with humans or other Lycans. But, again, I didn't say that out loud. Jeffrey still thought *I* was normal. He knew there was something weird about Justice, and he probably suspected Timothy wasn't all there, but he still thought *I* was a regular, normal woman. Admitting I was surrounded by freaks would make him wonder.

"Maybe you're a virgin magnet," he said and then laughed. "Maybe you've got some kind of magic spell over all the pathetic little virgin men in the world, huh?"

He'd meant it as a joke, but he was half right. The Seduction, one of my least favorite gifts, attracted people to me whether I wanted it or not. I'd learned to suppress it just recently. Zia thought I was stupid for keeping the Seduction at bay since she used it every day to get whatever she wanted. That was the "spell" she'd used on Boad. That and Suggestion, which, thankfully, I didn't have.

I didn't want to be like Zia, controlling people with the false promise of sex or affection. I'd had a hard enough time finally having sex with Justice after a year of being a couple, I certainly didn't need a trail of lust-sick men and women following me everywhere I went.

No, the Seduction wasn't always about sex, but it often turned to that when dealing with certain people. The Seduction promised my targets whatever it was that their hearts truly desired. For a lot of adults, that was sex.

"Wow, tough audience," Jeffrey said as he poked my shoulder with one finger.

"I'm sorry," I said. "I was just thinking."

I laid on my back and looked up at the dark ceiling. Jeffrey joked with me and played around and talked to me as if I was normal. But there hadn't been a day in my life that I could have called normal, nor a moment in my life that I could say I'd *felt* normal. . . except when Jeffrey was around. What I would give for just one day without psychic gifts and supernatural beasties. What would my life have been like if I'd been born mundane?

"Did you have a good childhood, Jeffrey?" I asked. "I mean before the Djinn came along. Do you remember being happy?"

He laughed. "Yeah, actually. I had a great childhood before all this crazy stuff started happening."

"Tell me about it?"

"What is there to tell? It was nothing special. I mean, everyone has birthdays and holidays and family gatherings, right?"

"No," I said. "No, not everyone."

He was quiet a moment, and I wondered what he was thinking. Had I shared too much? Would he stop seeing me as normal? Would he ask questions? He'd find out my secrets and then pass judgment like he'd done to Justice. Shit. I was really screwing this up tonight.

Before I could try to fix things, he said, "I won't ask. I can tell you don't really want to get into it, and I can respect that."

My throat went tight. I wanted to burst into tears. I'd assumed he'd react like Justice always did—pushing, probing, insistent that he knew best. But Jeffrey wasn't like Justice. While a small part of me was ashamed for even thinking he *could* be, another part of me was angry at Justice for making me believe for so long that his behavior was okay.

"So, what did you want to hear about?" Jeffrey asked.

I breathed a small laugh and said quietly, "Start at the beginning. Tell me everything."

We spent the next couple of hours talking about trips to the zoo and games in the backyard. I listened to Jeffrey's happy stories, and I imagined myself there with him, playing with his dogs and his little brother. Eating birthday cake and getting messy in melting, sticky ice cream during summer. Movie nights with mom and dad. Sleepovers, picnics, going to friends' houses for dinner. . . And laughter. Always laughter and smiles and love. All the things I'd never known.

"It sounds wonderful," I whispered. "Thanks for humoring me."

"I was happy to. Besides, I think I needed that."

"Oh?"

"With all this weird stuff going on, it was nice to just remember the good parts. Even if it was just for a little while and nothing has really changed."

Oh, plenty had changed. He might not have realized it, but he'd changed things for me. Thanks to him, I had some happy memories to cling to now, even if they weren't my own. Even borrowed from a friend, these memories could help chase the bad things away, and I owed Jeffrey for that. I'd pay him back somehow, I promised myself.

Smiling and finally at peace, I started to drift off to sleep, anticipating good dreams for a change.

But Jeffrey's soft voice pulled me back to waking when he said, "Don't ever lie to them, Mina."

I nudged his arm with my forehead. "Lie to who?"

"Your kids."

That peaceful feeling dropped away and I plummeted into sadness once again thinking about *that* day.

I said, "I don't have any kids, Jeffrey." What I didn't say, is that I *should* have a child. But my child never got to take a breath, never got to see the world because the bad guys had stolen his or her life before it ever really began, and it was *my* fault.

"I know," he said. "But when you do have kids, don't ever lie to them."

I shook my head, trying to knock the memory from my mind and focus on the conversation. "What brought this up? What are you talking about?"

"The monsters," he whispered, and he sounded small, scared. "Don't ever tell them the monsters aren't real, because the monsters *are* real, and they're always listening."

"Jeffrey. . ."

"Promise me, Mina. Promise you won't lie to them."

I shook my head. "I won't lie to them."

And it was the truth. I wouldn't tell my future kids, if I had any, that the monsters weren't real, because I knew it was a lie, too. But not in the same way Jeffrey knew it. Not in the same way he meant it. I would tell them that the monsters were real, because *I* was one of the monsters, and they would be, too.

~~

Summer sun streamed in through pale white curtains, leaving long, golden streaks on the floor. A gentle breeze blew in off the ocean and moved Justice's drying hair across my face. Our wet clothes were piled next to the bed, still smelling of sea water and sand. He kissed me, holding me tight against his body.

I ran my hands over his chest, brushing his nipples with my fingertips. His skin was still cool from our impromptu swim, and the sensation sent shivers through my body. He sighed and threw his head back as I kissed his chest, nibbling my way down his body, licking the sea salt from his skin. I steadied myself with hands on his slender waist and went to my knees kissing down his belly.

Stop, a far off voice called.

My mind struggled with the scene. This wasn't right, but I couldn't put my finger on what was really happening, and I was compelled to kiss lower.

Stop! Look!

The smell of fire and a musty, acrid scent wafted through the window. I looked up to find Justice's golden eyes looking down at me, but they weren't in his face.

With a gasp, I moved my head back, may hands still on his waist. The giant serpent towered above me, a red forked tongue flicking between scaled lips. Not black. Silver, gold, red. The sheen of vibrant colors on bright metallic scales, shimmering in the light from the window.

"Justice?" I whispered, though I knew it wasn't him.

Something moved under my hands and I looked down. Justice's firm belly had morphed into an undulating scaled body. Long, thick, heavily muscled. Barely contained power.

Yanking my hands back, I looked up again. The snake opened its mouth and drew back, long white fangs dripping with liquid fire.

~~

I snapped my eyes open and jumped from the bed. Confused, I tripped over something on the floor and fell. I scrambled on hands and knees to the door, my heart racing. The room spun and I swayed. I rubbed my eyes, then struggled to my feet, the remaining sleep-haze draining my coordination. For a moment I fumbled around the wall for the switch, terror fogging my thoughts. Then bright light burst through the room as the light bulb fired to life, but the nightmare continued.

Cardboard boxes had been tipped on their sides, and

shredded papers decorated every surface in the room. Clothing had been dumped from drawers, and Jeffrey's small collectibles had been smashed and ground into the dingy carpet.

I scrubbed at my face, forcing myself to fully wake. My heart hammered in my chest, threatening to burst through. What the hell happened?

"Jeffrey?" My voice cracked.

The bed was empty. I reached behind me and fumbled at the doorknob with shaking hands. I'd lost Jeffrey. It was my turn to watch him and I'd lost him.

"Shit," I said as I slipped out into the cold living room.

It was still dark out, not even a hint of dawn in the air. Clouds had moved in while I'd slept, muting the moonlight and darkening the apartment. But I didn't need a lot of light to see that the rest of the apartment was a jumble of papers and smashed dishes. The card table had been turned on its side, the ugly Naugahyde topper shredded to bits.

It didn't take a detective to figure out that someone had been here searching. But for what? And where was Jeffrey? And how the hell had I slept through all of this?

Pounding on the front door pushed a surprised yelp from me, and I covered my mouth with one hand. Calm down. I had to calm down and think straight.

More pounding. "Open up!" a familiar voice came from the other side of the door.

Tripping over a carton of torn books, I went to the door and pulled it open.

"Mina?" Detective Richards looked into the apartment, confused. "What—"

"What are you doing here?" I said.

"I was going to ask you the same thing." Detective

Richards shook his head. "When did you get here?"

"A few hours ago." Narrowing my eyes, I said, "Wait a minute. You've been following Jeffrey, haven't you?"

"Apparently not close enough."

I frowned. I just didn't get Richards sometimes, but now wasn't the time to ask for explanations. Jeffrey was gone and his apartment had been ransacked. And I'd slept through the whole damn thing.

"What's going on in here?" Richards asked, not looking at the disheveled room, but staring down at *me*.

"It isn't what it looks like," I said. For some reason I felt like I needed to assure the detective I wasn't having sex with Jeffrey. Not that it was any of his business.

"Yeah? What do you think it looks like?"

"What are you doing here?" Confusion quickly melted into anger. I should have been thankful Richards was here, should have asked for his help in figuring out what happened while I'd slept. But I was mad because he was jealous or annoyed—or whatever he was—and I didn't know why. I didn't owe him anything. We weren't lovers. We weren't even friends. I already had my hands full of needy, confusing men, I didn't need to add another.

"Fine," he said. "Bragg has been under surveillance."

"Why?" I folded my arms over my stomach. "You questioned him and let him go. You said you trusted me."

Detective Richards' deep brown eyes flicked around the room and then settled on me. "I did."

"What's *that* supposed to mean?" Shaking my head, I held up one hand. "Forget it. Lets concentrate here. If you've had Jeffrey under surveillance that means you should have seen where he went."

"Went?"

"Yeah, Einstein, he's gone." I kicked at one of Jeffrey's folding chairs. It was bent and the padded seat had been ripped open so yellowed foam burst from the sliced cover. "Someone came in here and royally fucked his house. Did you see anyone come or go?"

Detective Richards shook his head. "No."

"Then what made you come up here?"

"It looked like someone was struggling. I saw figures in the window not five minutes ago."

My blood went cold. Five minutes. I'd missed him by *five stinking minutes*. That meant he couldn't have gone far.

"The back," I said and spun around to face the tiny kitchen.

Jeffrey's kitchen opened up to a small deck. Hanging off the railing was an emergency ladder, usually all rolled up. Tonight it hung down to the ground floor.

TWENTY

~~

"Gone?" I shouted. The cell door was closed, the lock still engaged. I stared in disbelief. "How did she get out?"

Justice shrugged. "I don't know. I came down to check on her and she wasn't here." He shook his head. "I don't even know how long she's been gone."

"It's more than a coincidence that Jeffrey and Nafeeza are both gone," I said.

"You think she went up to his apartment and *took* him?"

"What else could have happened?"

Justice shook his head again, avoiding my eyes. "She's half his size and can't weigh more than a hundred pounds."

Hands on my hips, I glared up at Justice. "You've seen *me* right? I'm only an inch or two taller than she is. Think I could kick Jeffrey's ass?"

"Without a doubt," Justice said. "But you have a little

more *oomph* to you than Nafeeza does."

"Psychic gifts or not, anyone can take down Jeffrey Bragg. He's a teddy bear."

"We don't even know for sure Nafeeza did it, Mina."

I glared at Justice harder. "Why are you defending her?"

He glared back. "Why are you accusing her?"

My eyelid twitched, and I had a sudden urge to kick Justice in the shins. But I didn't do it. Instead, I took a deep breath and held my fists out in front of my body. I put each finger up, one at a time, as I counted to ten.

Justice had seen this particular ritual more times than he could probably count. Interrupting my process never ended well, so he kept his mouth shut.

Fists uncurled and fingers flexing, I felt myself calm once more. I said, "Listen, I'm not accusing Nafeeza. I just want to talk to her."

Justice narrowed his eyes and crossed his arms over his broad chest.

"I know you're angry with me," I said. "I get it, Justice. But we can't do this. This isn't about *us*. This is about Presence and the oath we took. Our job is to take care of weird stuff like this Djinn, and we can't let our petty bullshit get in the way."

I searched his face for understanding. I even opened my mind to him and tested the psychic walls he'd put in place. Justice's jaw clenched and he looked away from me, emotions tripping across his face. Anger, hurt, annoyance.

"Fine," he said. "Fine. Concentrate on work. We'll discuss the other things later." Justice took a deep breath and looked back down at me. "I hear you, but I don't see any proof that Nafeeza's done anything wrong here."

I threw my arms up. "How about escaping the cell? Or tricking us into releasing the Djinn? Or lying to us about *why* she's here in the first place?"

Justice's lip curled. "Did it occur to you that maybe Jeffrey came and got Nafeeza? Maybe *he's* holding *her* hostage?"

It was so ridiculous I couldn't respond right away. I just blinked at Justice, my mouth agape. He could *not* be serious.

Finally, I said, "Yeah, Justice. Let's go with that a minute." I wiped a hand over my face and then looked him in the eye. "Jeffrey, who knows nothing about Presence and who *hates* even the *idea* that the supernatural world exists, just happens to know we threw Nafeeza in a cell down here below Oliver's shop. He not only broke into the shop without leaving a clue, but he got past the hidden door *and* navigated miles of dark, identical tunnels to come straight to the cell. Then he let her out without unlocking the door, and disappeared with her without you seeing him. *And* he did it all within the twenty minutes it took for me to get here." I took a breath and added, "Does that sound about right?"

Justice scowled at me, then spun around without a word and stormed down the hallway. Before he turned the corner he roared and drove a fist into the brick wall.

~~

A gray pinstripe suit and shined black shoes should have looked out of place amid the garbage and empty boxes. But Jacob Latrator's confident aura and relaxed stance made it impossible to think that he didn't belong *wherever* he happened to be.

Latrator had left his curly sable hair loose around his shoulders so it framed his face, and when he smiled, sharp canines gleamed in the light of the moon. That smile could melt your pants right off, and he knew it. He used it now as he came toward me, deftly straightening his tie despite the long black claws in his human fingers. It wasn't the fact the full moon was tomorrow night that made Latrator's wolf side show; he looked that way by choice every day. Maybe it was the Lycan in me, but the fangs and claws added a certain feral appeal to my pack leader.

Even nursing a broken heart, I could appreciate the fact Latrator was a nice piece of eye candy. I wasn't alone in my thinking either. In addition to the tempting wrapper, Latrator had a way with words that left most women swooning long after he'd walked away. I'd seen him flirt and charm and enchant his way through a crowd of people— men *and* women—but I had yet to see him *with* anyone. Latrator always went home alone, by choice. It made me wonder about him and his secrets, but not enough that I'd ever asked. We were friends and we'd been through a hell of a lot together in the short time we'd known one another, but that's where it ended, and I didn't feel like I had a right to pry.

Latrator took my hand in his and raised it to his soft lips. He placed a gentle kiss on my knuckles, his emerald eyes rolled up to look deeply into mine.

As fun as it was to be the current focus of Latrator's charm, we had business to discuss. I smiled and withdrew my hand as I said, "What's the verdict?"

"It's still in there," Latrator said. "Or it's in there *again*. I'm not sure which since our guard seems to have disappeared."

I glanced over at Timothy pacing the ground in front of the hole the snake had gone into earlier. The hair on his back was raised and a low growl rumbled around him.

"How long ago did the guard leave?" I asked.

"Maybe an hour," Latrator said. "We only had one

guard stationed."

"Why only one?"

"Before Timothy left, he said to look for a snake." Latrator shrugged broad shoulders and gave an apologetic grimace as he said, "How much trouble could one snake cause?"

"A lot," I said and started moving toward Timothy.

With one touch of his gentle hand on my arm, Latrator stopped me in my tracks. Static zipped across my skin as my wolf reacted to my pack leader's touch.

"We haven't seen you for quite some time, *Ma Cherie*. The pack misses you." He lowered his voice so it was nothing more than a rumble between us. "*I've* missed you."

The sound of his voice made my body tighten. We'd never had an intimate relationship beyond friendship and being pack mates, and I wasn't even sure his attention was an indication of any real interest in me. But that voice, that hair, those shimmering eyes. . . I'd had more than one naughty dream featuring Latrator in various embarrassing situations.

Well, I'd have been embarrassed if anyone *knew* about them, at least. If I had my way, nobody would ever hear about those fantasies, and they'd stay just that. *Fantasies.* I'd already screwed up one relationship with someone who was supposedly my boss, and a pack leader was sort of like a boss, so I wasn't about to mix business with pleasure again. Jacob Latrator was off limits.

Now, if I could just convince my quivering insides of that we'd be doing just fine.

"Later," I said—a little sharper than necessary—as I pulled away from Latrator's touch.

I half expected him to grab my arm and spin me around, demanding I pay attention to him or talk to him or to just listen while he screamed at me. But he didn't, and I was immediately ashamed of myself for even thinking that. Latrator had *never* done those things to me, or even indicated he was capable of being a bully like that.

Once again I was projecting Justice's bad behavior onto other people. It made me angry with myself, but I didn't have time to ponder it or work on fixing it. I had a job to do.

Timothy stopped pacing and wagged his tail when I came close. He chuffed and looked back at the hole in the side of the building.

"I don't suppose you've got a trail on Jeffrey, do ya?"

Timothy dropped his tail and whined.

"That's okay, we'll find him." I stood and looked at Latrator. "So where did the guard go?"

Latrator pointed to his left into the dense brush and tall trees. "He went in that direction. I've sent a search party but haven't heard back yet."

"Think he got spooked?"

"It was Damien," Latrator said with a kind smile. "Of course he got spooked."

Damien was just barely seventeen and new to the pack. He'd been a Lycan his whole life, but just recently combined his tiny pack with ours. Latrator had taken him under his wing and been trying to help the boy get some confidence. Damien and his whole pack were unusually shy, so Latrator's attempts at toughening him up weren't working very well.

Timothy snarled and began scratching at the concrete. Kneeling by Timothy, I flipped on my flashlight and directed the narrow beam into the hole. The concrete was cracked and crumbling all the way back until the tunnel took a sharp left. It wasn't more than a forearm's length before the turn. For a moment I actually considered sticking my hand in to see what I could grab, but years of watching horror movies had taught me to *never* put your hand in the hole.

"Why not send Justice in?" Latrator offered.

"Huh," I said as I stood and switched off the light. "The very nature of this thing centers around trickery and deceit. For all we know it could be sitting beyond that bend just waiting for someone to reach in and grab it." A small grin split my lips and I chuffed. "Tempting as it is to send Justice in there, I think we better come up with a better plan."

Latrator tipped his head and gazed at me. He smiled softly and said, "Do I sense trouble?"

My smile turned bitter and I said, "Maybe if we get this Djinn business under control I'll spill all the juicy details, but right now we need to find a way to get this damn snake out of the hole that doesn't involve a suicide mission."

~~

Sometimes it doesn't matter what you want. When Justice stood in front of the snake hole ten minutes later, I realized this. Not that him doing the exact opposite of what I wanted was anything out of the norm, but this time I couldn't help but think he was doing it to intentionally piss me off or to prove something to me. Either way, it was stupid.

"There's got to be another way, Justice." Goosebumps prickled up and down my arms.

"If you can think of one, now would be a good time to share it," Justice said.

Before I could open my mouth to take a breath, he was gone.

I'd seen him shift into mist many times, and every

time I wondered what that must feel like. Funny that I'd never asked before. I guess when you're fighting for your life those little questions slip your mind. And now that we were no longer an item I didn't think I had the right to even ask the questions. In fact, whether it was questions, work conversations, or social situations I wasn't really sure how to handle Justice at all anymore.

Most people learn to deal with breakups when they're teens, so by the time they're adults they can handle things a little better—theoretically, at least. Not me. My first relationship didn't happen until I was well into my thirties. It left me dazed. I hated how the thoughts invaded my every moment. I hated how lost and guilty I felt, while at the same time I felt lighter and free.

Surely, that feeling of freedom should tell my weeping heart that the relationship hadn't been healthy. But the heart hears only what it wants to, and reason doesn't even play into the equation.

And why was I thinking about that now? There were a lot more important things to deal with than what a screwed up relationship we'd had.

Justice swirled around the snake hole, churning and tumbling over on himself, almost as if contemplating something. Maybe he was thinking about me. Maybe he wasn't. It didn't really matter, did it? As if in answer, he flowed inside the hole and out of sight, and my shoulders went tense.

We were no longer lovers, but that didn't mean I'd stop loving him. And it definitely didn't mean I'd stop worrying when he was on dangerous missions. My stomach flipped and flopped, tying itself into knots as the seconds ticked by. Justice could hold the mist for several minutes without straining himself. I hoped it took him less than that to see what he needed to see and then get out.

A car sped by, its lights playing along the side of the building for a moment then fading away. Even in a town as small as Port Orchard, there's never really middle of the night silence. The thump of dance music drifted in from the dance club over the hill. Wind rustled the leaves in the trees, and some little creature scurried under the bushes behind me. Even with all the noise I could hear my heart thrumming in my ears. Too fast, too loud.

A voice whispered close to my ear, "I can taste your fear."

I jumped back and spun around. "That's creepy, Latrator."

"I thought you might say that." He smiled, canines glinting.

"Don't sneak up on me like that."

Latrator smirked and said, "How *should* one sneak up on you then?"

Pursing my lips, I crossed my arms under my breasts, but my stern look and defiant posture didn't faze him.

He leaned in slowly as he said, "You should be paying closer attention to your surroundings instead of listening to your own. . . heart. . . racing." He whispered the last word so close that I felt his warm breath on my cheek.

I gently pushed him back with both hands on his chest. "Are you flirting with me or scolding me?"

He grinned and raised one eyebrow. "A little of both." Then his playful smile softened, and he said, "Honestly, *Ma Cherie*, I was only trying to lighten the mood. I can feel your pain. . . and it disturbs my soul."

"Why's my pain matter to you?"

Latrator reached out and took my hand in his, stroking the back of my hand softly with his thumb. His deep green eyes trapped my attention. "As your pack leader I am compelled to do whatever I can to ease your suffering.

Be that laughter or distraction. . . I am your man."

I looked down at my hand in his and felt warmth spread over my cheeks. "As my pack leader?"

"And. . ." Latrator said, "as your friend."

We shared a quiet moment with our gazes locked. I thought he was going to kiss me then, and I wasn't sure how I would respond to that. He was hot and he was charming and most importantly he was honest. But I'd once thought all those things about Justice, and look how that had turned out.

Seconds ticked by and I had an urge to lean in for the kiss myself. But before I could decide, Latrator released my hand and turned away. Part of me wanted to rush to him and plant a kiss on those soft lips. But how much of that was my broken heart reaching for anyone to ease my pain? How much of that was my need to plug that gaping, painful hole in my soul? How much of that was the dreaded rebound effect after a nasty break up? I wasn't willing to damage my friendship with Latrator to find out.

Frowning, I watched him walk slowly toward the bushes, his hands deep in his trouser pockets. I shook my head, then went to stand by the snake hole.

Timothy sat patiently like all good dogs do. He thumped his tail once on the ground when I came near, then turned his attention back to the hole.

It had been at least ten minutes, I was sure of it. I looked at my watch. Only five had passed. Shit.

Another car drove by, this time with those bright, blue-tinted headlights. Those always made me look twice. They just didn't seem right. Almost like the cars were supernatural, like they had some kind of special powers that other cars didn't.

Maybe I was just paranoid.

A soft whisper and a damp breeze around my ankles

brought a rush of relief. The dark mist of Justice bubbled up and up until it was the right height, then Justice's upper body materialized before me, his lower half staying misty.

"It was there, but not anymore," Justice said.

"But Timothy's been out here watching," I said. "Nothing came out of that hole."

Justice shrugged. "Maybe it left when the guard disappeared?"

"We've had Lycans passing the shop all day and night. Someone would have seen something. Besides, both Timothy and Latrator said they smell it here still."

"It's not in there, Mina. It must have found another way out." He grabbed his pants from the ground and as he slipped them on I saw his lower body solidify.

"This is ridiculous!" I threw my hands in the air. "We can't chase this thing all over. We've got to find Jeffrey."

"Find Jeffrey and we find the Djinn." Justice nodded as if agreeing with himself.

"What about Nafeeza?"

"Nothing," he said, his face tightening. "Not a sign of her anywhere. I asked everyone before I got here. No one has seen or heard from her since we put her in the cell."

"I knew there was something funny about her, Justice."

His brows came together. "She isn't gifted, Mina. Oliver would have sensed it years ago. She uses spells and scrolls and reagents, not psychic gifts."

"Then tell me how she got out of that cell. Tell me how she got into Jeffrey's apartment and took him away."

"You don't have any proof she was the one who took Jeffrey. In fact, you don't even know that Jeffrey didn't just leave on his own. He was in the living room while you were sleeping in the bedroom. He could have slipped out the back at any time and you'd have slept right through it."

"No," I said, shaking my head. "He was in bed with me—" The sudden mask of anger on Justice's face stopped my words.

"*Really?*" he said. "Now that's an interesting development."

"It's not what you think." Funny that I felt I had to explain myself twice in the same night. I was on a roll.

"Could we save the lovers' quarrel for another time, perhaps?" Latrator had come up behind us, his smile not all-together friendly.

Justice spared me a quick, unreadable glance before he turned his attention to Latrator. "Ideas?"

Latrator nodded. "I've got a small group from our pack willing to go wolf and track Jeffrey from his apartment. Do you think you can clear us a path so we're not. . . apprehended?"

He meant, could I keep the cops busy so they wouldn't shoot my pack mates. I nodded.

~ ~

Officer Bruno Harms was one of the meanest men I'd ever met. He looked like a tough guy should: Thick neck, dark buzzed hair, wide, crooked nose. He hated me and I never could figure out why. When he saw me come up to his unmarked car, he glowered at me through the tinted window. He didn't know, thanks to my Lycanthropy, I could see through the tint and sense his disdain a mile away.

I put my best friendly smile on and tapped his window with my fingertips.

"What do you want, Jewel?" he growled as the window slowly lowered.

"Can I bring you anything, Officer?"

He squinted at me, checked his watch, looked at me

again, suspicion plastered all over his face. "What are you doing out and about at three a.m. anyway?"

I batted my eyelashes. "Why, I didn't realize grown women had curfews in this town."

"Don't play coy. If *you're* out at this hour, you're up to no good."

"Is that your professional assessment, Officer Harms, or a personal opinion?"

"Don't matter, do it? I'm right and you know it."

I leaned against the car and smiled down through the open window. Somewhere in the back of my head I knew I must look like an overdressed and unsuccessful prostitute. Just something about the position and the situation. It made me giggle. Me, a prostitute, when it had taken Justice more than a year to get past a little heavy petting. And even then he'd only gotten laid once.

"Why are you smiling?" Harms moved his head back as if I were about to throw something dangerous in his lap.

"Just the situation, that's all."

He shook his head. When he looked at me again his eyes had softened some. His attention flicked from my face, down to my chest, then as far down my body as he could see without getting out of his car. He blushed a little and snapped his attention back up to my face.

"You know," he said, some of the gruff, hostile tones softening. "I'm not supposed to be talking to anyone while I'm on duty tonight."

Smiling sweetly and meaning it this time, I leaned over and rested my arms on the open window. "I don't think Richards will mind if you talked to *me* a little bit."

Harm's eyes went wide. "Oh, yeah he would. Especially if he saw—"

"Saw what, Bruno?"

He cleared his throat and shifted in his seat. "If he

saw how you're leaning in the window like that and getting all friendly with me."

Police officers didn't usually like dealing with private detectives, but the way Harms said it made the whole thing sound deeper. Why would it have bothered Detective Richards to see Harms talking to me? What kind of crap did the police say about me when I wasn't around to defend myself? Whatever it was, maybe that's why Officer Harms seemed to hate me so much.

I tried not to let my questions show on my face as I opened up and let my Seduction pour in through the window. Officer Harms closed his eyes and breathed deeply like something in his car smelled delicious.

The Seduction allowed me to feel people, their minds, their desires, their deepest wishes. Right now, my Seduction told me that Bruno Harms wanted something simple. Something surprising. More than anything in the world he wanted to be noticed and appreciated. He didn't care *what* he was appreciated for, just as long as it was sincere and he could feel special for once.

I smiled softly and said, "I want to thank you, Bruno."

He looked at me with heavily lidded eyes, and tipped his head. "For what?"

"For being you." I reached out and poked his shoulder with one finger. "I appreciate what you do every day. You keep us all safe. You make sacrifices so people like me can run around and act like fools, knowing you'll jump in and save our asses." I grinned.

At first he didn't respond. I thought maybe I'd missed the mark with the Seduction. But then his eyes moistened, and he looked away. "Damn, Mina," he whispered.

It was the first time he'd ever used my first name. The sound of my name coming from his mouth and the feel of his sudden welling emotion threw me off for just a moment, and my Seduction slipped. Harm's eyes flashed to life in that instant and his head snapped in my direction. "Get the hell away from me!"

Before the tinted glass slipped up completely, I saw something like fear cross his face.

I shrugged and turned toward Jeffrey's apartment, hoping I'd bought the Lycans enough time to start sniffing.

TWENTY-ONE

~~

By six a.m. the Lycans had tracked Jeffrey to the same field where the five missing teens had been found. We'd walked through the crime scene and twenty minutes farther to the edge of the clearing. The dew on the grass soaked into my sneakers, drenching my socks. My cold feet made my whole body feel stiff and uncomfortable, but I felt worse for the Lycans who were basically tromping through the cold, wet grass stark naked.

Alfred, the largest wolf in the front of the pack, sat and panted. His front paws and legs were soaked so thoroughly I could clearly see his pink skin through it. The dark fur on his belly had matted tight against him and rivulets of dew ran down his body and pooled at his feet. I'd only seen Alfred fully human one time. Nature and genetics hadn't been kind to him. Even soaking wet and smelling like any wet dog does, he was still more appealing as a wolf.

"Is this the end of the line, Alfred?" Absently, I scratched behind his ears.

I used to worry that my automatic reaction of petting someone in full animal form was upsetting. But after receiving a few pats and scratches and belly rubs myself, I knew it was actually quite pleasant. Maybe being full wolf gave you extra sensitive "pet-me" receptors.

Alfred wagged his tail and looked over his shoulder at Latrator who came to a halt beside me. Latrator nodded down at Alfred, and the big black wolf stood and sauntered off the way we'd come. The other wolves followed silently.

"They calling it quits?" I asked.

Latrator nodded and put his arm around my shoulders. "Three hours is a long time to trek through a damp field."

Several feet in front of me the field gave way to thick bushes and deep shadowed woods. I asked, "Does the trail end here?"

"It goes beyond the trees a bit." Latrator stepped in front of me and leaned in close. "Aren't you feeling tired, Mina? You've been up all night."

"Not really. I got some sleep at the apartment before Jeffrey disappeared."

"You aren't ready to quit? No rest for you?"

I shook my head, eyes already scanning the forest ahead, planning my route through the brush.

I'd expected him to insist I sit down and rest or that I go home and sleep. I'd expected him to tell me not to be stupid or stubborn, and that he knew what was best for me. Once again, I'd expected him to act like Justice.

Instead, Latrator said, "Then I'll join you on your hunt."

I smirked. "We're not gonna *eat* Jeffrey."

"Pity," Latrator said, turning to gaze at the woods.

I'd just raised my hand to give a soft thump on his shoulder when he turned and winked at me, a mischievous grin on his lips. I laughed softly and started toward the woods.

~ ~

The sun was shining, but the treetops soaked in all the heat before anything could reach the ground where Latrator and I picked our way through dense bushes and overgrown trails.

"If you shift," he said, "we can maneuver much faster and track much better."

"And then I ruin my favorite pair of jeans," I countered.

Latrator grinned and raised his eyebrows. "You could always strip beforehand."

I rolled my eyes and kept walking.

In human form my sense of smell was only a little better than a normal human. Latrator, since he always walked around with claws and wolfy teeth, was better equipped to sniff the trail. He was right though, if we shifted completely we'd have the same scenting abilities as a natural wolf, with the bonus of human intelligence. However, the full moon was thirteen hours away and I would be forced to shift then. I was in no hurry to do it early.

That's not to say I didn't like being a werewolf; it certainly had its advantages: Incredible strength, heightened senses, faster healing. But the disadvantages were nasty. A severe allergy to silver which could kill you instantly or slowly and painfully; being controlled by the moon restricted some of your activities; and being hated and feared by most humans was just plain miserable. At least I never got fleas.

After another half hour I stopped and sat on a fallen tree.

"You need a rest?" Latrator asked, sitting next to me.

"Are we any closer?"

He nodded and gazed in the direction we'd been heading. "They came through here." He lifted his face to the wind and inhaled deeply. "They even stopped in this very spot."

"Think we're moving faster than they are?"

"Jeffrey is human and so is limited to human speed. The Djinn may be faster on its own, but it will have to wait for Jeffrey to catch up," Latrator said as he shrugged. "Or, so I'm guessing. I don't know how fast they were going, only that they disturbed little on their way through."

"If they'd been moving fast, or if it had been dragging Jeffrey along, we'd see broken branches and a bigger trail." A thought hit me then. "Hey, Latrator?"

"Yes, *Ma Cherie?*"

"How many snakes did you smell today?"

"I could smell two distinct reptiles behind the store."

"That's what I thought." I nodded. "Yeah, me, too."

"Why? Is that important?"

"Only very," I said and turned to look him in the eyes. "We should have smelled one snake, not two. There's only one Djinn."

"Justice's animal shape is that of a large cobra, is it not?"

"Yeah, but he's not a Lycan. Justice is a Shapeshifter. He changes shape, he doesn't *become* the animal."

"Is there a difference?"

"When we change with the full moon we *become* the wolf, we *are* the animal." I chewed my bottom lip for a moment. "I've only seen Justice shift into that snake once, and I don't really remember a smell because I was only human at the time—I didn't contract Lycanthropy until a year later. But I do know that when he shifts he isn't *really* a snake. So he shouldn't smell like one, right?"

Latrator shrugged again. "I only know about Lycans. I'm afraid my knowledge of shapeshifters runs about as deep as my knowledge of the Djinn."

I scowled. Not at Latrator, just at the situation. I'd never liked unanswered questions, and I wasn't really in a position to find answers at the moment either.

"Perhaps," Latrator offered, "Justice has been spending a lot of time as a snake when you're not around? Maybe spending more time in his animal form grants him more of the animal's natural features."

"Like their smell?"

Latrator shrugged again. "I'm only guessing."

"Well, I know he's been showing off for Nafeeza since she got here. Maybe he's been playing snake, too."

~~

We'd been traveling for at least another hour before Latrator stopped. He pointed through the trees ahead to a small clearing. A ramshackle cabin stood about six yards in front of us, windows dark and smeared with years of grime and mold, roof tiles all but gone, leaving bare, grayed wooden slats. I'd have said the place had been forgotten for years if it weren't for the mess of shiny, empty beer bottles, potato chip bags, and syringes laying around the ground. Someone had even left a fairly new radio on the stump by the front door.

I whispered, "I think this is where the kids have their parties."

Latrator raised his eyebrows and nodded. "I think you're correct. That means the Djinn has been here before."

"And probably is now."

Latrator raised his face to the sky and sniffed for a moment or two. "Jeffrey is here."

I smelled the air, too, but couldn't pick up much. The smell of the blooming flowers and rich soil masked anything peculiar. Silently, I kicked myself for not shifting at least partway like Latrator. If I'd shifted some I wouldn't have needed help finding Jeffrey. Of course, then he'd know I wasn't human.

Why did that still bother me? Why was it so important that Jeffrey thought I was human?

I scoffed and closed my eyes for a moment. I *wanted* to be normal. Even if it was all just in Jeffrey's head, I wanted to be normal.

Latrator put a hand on my shoulder and gave a gentle squeeze. "We'll help him, Mina. Don't worry."

I was glad Latrator couldn't read minds. If Oliver had been here he would have known what I was thinking. He would never say anything about it, but he'd have known and that would have made me feel even worse. Did that mean I didn't like who I was? Did I hate myself and all others like me? The thought made my stomach tight.

Presence was full of understanding, generous people. They'd helped me recover from abuse, discover my gifts, and harness my inner strength. Latrator and his pack had helped me cope with my Lycanthropy and taught me to be proud of who I was and to accept people in all forms. My gifts and my Lycanthropy had helped me locate and save dozens of kids. I couldn't have done that without my gifts. Yet, here I was wishing I was *normal*.

A scream came from inside the cabin. Jeffrey's scream. The sound brought me back to reality, and I crouched behind the last bush before the clearing.

"Go get Justice and tell him how to get here," I whispered.

"I won't leave you alone."

"I won't do anything stupid, I promise."

Latrator grinned and shook his head. "Don't make promises you can't keep, *Ma Cherie*." Then he leaned in, kissed my cheek, and took off toward town at a dead run.

~ ~

What took Latrator and I two hours to cross would take a fully shifted Lycan only fifteen minutes. Fifteen minutes to town, five minutes to shift back to human—or as human as Latrator ever got—maybe another ten to track down Justice. If he did his little floating deal, Justice could be here in thirty minutes, faster if he went misty. Of course, then he'd be naked.

An hour of sitting here listening to intermittent screams from Jeffrey. Would he still be alive by the time Justice arrived? Could I just sit here and listen to him being hurt?

"No!" Jeffrey screamed. "No, stop!"

"Ah, shit," I said under my breath.

Who was I kidding? I couldn't sit here and do nothing. Crouching lower, I touched the ground with my fingertips and moved around the cabin, still sheltered by the brush. From the shape of the outer walls and placement of the windows, I guessed there were at least three individual rooms. When I'd done a complete circle, I stopped and closed my eyes, trying to isolate the sounds from inside the cabin.

I concentrated on blocking out all the sounds of the forest, the sounds of life and nature. After a few long, slow breaths, I'd pinpointed Jeffrey's voice. I could hear him inside the cabin speaking in a soft, frightened tone. He was in the room closest to the front door.

My eyesight would be messed up for a few precious seconds after leaving the daylight of the clearing and entering the dark cabin. Whoever held him captive would have the jump on me while I stood there blind. There were no back ways into the house and none of the windows were big enough for me to squeeze through. I'd make too much noise climbing to the roof, and I wasn't even sure the thing would hold me anyway. I hated it when I was left with no options.

I took a deep breath and stood. I walked toward the front door, almost casually. No need to run in screaming, no need to sneak. As soon as I opened the door, they'd know I was here.

The door squealed as I pushed it open. Besides the darkness, the first thing I noticed was the dank smell of old rotting wood. The whole place was going to crumble in on us. The second thing I noticed was the smell of something sweet and exotic wafting through the air just under the damp smell of rot.

"Nafeeza," I said into the dark.

"Very good, Mina."

By the time my eyes adjusted to the dark, Nafeeza was standing a few feet ahead of me. Broken streams of sunlight came in through the spaces in the roof, lighting small portions of the floor. Some trick of the light made Nafeeza appear to be on fire.

"Where's Jeffrey?" I said, taking a step forward.

"He is with us."

"Us?"

"You still have not figured it out?" Nafeeza laughed. "And Oliver spoke of how *sharp* you were."

The insult didn't ruffle my feathers. Bad guys always try to screw with your head. Getting you angry made you do stupid things. I'd promised Latrator I wouldn't do anything stupid. Though honestly, traipsing in here alone had been pretty stupid.

"Who else is here?" I asked.

Nafeeza just smiled and motioned deeper into the room, an invitation for me to go and look for myself. I hesitated, watching Nafeeza's irritatingly smug face.

I sneered, then moved toward the back of the room. The air was thicker somehow, harder to bring into my lungs, harder to push back out. The suffocating smell of damp decay and Nafeeza's strong perfume mixed into an almost unbearable haze. I could feel it around me, touching me, soaking into my hair and clothes.

Nafeeza glided next to me, brushing me with her hand and suddenly I smelled it.

I'd smelled it when I first met her, but it was masked by all that perfume. I'd smelled it in Jeffrey's apartment while I slept.

I froze in place, the hairs on my arms standing at attention, ready to bolt at the first sign of trouble. Nafeeza stopped moving, paused, then turned slowly. An evil, wicked smile crept across her lips and her dark eyes glinted with an inner fire.

Under all that perfume, all those spices and exotic aromas, was the unmistakable musk of snakes.

TWENTY-TWO

~~

Funny, but I'd been in cages before. This one wasn't too bad when compared to the others, but I'd definitely been in nicer ones. At least there were blankets so our butts didn't get splinters from sitting on the creaky wooden floor. Granted, the blankets were full of holes and felt stiff and scratchy with years of grime and who knows what else, but I'd try not to think about that too much. The cage wasn't more than six feet square. The dull metal bars had lost their shine over time, but they looked solid. Nafeeza hadn't brought the cage here; it had been built into the cabin. The bars came up through the floor, probably secured to a metal base buried under ground. Who would have built such a sturdy cage out here, and why?

Before I'd even stepped into the cage, I'd known Nafeeza was going to lock me in it, but she wouldn't let Jeffrey out, so in I went. Stupid to walk into the cage, I know, but I had to see for myself that Jeffrey was okay.

Jeffrey huddled against the bars in the far corner, arms wrapped around his knees, pulling them closer to his body as I approached. The whites of his eyes were bloodshot, his face pale, his lips pulled tight in a grimace. A deep purple bruise on his left cheek screamed for attention.

"Did Nafeeza hit you?" I asked.

Jeffrey nodded and ducked further behind his knees as if the very mention of her name would cause more pain.

I reached out to touch his shoulder, a comforting gesture that had worked on him before, but he pulled away with a whimper.

"I'm gonna get you out of here, Jeffrey," I said. I just didn't know how.

Turning, I scanned the cage one more time, hoping to catch sight of a weakness. It seemed solid enough, but the bars weren't silver; I could probably bend them if I shifted to partial wolf. But then Jeffrey would know my secret.

Immediately, I was ashamed of myself. Was my illusion of normalcy that high on my list? Even seeing the desperate situation we were in, was my own selfish need to seem human more important than getting out alive?

It was an ugly realization, but there you have it. I wasn't proud of that fact, but it wasn't something I could change at the drop of a hat. Jeffrey made me feel normal, and I'd do whatever I could to keep that feeling. As ashamed as I was to admit it, I might even cost us our lives to retain the illusion.

However, giving up was not an option. I had to at least try.

"Nafeeza!" I shouted. "Others will come. They won't ignore my disappearance!"

Nafeeza appeared out of the shadows. "I am counting on that," she said, then backed into the dark again.

"She's been waiting for you to come, Mina." Jeffrey's voice was dry, strained. "She's been waiting for both of you." He looked at me then, his face contorted in a mixture of anger, sadness, and fear. "She told me all about you. She told me *everything*."

Maybe it was my look of surprise, maybe it was my silence, but Jeffrey shook his head and gave a loud, barking laugh. "Of course. I can't have normal friends can I? My whole life has been one big horror story. Now I'm surrounded by demons, psychics, and fucking werewolves."

"Jeffrey, I—"

"God, Mina," he said. "Just stay away from me."

My heart dropped to the bottom of my stomach and tears threatened to come, but I said, "I'll set you free, Jeffrey. I promise. You can hate me later."

I saw him shudder and look away. I felt sick. Nafeeza giggled from somewhere in the dark and I was angry again, my despair forgotten in the rush of adrenalin-fed Fury.

I gripped the bars and gave them a light tug. The ceiling creaked and splinters of rotted wood fell to the floor. I shook the pieces out of my hair and looked up. The bars were bolted tight, and at one time this cage would have held me, but not today. Time and neglect had made the cage a joke. Strong bars and bolts are useless if the house around them is falling apart.

Holding my breath, I gave the bars another tug, this time with more force. The ceiling groaned and more wood fell to the floor in bigger pieces. Jeffrey mumbled something and pulled himself into a tighter ball.

"Naughty little Mina." Nafeeza stepped into the dim light again, shaking her head. "You would do well to sit still and wait."

"Yeah?" I said, my upper lip twitching into a sneer. "You'd do well to shut the fuck up."

"Or what? Will you pull the bars from the cage and eat me up like the big bad wolf from your fairy tales?" Nafeeza laughed.

I replied, "Something like that," and gave a cold, empty smile. I let an inhuman growl rumble deep in my chest and fill the room.

"You think I fear you?" Nafeeza moved closer, just out of reach. "You think a little werewolf can beat the mighty Djinn?"

"When did you possess her? During the ritual at my house? Behind the shop? How long have you been in Nafeeza's body?"

She laughed again, loud and explosive. "Nafeeza's body? I *am* Nafeeza!" She spun around, arms raised. "I've always been Nafeeza, always in control of the girl. And before Nafeeza, it was her mother, and her mother before her."

Fire erupted from her skin and she laughed again. The bright flames were a shock in the near dark of the cabin. They burned my eyes and I had to cover my face as I stumbled back. Jeffrey sobbed, the sound muffled by his knees.

"You see?" Nafeeza said. "You see how powerful we are? You see why you and your gathering of freaks cannot even think to defeat us?"

The blinding light faded and I lowered my arm. She was back to sweet Nafeeza again, petite, quiet, reserved. She looked so damn human.

She held a finger to her mouth and said, "*Shhh*, your lover approaches."

A moment later Justice was in the room. He was dressed, so he hadn't gone misty to get here. How long had we been in the cage?

Justice looked at Nafeeza standing with her dainty

hands folded in front of her, and then his gaze moved to Jeffrey and I locked in the cage.

"It doesn't have to be this way, Nafeeza," Justice said. "You can take the Djinn and go home."

"Justice, no," I said.

He held up his hand to silence me and turned his attention to Nafeeza. "We won't stop you."

Nafeeza smoothed her hair back from her perfect face. "I appreciate your offer. However, I am not here just for the Djinn."

"What?" I said.

Nafeeza spared me a glance and then turned back to Justice. "I came to retrieve our Djinn, yes. When I arrived, I found another treasure that I wish to bring home." She moved to where Justice stood and touched his arm. "I wish to bring you home with me, Justice. You belong with us. With *me*."

Justice stepped back. "No, I belong here. I told you before—" he took two steps toward the cage, his eyes still on her—"I belong to Mina."

Nafeeza's power filled the room in a rush of heat. The smell of warm herbs and incense moved over my skin like molten lava burning me from the toes up. Jeffrey cried out behind me.

"You are no different than us, Justice." Nafeeza glided across the room with liquid grace, swirling red and orange silk, and smooth black hair. Justice turned his head to look away but she was there in a flash of blinding scarlet light.

"I'm nothing like you," Justice said.

"Ah, but you are." She breathed the words, barely speaking, but I heard. "We become the smokeless fire, essence of the desert. You become the dark mist, essence of the deepest night. We become the shining desert viper, embodiment of the sun and heat. You become the obsidian cobra, embodiment of darkness and cold."

Nafeeza brushed fingertips across Justice's cheek. He shuddered and looked away.

She laughed and said, "Two pieces. Light and dark. Heat and cold. One does not exist without the other."

"No." Justice shook his head.

Nafeeza went on her toes and steadied herself against Justice's chest. He didn't move away.

"Your eyes," she whispered, "are the eyes of a serpent, not a human. You are not one of them. They do not appreciate what you are or what you can do. They do not find you beautiful as I do."

"Bullshit!" I shouted before I could stop myself.

As soon as I spoke, Nafeeza's power surged into me. It burned me from the inside, scorching my mouth and throat as it shot down into my body. I fell back, struggling for breath, gagging on the thick heat. Jeffrey scurried from the corner and came to me, tried to touch my cheek but drew his hand back when another surge of hot power flowed into me. I choked, coughed, gasped as the thick fist of fire sealed my throat shut. Stinging tears ran from my eyes as panic gripped me. I thrashed my arms and legs in a vain attempt to loosen the tightening power, to shake free of its grip.

"Enough, Nafeeza!" Justice grabbed her wrists. He held her tight and stared down into her face. "Take your Djinn and leave."

"That is your final word?"

Justice nodded.

The burning power receded. I gagged, sputtered, my body racked with convulsions as the heat-fist slowly pulled out of my throat. Jeffrey held my face in his hands, a comforting touch to ease my panic. I stared up into his eyes and willed myself to calm. He wiped my tears away even as his own tears shimmered on the edge, ready to spill over, his mouth trembling as wordless sounds tumbled out.

And then I felt the power leave me for good. I grabbed Jeffrey's shirt and pulled myself to sitting. The air filled my lungs finally in a sweeping, cold burst, and the searing fire died down. New tears streaked my cheeks and I sobbed. She would have killed me. A few more seconds and I would have suffocated. Or cooked in my own skin.

Jeffrey wrapped his arms around me and held me close. He sobbed, "I'm so sorry, Mina. I'm so sorry. I didn't mean any of it. Please. Please forgive me."

He crushed me to him, squeezing the air out of me again. I wasn't going to suffocate twice in one day. I pushed him back and sucked more air into my lungs. He sat back and stared at me.

"Okay," I wheezed. "Forgiven."

With fingers around the bars, I pulled myself to standing and staggered to the locked door of the cage. Justice came to the bars, then reached out and touched my hand.

"She's going to leave," he said.

"It's—" I shook my head and coughed. "It's never that easy."

Justice smiled but his eyes stayed concerned. "You never trust anyone."

"And you always trust everyone."

Nafeeza moved around the room collecting some items and placing them in a multi-colored sack. She glanced up, saw me looking, and winked. My skin prickled with heat, but this time it was my own power. I wanted her to die. She *needed* to die. And my Fury agreed.

"Let us out, Nafeeza," I said.

She shook her head. "Not until Jeffrey's Djinn comes

back. I will leave here when I collect my brother."

"Brother." I spat the word. Why didn't it surprise me that she was related to the demon? Things were making sense now.

Nafeeza put the last of her belongings into the bag and settled on the floor, crossing her legs. "I have been looking for my brother for many years. When the man brought the book back from my homeland, my brother was taken with it."

"You're talking about Walter Garrot."

"I care not for his name, call him what you will. The man took the book and my brother with it. But he took more than that. The virginity of that female child was stolen, and therefore my brother's vessel was stolen."

"Wait," I said. "Your brother's vessel was that girl?"

Nafeeza nodded.

"But you call him *brother*, not *sister*."

"We Djinn do not have genders in the same way you humans do. We refer to one another by the gender of our chosen host only in the presence of those who do not understand."

"And your brother couldn't take over the girl because Garrot raped her?"

"Correct," Nafeeza said with a single nod. "We. . . dislike the activities of your race. We find it distasteful how you must behave. But we do understand the necessity of your. . . mingling, and so when we are finished with our hosts, we release them and allow them to. . . *breed*." She said the last word with her nose wrinkled and lips tight.

"But you've been trying to get into Justice's pants since you got here." Saying it out loud brought a wave of jealous anger through me, and my cheeks went hot. Not that it should matter. Even if we survived all of this, Justice and I were still broken up.

"I care nothing for such activities, however my host is of age, and she finds Justice a suitable partner."

"And if he had said yes, and he went back with you, you'd have had little baby *vessels* with him so all your Djinn buddies could possess them, too?"

"I sense your hostility, Mina."

"Gee, Nafeeza, I wonder why? Why are you telling me all this after trying to boil me alive, anyway?"

Nafeeza shrugged. "I do not hate you. Perhaps I hope that your understanding of our nature will allow your kind to forgive us for what we must do."

"And what must you do?"

Nafeeza didn't answer, but I was fairly certain I wouldn't have *liked* her answer anyway. Unlike Justice, I was pretty sure she had no plans of letting us out of this cabin alive. Knowing that, I didn't really give a shit how forthcoming she was being, I definitely wasn't about to forgive her. But she obviously didn't realize that, because she kept talking. Fine with me. The more info she wanted to spill, the more likely I'd be able to find a weakness to exploit.

"I thought at first my brother was stolen from us," she said. "But when I arrived here I realized he had attached *himself* to the book and encouraged the man to bring him to America." Nafeeza shook her head and gazed at her hands folded in her lap. "Why my brother would leave our land, I did not understand at first."

"Maybe he was trying to get away from you."

Nafeeza glanced at me, raised an eyebrow, then looked to Jeffrey who'd come up behind me. "My brother will come back for you, Jeffrey Bragg."

"How do you know that?" I said, sliding left to obscure Jeffrey from Nafeeza's gaze. Best to keep her attention on me. I could survive the attacks better than

Jeffrey could. Yeah, it would suck and probably hurt a whole hell of a lot, but I refused to sit in here and watch Jeffrey die if I could take the brunt of her anger and save him any further pain.

"My brother will come back because he *has* to."

"What if he doesn't?"

"He will die."

"So much for being more powerful than the humans, huh, Nafeeza? You sound like a bunch of parasites to me." That's right, antagonize the demon.

She glared at me, the glint of fire behind her dark eyes. Justice moved in front of the cage and blocked Nafeeza's gaze.

"That's enough," Justice said. "Just call your brother and get out. My patience is wearing thin." Justice's voice was still smooth and soothing as always, but I could feel his energy rising in the room, cool and damp, like a chilly October mist.

"You deny my host her desires," Nafeeza said, "then command *me*? I think not."

Nafeeza's power pulsed once and the room went devilishly hot again. Sweat trickled between my breasts and down my face. Another pulse and the room was cool again like the blast from an air conditioner. I shivered as the sweat gelled on my skin.

"Ah, Jesus, Jesus," Jeffrey mumbled.

"Calm down, Jeffrey," I said.

It took all I had to keep my voice even. I took a slow, steady breath and let it out. What I wanted to do was scream and run out of the cabin, but that wouldn't help Jeffrey. Watching the sweat bead on his brow and the wild shaking in his hands, I knew he needed all the help he could get. He was in over his head.

Hell, *I* was in over my head.

TWENTY-THREE

~~

Justice and Nafeeza faced off in the center of the room. It was like an old western where the good guy and bad guy stood in the center of a dusty road waiting for the other to flinch before they'd pull a gun and shoot them dead. Only there were no guns here, no extras hiding behind the water trough or peeking through second story windows. That, and the good guy was wearing black.

"Back up," I whispered.

When Jeffrey didn't move, I took hold of his upper arm and dragged him to the back of the cage. Despite his mumbled objections, I pulled him to the floor. Once he was firmly planted on the blanket in the far corner of the cage, he turned wide, frightened eyes to me and I thought how very much like a little boy he looked. A scared little boy watching the thing under the bed eat his parents just after they'd promised him the monsters weren't real.

"Don't move." I touched fingertips to his cheek, then

turned and moved to the front of the cage.

Justice floated inches off the ground, his hair rippling behind him. Swirling clouds of dust churned under his feet as the air held him suspended. Nafeeza laughed and threw her hands out to the sides. She rose off the floor, her skin turning translucent as her veins began pumping, not blood, but white-hot fire around her body.

With a crack of thunder, Justice and Nafeeza were wrapped in shadows and light, cold wind and searing fire. Nafeeza's hands shot forward, wrapping around Justice's throat, her tiny fingers trying to squeeze the life out of him. Justice winked out of existence. Just like that, he was gone, his clothes left rumpled on the floor.

Nafeeza screamed in frustration and looked all around the floor. She knew he was there, a misty presence on the shadowed floor, waiting for the perfect moment to rise up and strike her down, but she couldn't see him. Neither could I.

Nafeeza didn't wait. She sent a stream of fire from her fingers to the floor directly under her, and I felt the heat wave hit me like running face first into a brick wall. It knocked me back and I stumbled over the blankets on the floor.

Another blast of fire and Nafeeza was searching the floor, moving the stream of flames along the ground, back and forth. Justice was nowhere to be seen.

"Do not hide from me!" Nafeeza's voice was a banshee's scream over the roar of flames.

Justice's voice came from all around, "The shadows always avoid the light."

I gave a short laugh. Always logical, my Justice.

I could feel him brushing over me, a cooling touch in the inferno of the cabin. He'd spread himself so thin he was everywhere. So thin the fire couldn't touch him. Or so I hoped.

Nafeeza turned blazing eyes on me. I scrambled back, my butt dragging along the floor until my back hit the bars at the end of the cage. Nafeeza floated toward me, a nightmare of crackling flames and scorching heat. I shook my head and clamped my mouth shut, holding my breath.

Nafeeza raised her hand, slowly, making the moment last. A wicked smile uncurled on her lips and her hand began to glow. The air grew even hotter and I had to shield my eyes for fear of them drying up and bursting into flames. I braced myself for the blast of fire that would melt me into a puddle of boiling flesh.

Instead of heat, I felt the rush of cold air against my face. The cooling breath of icy wind blowing my hair. When I opened my eyes I saw Justice inside the cage with me. He floated above the floor, his lower half nothing but swirling mist, his upper body naked and glistening. His arms were spread wide to shield me, the cold wind of his power rushing from his body and holding back the roaring blast of hellfire Nafeeza directed toward us.

"Dearest sister!" Jeffrey shouted above the noise of the battle.

Nafeeza dropped her hand and stared. Justice let his arms fall to his sides and his misty feet touch the ground. He swayed for a moment then steadied himself and sat. He pulled a blanket into his lap. Modesty, even under pressure.

Jeffrey pushed past me, past Justice, and grabbed the bars of the cage. "Let me out, Sister."

Nafeeza backed away, shaking her head. "Let yourself out. Release the human and agree to come home quietly."

"Never!"

"Then you will stay in that cage until the human rots and you are forced to find another." Nafeeza sat on the ground, hands resting on dainty knees. "I will wait."

"Nafeeza, Nafeeza," Jeffrey said in a voice that wasn't his. "All this time and you still do not understand the freedom of this country. I am no longer forced into servitude, no longer doubted. These Americans *believe*, and they *fear!*"

"Our masters demand your return."

Jeffrey laughed, but it wasn't his laugh. It was too deep, too sinister to be my sweet, kind Jeffrey.

"I serve no one," he said.

"Mina!" Detective Richards' voice came from outside the cabin.

"Oh, God, no." I looked at Justice letting the fear fill my eyes.

Before Justice could do anything, Detective Richards burst through the door, gun held in both hands, pointing at the ceiling. He took a moment to blink into the dark. When his eyes adjusted he scanned the room and found the three of us caged and Nafeeza sitting in the middle of the room in a pool of sunlight coming in from the broken roof.

"What's going on here?" Richards said.

"You've got to get out," I said. "Leave, run!"

"I do not think so," Nafeeza said quietly as she stood. She pointed to the door and it slammed shut, the lock turning and clicking into place.

"What the hell?" Richards said.

He turned his head and looked at the door. He didn't see Nafeeza rise off the floor. He didn't see the bolt of fire from her fingers. It hit him with a crack that left me temporarily deaf. The blast knocked Richards flat on his back. The gun flew from his hand and skittered across the floor, coming to a halt by the cage. When the flames died down, his clothes were smoldering and large blisters had already formed on his face and chest.

"Richards!" I screamed and gripped the bars of the

cage. "Randal, get up!"

Detective Richards lay still, smoke moving upward from his body in wispy, lazy swirls.

Jeffrey screamed beside me. I spun to look just in time to see him grab his head, his teeth grinding together.

"Get out, get out, get out!" Jeffrey grunted.

He fell to his knees, hands over his eyes, his face straining. In the next moment I saw the double image again. The translucent orange Djinn struggled to stay connected, hands around Jeffrey's throat, eyes blazing. Jeffrey screamed again and went to his hands and knees. The Djinn floated above him, left hand around Jeffrey's throat, right hand slashing at his back and neck, leaving long bloody lines and shredded clothing. A wisp of orange light connected the Djinn's misty bottom half to Jeffrey's belly, a frail, ethereal umbilical cord growing thinner the longer Jeffrey struggled.

"Brother!" Nafeeza shouted.

The Djinn let go of Jeffrey and turned. He snarled and let loose a rumbling scream that shook the cabin. Justice took hold of me and kept me standing as the floor shook beneath us.

"Time to go home, Brother." Nafeeza lifted the beaded sack and pulled Jeffrey's book from inside.

"No!" the Djinn screamed. "Not now, not ever!"

He curled his hands into fists and moved them in front of his body creating an X with his wrists. The temperature rose again, this time from the Djinn floating a foot in front of me.

I backed to the wall and concentrated on the cool energy blowing off of Justice again. I pulled it to me, surrounded myself in it, making a cocoon of cold air to shield me from the inevitable blaze. Justice nodded once and then shifted to mist. He moved along the floor and out of the cage, positioning himself behind Nafeeza.

"What are you doing, Brother?" Nafeeza dropped the beaded sack and the book, her eyes narrowing. A second later she clutched her chest and gasped. "No," she breathed. "You would not."

Brother Djinn nodded once and sneered at Nafeeza. He lifted his crossed arms above his head and then brought them down hard. As he did so, Nafeeza screamed and collapsed to her knees. Orange liquid blossomed on her dress. It steamed and sizzled through the fabric. Tainted blood. She pulled her blood-smeared hands away and looked at them, shaking her head. Just then the front of her dress exploded outward showering the ground with bits of flesh and streams of fiery liquid. Fire poured out of the hole in Nafeeza's chest and one last scream died on her lips as she fell back. Her body convulsed once and the fire died out. The blood continued to leak out around her, a shimmering, steaming pool of liquid fire.

TWENTY-FOUR

~~

"It's over," Jeffrey said.

I spun to my right and found Jeffrey leaned against the bars, Detective Richards' gun in his right hand and pointing at his temple.

Jeffrey laughed, shrill and crazed. "It's over, you fucking bastard."

"No, Jeffrey!" I screamed.

Before I could go to him, the Djinn reached out and made a fist in the air. Jeffrey jerked back and dropped the gun. He began to rise off the floor, his legs kicking, hands clawing at his throat.

"You need only draw breath, nothing more," Brother Djinn said, then tossed Jeffrey to the back of the cage.

Jeffrey's head hit with a dull *thunk* against the bars and he slid to the floor. Eyes barely cracked open, he met my gaze for a moment, a trickle of blood rolling from the corner of his mouth. He lifted his head a bit, then lurched forward, crawling toward the gun. Before he could reach it I heard a wet snap and saw Jeffrey's forearm bend up, the bone broken in two and pushing through the skin. Blood poured out and seeped into the rotting floor boards.

Jeffrey howled and rolled onto his back, his broken right arm flopping limp at his side. Another crack and his left arm lay crooked and useless, too.

I knelt by Jeffrey and tried to comfort him, my mind racing. Brother Djinn smiled triumphantly down at us, and I hated him more than ever.

Justice's energy chilled the air again and he sank to the floor outside the cage. In the blink of an eye, he was gone. I was confused for a second until I saw movement in the shadows where Justice had once stood. I smiled coldly and glanced at the Djinn still floating above us.

"You have company," I said.

Brother Djinn frowned and looked toward the shadows as a dark shape slithered from the center. Made of swirling black smoke at first, the shape shot up from the ground and solidified before our eyes. The filtered sunlight shimmered off of Justice's sleek black scales and glinted off his golden eyes. His flat head almost touched the ceiling, his cobra hood more than four feet across. Massive black coils slapped the floor, heavy, thick muscles working beneath the gray belly scales. A shining black tongue flicked out between his lips and a hiss filled the room.

"A fight then!" Brother Djinn said and sank to the floor. He snaked out through the bars toward Justice, leaving his wispy trail attached to Jeffrey's navel.

Brother Djinn's transformation was almost identical Justice's. He disappeared for a heartbeat, then reappeared in his new form. Instead of smoke and mist and shadows, Brother Djinn's snake appeared in a flash of fire and bright light. It rose up from the flames, golden scales shimmering and glossy.

The two serpents crashed into one another, fangs flashing, tails whipping, strong bodies wrapped tightly around each other.

Justice wasn't going to win. His snake was impressive to look at and even powerful, but it was only Justice inside. He wasn't a Lycan, wasn't really a snake. He may as well have been Justice the man going hand to flaming hand with the Djinn.

I watched, horror-struck, as my former lover, my best friend, fought an impossible battle.

"A way out," Jeffrey groaned. I looked down and his face was white, bloodless, pain glazing over his eyes. He flicked his attention to the gun laying against the bars.

Realizing what he meant for me to do, I shook my head, the hairs on my neck standing up. "No," I said.

"Please," Jeffrey begged between ragged breaths. "Save me. You promised. . . to set me. . . free."

I could hear Justice and the Djinn fighting, whipping serpentine tails, fangs clashing, muscled bodies slamming into the walls. Justice wouldn't last forever. He was growing weaker the longer he stayed a snake. The Djinn would kill Justice and then come for me. Jeffrey would be forever trapped with the demon inside of him. He'd be forced to watch as the Djinn played his killing games, sucking in the fear and screams of his victims forever.

I looked down the long line of Jeffrey's body, his ruined arms limp and bloody at his sides. The thin, wispy light that bound the Djinn to Jeffrey glowed brighter, stronger, sucking the life force from Jeffrey to boost its own strength and kill my Justice.

There was no other way.

Tears streaming down my cheeks, I lifted the gun in shaking hands. It was so heavy, so powerful. All it would take to end this nightmare was one move. Squeeze the trigger and all Jeffrey's suffering would be over. Squeeze the trigger and Justice would live. Squeeze the trigger and the children would be safe.

Squeeze the trigger.

The memory of Cadric's gun was so vivid I could feel it there, pressed against my forehead, pressing hard enough to bruise. I could hear the click of the empty gun. I felt the puppy's blood spattered on me, saw it stain the fresh white snow.

I shook my head and set the gun on the floor. "I can't do it!"

Jeffrey closed his eyes tight, his face a grimace of pain. The binding light of the Djinn pulsed rapidly as blood poured from the wounds in Jeffrey's forearms. I heard one of the snakes squeal. The sound rattled my bones, chilled my blood.

Justice was dying.

"I'm so sorry, Jeffrey," I sobbed and picked up the gun.

I pressed the barrel to his forehead and he opened his eyes. The pain, the torment, the nightmares, all plain to see in those clear, pale eyes.

"I love you, Mina," he said. He shut his eyes and clenched his teeth.

"I love you, too, Jeffrey," I said just before I squeezed the trigger.

TWENTY-FIVE

~~

Blood. Gore. Bone. That's all I could see when I shut my eyes. *This* would be my newest nightmare, the newest thing to make me wake, screaming in the night. This moment would haunt me for eternity.

Jeffrey's body went limp against me. The room grew colder. My sweat and the splattered blood began to cool on my skin almost at once. It took all I had not to be sick, not to wipe the cooling liquid away. I knew if I touched it I'd smear it and make it so much worse, and I didn't want it on my hands. I didn't want to see Jeffrey's spilled life drying on *my* body.

It was the sound of struggling and a high-pitched squeal that made me open my eyes. I dropped the gun without looking down at what was left of Jeffrey, at what I had done. The screams were inhuman, garbled, ending in hissed curses.

Sobbing, I crawled away from Jeffrey's body and

toward the screams. Funny that I should crawl closer to a shrieking, angry Djinn instead of cradling the body of my friend.

No, not funny at all. *I'd* killed him. It was my fault Jeffrey was dead.

My fault.

My stomach knotted at once and I threw up. My head spun and my body shook. I was a killer. I'd murdered an innocent man. My humanity was slipping away and I couldn't do a damn thing to stop it.

The naysayer whispered, *Add another notch to your belt, my girl.*

Tears stung my eyes, but I opened them. I had to see. Please let Justice be alive.

I had to blink away the tears to see clearly, but Justice was standing, as a man, in the center of the floor. A glowing puddle of thick yellow and orange liquid swirled at his feet. An occasional flash of fire erupted and then died away as the ooze steamed and bubbled.

"Justice?" My voice was harsh, the muscles tight with despair, sorrow, self-loathing.

He turned those golden eyes to me and I noticed he was shaking. He was so pale, so weak he could barely stay on his feet. He didn't even have enough strength to put his clothes back on, so he stood there, bare and vulnerable.

"We won," he whispered.

We'd won, but at what price? Had Justice seen me shoot Jeffrey? Had he watched me pull the trigger and the blood splatter? What did he think of his precious Mina now?

My world swam and I laid on my side, my cheek resting on the rough floor of the cage. Justice was moving on the other side of the bars but I didn't care what he was doing. The darkness behind my eyelids was a comfort.

Leave me in the cage, Justice. Leave me in the cage to rot with Jeffrey's corpse like I deserve. But I couldn't even call the strength to say it out loud, so I just lay there. The lock clicked, and I heard the door swing open with the creak of old metal.

"Come on, Mina." Justice's voice was soft. I felt his cool fingers brush my face, felt the tremble in his hand.

I didn't move. *Couldn't* move. I felt Justice walk around me, lay on the floor behind me, scoot in close and put his arm around my waist. He hugged me close and nuzzled the back of my head. We weren't lovers anymore, but this wasn't about sex. This was about comfort. Mine or his, it didn't matter.

I imagined what we must look like. Me covered in blood and pieces of body, Justice naked and spooning against my back. Jeffrey sprawled only a few feet away, broken bones, splattered brains, and spilled blood. Nafeeza and her ruined chest, the puddle that used to be Brother Djinn, and poor Detective Richards outside the cage, blistered and ruined.

TWENTY-SIX

~~

I'd killed men before. Several, actually. Why should killing Jeffrey have been any different? He was just a man, made from the same stuff as the others I'd killed. Why did it matter? Why was I hurting?

Because he'd been my friend. All the others I'd killed had been trying to kill me first. Trying to hurt me and then kill me. Jeffrey wasn't trying to hurt me. He'd never hurt me. All he ever offered me was friendship, while he hoped for so much more.

I killed my friend to save countless other people. Didn't that make me a heroine? I'd sacrificed my own morals, my own sanity, my own humanity to save the lives of strangers.

Somehow, I didn't think I'd be getting any awards for my "good" deed.

Bruno Harms scribbled something in his notebook, turned to his computer, and punched a few keys. He typed like he didn't know what he was doing. Two fingers, slow.

Peck.

Peck.

Peck.

My eyes stung and my face felt raw from wiping away the unstoppable flood of tears. I'd been allowed to clean up in the station bathroom after they'd poked, prodded, swabbed, and bagged their samples as evidence, but I still felt dirty. I'd never come clean. Not after this.

"What did you say happened to the woman?" Officer Harms asked.

I'd already told him a hundred times. I'd told him the truth. I'd shot Jeffrey to save Justice. Did he believe me? Hell, I wouldn't have believed me if I were in his position.

"Nafeeza was killed by her brother," I said.

"Uh huh," Bruno said. "The genie, right?"

"Djinn," I corrected.

My eyelids were so heavy, my body aching. Justice had been rushed to Divine Hope Hospital after Bruno and his men found us in the cabin. Justice was unconscious. The police didn't know why, but I did. He'd pushed himself too far. He'd done something similar not long ago. And again, it was *my fault* he'd done that. The man had lived for two hundred years without a hitch, he meets me and almost dies twice.

I started to sob. My hands smelled like burning sand, warm spices, and something else under it all. Something neck ruffling and cold. No soap could wash the smell of snakes off my skin.

Bruno stopped pecking at his keyboard and glanced at me. I sniffled and stared at my lap. My favorite pair of jeans was soaked with blood and torn at the knees. The sight of my jeans made me burst into tears again.

"Go home, Ms. Jewel," Bruno said. "Just go home.

When Richards wakes up, we'll ask him what he wants to do."

"What?" I looked up at the officer, my eyes still leaking tears.

"Go on," he said gruffly.

"I'm not going to jail?"

Bruno locked his gaze on mine. "No. Not today." He glanced at his watch. "Besides, if I put you in jail, come nine o'clock you might eat the other prisoners."

I stopped sniffling and stared at Bruno. My upper lip twitched. "How did you know?"

Bruno gave a bitter smile. "I can smell it on you."

"You. . ." My eyes went wide. "Shit, Bruno!"

He nodded his head once on his thick neck. "Yeah."

I leaned in close to whisper. There weren't any other police officers nearby but I didn't want to be too loud anyway. "What kind?"

Bruno blushed and mumbled, "Tiger."

I grinned and poked a finger against a small stuffed Tigger doll resting against his monitor.

Bruno laughed and turned off his computer screen. "Go home, Jewel. Or wherever you puppies go at night."

~~

I didn't go straight home. Divine Hope was almost glowing in the early evening light. The sun was working its way down, sending its last fiery rays out along the horizon. I had a couple of hours before I had to be somewhere safe.

Justice's room was cool and quiet, the hush of the air conditioner a calming presence. He lay in the middle of the white bed, his hands folded over his stomach, his long hair spread out around him in dark sheets. Someone had brushed his hair while he slept so now it shimmered, almost liquid-looking against the white bedding.

I kissed his forehead and ran my fingers down his cool cheek. He looked peaceful. I hoped he was having good dreams.

Detective Richards' room was three doors down on the same floor. He was awake when I came in. His face was bandaged and his hands were wrapped to look like thick white boxing gloves.

"Hey, Detective," I said from the doorway.

"It's good to see you, Mina." His voice was a little muffled by the bandages, but I was just happy to hear him talking.

"How you feeling?" I asked.

"Surprisingly good. Dr. Stevens seems to think there won't be any scarring."

I smiled. I'd asked Bernie to make sure Detective Richards looked as handsome and dashing as before the incident. The bandages were mostly for show. By the time they came off, his burns would all be healed.

"How are you, Mina?"

"Fine."

"You can't lie to a cop."

"Yes, I can," I said with a grin. "I just can't make him believe it."

He laughed. "Seriously, you going to be okay?"

I paused, shrugged. "Probably."

I didn't say yes, because I wasn't sure I would be. This whole ordeal might just have been the thing to finally break me. You can only handle so much before you finally snap, before you reach the end of your own strength.

Detective Richards watched me through the bandages, his eyes sparkling. He had questions, I could see it in his eyes. But he wasn't going to ask. Maybe he didn't want to know the answers. Not really.

~~

The last light of the sun faded away and darkness bled across the sky like spilled black ink. All around me I could hear clothes ripping or being pulled off, joints snapping, the wet slide of muscles and ligaments moving and fusing back together in their new places. All the sounds, and I didn't look around.

Latrator came up behind me and ran his clawed fingers through my hair. "I'm so glad to see you with us tonight, Mina."

"It's good to be here," I said, and I meant it.

"Can you feel her pull?"

My gaze was locked on the moon shining in the night sky. I nodded. "Yeah, I feel her."

"Then let yourself go. Let the Great Mother bring you to life. Let her light cradle you as you remove your mask and become one with us."

I laughed and looked at Latrator. "You're always so poetic."

He bowed deeply, then straightened and put his arm chastely around my waist. He gazed up at the moon, but said nothing else.

"Will you shift tonight?" I asked after a few quiet moments.

"Do you wish me to?" He turned and stepped in front of me, lifting my hand to his lips. He laid a gentle kiss on the back of my hand, so gentle I couldn't feel his fangs.

Did I wish him to? It seemed like a question meant to ask something so much deeper than that. My brain was tired, my body aching. I didn't want to deal with Latrator and Justice and Timothy.

At least I didn't have to worry about Jeffrey trying to

get romantic anymore.

I sat on the ground and buried my face in my hands and wept quietly. Latrator sat beside me, a comforting arm across my shoulders. He didn't say a word, he just held me, because that's what I needed.

A few minutes passed and all the sounds of my pack shifting had ceased. Everyone had taken off to play in the woods, hunt animals, enjoy a night of furry pleasures, and I was still sitting here, furless.

I wiped my eyes on my sleeve and looked at the back of my hands. "Why haven't I shifted yet, Latrator?"

He shrugged. "I'm unsure, *Ma Cherie*." He looked up to the sky, the moonlight spreading over his face, drowning out all color. "Perhaps the Great Mother has taken pity on you this month. Perhaps you will not be drawn to the change."

I scoffed. "You mean maybe something good will actually happen to me for a change?"

Latrator looked at me and smiled. "Many good things happen to you. You have but to acknowledge their existence."

"More poetry," I said with a shake of my head.

After an hour of sitting with Latrator and not feeling another twinge of need, I stood and brushed off my sweat pants. "If I'm not going to shift tonight, I think I'd like to go home."

"Your house will be empty this evening."

I sighed, my heart suddenly aching again. "Oh, yeah."

Justice was still in the hospital, and even if he wasn't, he didn't live with me anymore. Timothy would be out all night with the pack. And Jeffrey was laying in the morgue freezer. I'd be home alone until early morning. Unless. . .

"Jacob?"

Latrator looked at me, surprised. "Yes?"

"Would you come home with me tonight?"

More surprise on his face, then a quick blink. "It would be an honor."

He offered his arm. I slipped my hand under his arm and let him lead me out of the woods.

TWENTY-SEVEN

~~

The cat was a warm weight against my thighs. He purred and breathed and moved under my touch, and I found comfort in that closeness. He demanded little of me outside of food and water and a warm place to sleep, and I appreciated his company in my otherwise empty house. His presence made my blood cool and my tension slip away, which in turn made my mind slow down long enough to get through what I needed to do.

I looked down at my open journal laying next to me on the bed, touched the empty page, and watched the words flow out from under my fingers.

I know I said I'd write more, and I really meant it. But life gets in the way sometimes so you'll have to forgive me if battling demons (both inside and out) prevents me from staying on top of this journal. Bernie says writing is good therapy. I told him he's just tired of hearing me bitch. He scowled at that. Nice to know I can still irk him a little.

I'm happy to report that Detective Richards was able to bury the incident—and my part in it—under mountains of paperwork. He worked the media and put all the focus on the fact Evan had survived and come home, and that the murderer had been taken down for good. There will be no more exploding hearts in Port Orchard. . . We hope. I told Richards if there *were* any more, not to call me.

All of the deaths were blamed on Nafeeza. I wanted to torch her remains, but I got vetoed, and her body was shipped back to her homeland. There wasn't enough left of Brother Djinn to fill a shot glass, but we sent that with Nafeeza's body, too.

I got a letter a week or so after the incident with Brother and Sister Djinn. I'm not sure who it was from but it gushed with apologies for those who'd died, and well wishes for those who'd been touched by the Djinn and survived. The letter explained how certain families had been coexisting and working in secret symbiotic relationships with the Djinn for aeons—basically, confirming what Nafeeza had told us. It ended with a short and simple promise that "they" would make sure no other Djinn escaped.

I doubt "they" can stop it, but it was a nice gesture.

With both of the Djinn dead and Jeffrey long buried, we have no way to know for sure why the teens died and who wrote the notes to get them to the party in the first place. I really thought the Congregation had a hand in this one, but we've hit dead ends everywhere we've looked since the incident. It's hard enough catching those bastards *with* evidence, I won't be able to prove my suspicions to Presence without *something* to show them.

Looking at the whole fiasco in retrospect, the fact I tried so hard to pin it on the Congregation kinda bothers me. Nafeeza gave off every clue that she was involved, but I was too blinded by my own bias to see it. While there is no doubt that the Congregation of Truth needs to be obliterated, if I'm ready to blame every missing kid on them without evidence, does that mean my judgment is impaired? Just because I can't get over what Cadric and his Congregation flunkies did to me when I was a kid, does that mean I'm hindering cases rather than helping to solve them?

Those questions and the resulting realization has put me on notice. I promise, I'm going to be more careful in the future. I'm going to look at all the clues for what they are, and not try to fit them into my automatic suspicion of the Congregation.

But back to the kids. If I had to wager a guess, and leave the Congregation out of this one, I'd say that the teens' deaths were just the Djinn having a *good time*. Sure, Brother Djinn came here for revenge at first, but I think after he screwed with Walter Garrot's life and family, he actually enjoyed the killing. I say that because of the way Brother Djinn spoke about the freedom here in America, and the way we *"believed* and *feared."*

I've heard that same kind of hunger in voices before. Human, Djinn, gifted, or mundane, I guess evil doesn't care what species you are.

Evan, as it turns out, has a touch of psychic abilities of his own. Bernie guessed that it was his inner strength, his gift of Resilience that kept the Djinn out of his head and body. He'd survived not only by luck, but by design. Evan would survive this and anything else thrown at him—as long as he pays attention.

Is he indestructible? No, just very hard to hurt. Presence has taken him under our collective wing and begun teaching him to hone his ability. His mother thinks I'm simply being a good mentor and helping her troubled son to learn a profession early. She thinks he'll grow up to be a police officer or a private eye like me.

We let her think that.

I know what you're waiting for, dear reader. I've

already spent years putting my personal life onto these pages, so why hesitate now? That's the juicy stuff, right? My screw ups? My drama? All the times where you say to yourself, "That was stupid, Mina!" or "I'd never have done it *that* way."

If you're reading this, I'm dead and gone, so what does any of it matter? Why do I care that you'd be disappointed if I suddenly stopped retelling all the goodies and stuck to just the rundown of my oddest cases? Well, I've disappointed enough people, so I'll throw you a little treat. And though you and I will never meet, at least I can tell myself that someday in the future, someone somewhere won't think I'm a total fuck up. At least I've succeeded in entertaining you, if nothing else.

Let me start by saying that Latrator was a perfect gentleman the night of the full moon. We cuddled and we talked, and then we slept until dawn. No monkey business, no funny stuff, not even a twitch from his lower regions. It was exactly what I'd needed. . . Though I admit, thankful as I am that Latrator really is a nice guy with control over his libido, I'm a little put off by his lack of interest. Put off, yes, but, staying on par with my ever-conflicting self, I am also impressed he didn't take advantage of a tempting opportunity: Poor, sad Mina, vulnerable and easily swayed in her heartbroken state.

Maybe I *am* just another pack mate to Latrator. Not sure why I care though. Men suck, as has been abundantly proven by my experiences with them.

On the less-than-happy front, Justice is out of the hospital, but not good as new. The fight with the Djinn has left him almost crippled. He can walk and talk and all that, but his powers are a shadow of what they'd been before. Bernie isn't sure why, and he isn't sure Justice will ever fully recover.

Justice and I haven't talked about the breakup, or even tried to reconcile. I'm not sure if he's finally accepted the truth, or if he's just too worried over his own health to even bother with the subject. He spends a lot of time in his little room down at HQ, and misses some of our meetings, too.

I worry about him, of course. You don't stop loving someone just like that, but I'm trying my damnedest to move on and learn from the situation. I will not be tricked again. A handsome face and pretty words can't hide the truth when a piece of your soul is black and full of hate. A soft, comforting hand can't take away the pain of controlling and cruel words.

Bottom line? Like I told Bernie before, I'm done with men. They're not worth the effort. They're not worth the stress or the heartache. I know not all men are creeps, but I just don't have the desire to dig through the assholes to find the one shining gem. I figure I lived a few decades without a love-life before Justice came along, I can do it again.

I snapped the journal shut, and the cat opened his large, aqua eyes. He blinked once and purred at me, turning onto his back to expose his white belly fur.

"I don't need a man," I said, running one hand down the cat's soft tummy. "Isn't that right, Jeffrey?"

Sneak peek of book four
Presence: Into the Dark

ONE
~~

"Shut up!"

Harsh words crashed through my sleep, yanking me to consciousness. As if to accent my sudden awakening, Thomas screamed, his tiny voice riding on the static crackle of a bad wireless connection.

My eyes snapped open and I sat up, my heart thundering in my chest. It took only a moment for my senses to sharpen, focusing on the baby monitor receiver on the nightstand next to me.

"Stop it," came the voice again, and the receiver lights turned from green to red, indicating a loud noise. Or someone speaking next to the transmitter attached inside the crib.

My stomach jerked and my sluggish, sleep-impaired brain struggled to make sense of the situation. Justice was out on assignment and Timothy was hanging out with the other werewolves. That left Thomas and I alone in the house. Or at least we should have been alone.

Quietly, I swung my legs over the side of the bed, trying not to panic as I listened to Thomas struggling, grunting, and whimpering.

My little one had nightmares. Dr. Bernie Stevens said it was just normal baby stuff and he probably wasn't really having bad dreams at all. But I could never quite shake the feeling that Thomas *was* in distress. It was that feeling that made me wake every night, thinking I heard someone walking the hall toward his room, whispering to Thomas over the monitor, or laughing softly with sinister intent.

But that was ridiculous. Surely, I'd imagined the

gravely voice, the rough commands, the scraping sounds of something brushing against the transmitter in the crib. My logical side told me it was all in my head. I'd had this nightmare before, and it always ended with me fully waking, realizing the truth that nothing terrible was happening inside the room across the hall where my baby slept.

Well, my logical side could stuff it. It could throw convincing arguments at me all night long, but I'd still need to see for myself that Thomas was safe.

I'd just slipped into my bathrobe and started reaching for my bedroom door when Thomas' squeal of terror struck me to the core.

I yanked the bedroom door open, took two long strides across the hall, and tore the nursery door open. I stepped inside the room in time to hear Thomas' strangled cry cut short. My heart riding in my throat, I jammed my left hand against the wall and threw it upward to hit the light-switch.

Light flooded the room. And in those precious seconds as my eyes adjusted to the bright light, I saw my baby's empty crib, shredded blankets thrown about the room, and Thomas' tiny, pajama-clad legs kicking wildly as they disappeared into the darkness under the crib.

~~